THE
SECRET
OF THE
STORMS

The Secret of the Storms
Copyright © 2022
Joseph Monteleone

ISBN: 978-1-957344-20-1

Cover design by David Warren

Published by WordCrafts Press
Cody, Wyoming 82414
www.wordcrafts.net

THE
SECRET
OF THE
STORMS

CENT'ANNI

(100 years)

JOEY MONTELEONE

WordCrafts Press

Foreword

If a family can have an anthem, *Family is Everything* belongs to the LeoMortes. In *The Secret of the Storms*, Mr. Monteleone chronicles the journey of a family who exemplifies that principle, albeit on a road that often strays from the straight and narrow. Secret mixes courage, fear, defeat, success, joy and agony then adds a dose of mystery and violence to a bread that takes one hundred years to rise! When the feast is over one concludes not only that family is everything, but also—families are forever. And if those dualities are true, where is the next chapter?

Vincent and Rosa, his wife, are the first in the family line to take the giant step across the sea from their small village in the south of Italy to the burgeoning metropolis of St. Louis. There, living in a second-floor walk-up, nearly penniless, begins the epic journey of a family that exemplifies the American dream. Sticking together, trusting only family is the only guarantee, the only thing they know will assure survival. Generations of LeoMorte pull the reader along through historical events of the early twentieth century.

As the family grows, Anthony (Big Tony) LeoMorte assumes the de facto role as family patriarch. His drive, ambition and cunning elevate him from the son of a bread baker to the pinnacle of his Italian neighborhood. His only motivation is his obsession with the success and protection of his family. His mantra "Family is everything" permeates his counsel to his children; it also is the impetus for falling on the other side of the law.

Monteleone weaves a gripping story with surprises that keeps the reader wanting to turn the page. And that's the essence of a well written tale. Kudos to him for having memorialized the journey of this family of immigrants coming to our wonderful country and having done so in a manner that would make his family as proud of him as they are of the Cent'Anni.

~Michael J. Vines

Chapter 1

The Dream

Cent'Anni, Italian for 100 years, a century. It could, under certain circumstances, seem like a lifetime, but in the history of the world, a mere blink of the eye.

After years of hard work, Vincent DeoMonte and his wife Rosa had built up a small grocery business and even managed some modest savings. Vincent started work early in life, and neither school nor education was a priority. Rosa attended school and learned English which she taught Vincent slowly, often their conversations were in a combination of Italian and English. They were residents of a small southern Italian village, Villa Cristo, and a small back room behind the store served as living quarters.

The store was a combination of smells. A dominant aroma of fresh garlic, along with green or black olives, fennel, oregano, and other spices all were displayed neatly on long tables. Locally grown vegetables added color and sold well to the residents of the village. Eggs, freshly baked bread, and a variety of cheeses all added to the sensory appeal of the store.

Marketing for meals was done throughout the day, as a lack of refrigeration, ice boxes, in most homes required frequent trips to the stores. A small brick oven in the rear of the store provided a place for Vincent to bake various styles of buns and hard crust Italian breads, and was a favorite of his patrons. His reputation as a baker brought customers from miles away to stock up only to return days later.

He had over the years perfected the art of bread baking,

especially loaves of Italian bread. During the noon hour he even developed a specialty, a warm loaf of freshly baked bread was sliced longways, olive oil was dripped onto the loaf, grated Romano cheese was added, and for a few cents more you could get olives, salami, and a small glass of red wine. The smell brought people in off the street to partake of the mid-day simple meal. In the colder months the baking oven served them well as an alternate source of heat for the backroom DeoMonte residence. A small selection of wine was displayed along the back wall and tempted his customers to move to the rear of the store.

During Catholic feast days and especially at Christmas some simple cookies were added to the other items available. The children visited and shyly stared at the carefully decorated simple cookies—they were often treated to the sugar cookies by the kindhearted Rosa who hoped to have her own children someday.

"I'm so proud of you Vincent. You've worked hard, and we have a good life; you're a good husband and provider."

"I knew early on I would make my living with my hands and physical labor. I'm satisfied to be a simple man, honest and dedicated to you my wife and to family."

In the Italian tradition, Rosa in early childhood had been promised to Vincent in marriage, a betrothal very common in the region and at the time. Their parents, lifelong residents of Villa Cristo were respected citizens—his father Antonino a shoemaker, his mother Gina a seamstress—and both devoted to family and church. Vincent's family included brothers, three of whom had left the tiny town for the larger Italian cities. Rosa was the only daughter of a well-established vineyard owner Thomasino DeNatali and his wife Lucia. Vincent and Rosa saw each other often and consistently on Sundays at the ancient stone church that was built at the base of a small hillside. Now 29 years old, Vincent was devoted to Rosa, 23, and his business.

He was a short man in stature, only five feet four inches tall, but his burly build was evidence of his willingness to labor and to his history of hard work.

Rosa was two inches shorter, slender, and always displayed the slightest hint of a smile on her face. Her tiny hands were like velvet, the opposite of Vincent's leathery hands. She dressed modestly, normally in dark colors. Stacked heeled shoes gave the illusion that she was taller. Her hair was always pulled back to reveal kind, dark-brown eyes, a oval-shaped face, and a pale complexion.

The stern Vincent had the hands of a working man; strong hands and bulging forearms were a testament to the manual labor he had always known. With dark hair and a receding hairline, Vincent's square jaw matched his ever-present serious demeanor. With a minimum of formal education, he had accepted his lot in life would be long days and short pay.

A look around their backroom residence revealed meager furnishings, a rickety pine table with seating for two was the scene of their meals. A handmade wooden shelf held a vase for wildflowers they occasionally picked on walks across the countryside, a delicate blown glass wishing well, a statue of the Blessed Mother, and a faded photo of Rosa's parents were carefully displayed and wore a coat of dust. A small bed barely big enough for the two made a safe little nest for this childless couple. Barren and bleak was the view of this shelter.

Rosa, a small but determined woman, suffered ill health most of her life. Her strength of spirit made up for her physical short comings. Her kindness and faith made her a favorite resident of the village. Rosa's formal schooling allowed her to keep track of the financial part of the business, though she was protective of Vincent, never wanting him to feel inferior. Vincent's pride in his craft gave him satisfaction, and he trusted Rosa to provide the help necessary to do business.

"We're a good team. Your hard work is paying off, our friends and neighbors love the bread, and the store will give us a future here."

"You know Rosa we'll never be rich; we'll get by but not much more."

"As long as were together, I'll be happy. I have you and maybe someday I can give you children. A simple life is all want."

"I love you Rosa. I know little about the world outside of here, but I want you to be happy, safe and satisfied."

Unanticipated trouble started in 1921, two large, darkly dressed men showed up at the store demanding a payment for their *protection* of the business.

"You have a good little business here, Mr. DeoMonte. We can help protect you—for a price."

"I'm Vincent DeoMonte. I was born here and almost everyone knows me. I don't need protection. Protection from what?"

"We can make sure bad things don't happen here, that you won't have an accident or lose your business. We just want a small token of respect, a few lire a week."

"Give some time, I'll think about your offer."

The Sicilian Mafia—*La Cosa Nostra*—had infiltrated the region and created fear with threats to the local businesses. Vincent, a peaceful man, asked for time to consider the situation. The thugs promised to be back in a week. Other business owners in the village urged him to give in and just pay the token of tribute. Vincent didn't want to frighten the frail Rosa with the threat, so he silently, nervously contemplated the situation. He watched the door each day thinking maybe the *mafioso* would not return. But true to their word, a week later the bell over the door rang signaling the entrance of someone to the store. They stared around the room and moved with purpose toward the store owner. Vincent felt his stomach knot and heartbeat increase as they approached the wooden counter.

"When can we expect payment of your debt?"

His face pale from fear, Vincent replied that he had decided to keep his hard-earned money. "I owe you nothing, there is no debt."

To convince the shopkeeper to comply the biggest of the two asked aloud, "Would you like to see your store destroyed, or maybe you don't care about the store. How about the woman? Is that your wife? Do you need a lesson in Italian justice?"

Vincent's fear instantly turned to rage, and he grabbed a large knife from behind the counter and leaped over it, chasing the fleeing felons. "Get out and don't come back, ever (*Esci e non tornare, mai*)!"

Rosa, hearing the disturbance, came quickly only to see her husband in pursuit of the two men. "What happened? Why would you pull a knife against those men?"

Vincent, still enraged, ignored her request for information about the incident. She knew the look of anger on his face was best left without additional conversation and certainly no more questions.

After a quiet, tense supper the couple prepared for bed without any mention of the day's incident. Before retiring Vincent nervously double-checked the door locks and put the same knife he had grabbed earlier beside the bed. Noticed by Rosa, she gave her husband a quizzical look that went unanswered.

"Vincent, I don't understand why you have brought a knife to our bed. Does this have to do with the men that came in today?"

"There are things you don't understand, things about the world we live in, things that shouldn't concern you."

Despite the extra precautions, she trusted Vincent but also knew not to ask anything further. A sick feeling gripped her; a dry throat accompanied by a nervous stomach would be her bed partner that night. Rosa eventually dropped off to sleep as her husband tossed about and realized troubled sleep for only minutes at a time. Late in the night, Vincent, exhausted from the day's events, drifted into a dream, maybe more appropriately a nightmare—one that seemed from every aspect, real!

Clear and colorful, in a view from above, Vincent sees himself walking the edge of the mountains. Moving quietly, he spots a lion in a small opening in the trees and draws back a bow, firing an arrow, striking the lion. The beast falls writhing, thrashing, snarling and biting at the arrow in its side, blood spurting from the gaping wound. As Vincent cautiously approaches, the lion's breathing grows labored, and it's clear that the massive creature is mortally wounded. As he kneels alongside the lion, as if from nowhere a deep, raspy, human voice begins. "Because of what you've done, your family will experience love and loss, happiness and heartache ,and unimaginable agony." Paralyzed by the ominous prediction Vincent can only think to ask, "For how long?"

As the lion gasps with its final labored breath it utters, "For 100 years. Cent'Anni!"

Waking in a panic accompanied by a cold sweat, Vincent feels the effect of his elevated blood pressure signaled by a thumping noise in his ears, and an unusual body heat becomes evident in his blood-red neck and ears. A life changing decision is made instantaneously.

"We've got to leave Italy!"

"Why would leave, this is our home? Everything we have, all that we know, is right here."

"Rosa, you must trust me. We have to leave here!"

"Leave family, friends, our future?" she asked tearfully.

"Our future is not here."

Rosa instinctively reached for her rosary beads. She trusted Vincent, but more importantly she trusted God.

Trying not to alarm Rosa, Vincent began to formulate an escape plan. Anticipating the return of the gangsters he decided to give the illusion of compliance by making the protection payment. A check of his available cash assets revealed a little over 700,000 lire, the Italian currency, equal at the time to around $430 in United States dollars. He would reluctantly pay and agree to the terms of 15,000 lire per week with the hope of secretly being gone by the next week.

The original two extortioners returned with two more men for a show of muscle and to convince their prey of their evil intent.

"I have reconsidered and will pay the money; I want to keep my business and family safe. You win, I don't want any trouble."

"You are a wise man Mr. DeoMonte, we'll be back next week and every week for your payment."

The payment was made, and Vincent watched intently as they

disappeared ominously down the village's main street. His rage hovering just below the surface, he turned back reluctantly to his business with mixed but intense emotions.

Where to go? Like many other Italians, Vincent had heard of opportunity in the United States. A new life, a new home, and he already knew of a few villagers who had made the trip.

As Vincent inquired around town, he heard many descriptions of the United States. "It's a land of wealth and even has streets paved with gold." Vincent's naivety allowed him to literally believe this story.

"You can live anywhere, make lots of money, have a big house," said another local businessman whom Vincent respected. A lack of education and an abundance of fear fueled Vincent's hope.

A fresh start, but it meant leaving everything and everyone they knew. Again the anger resurfaced as the shopkeeper contemplated having to relocate to a foreign land. So much to consider.

In many ways being essentially illiterate both Vincent and Rosa were dependent on others for assistance in many of their needs. Both knowing little English, their comprehension and second language skills had eroded from lack of consistent use. Vincent arranged for a late-night meeting with his boyhood friend Carlo who was a modestly successful carpenter. It was agreed Carlo would take over the business while Vincent went on what he described as a vacation.

"Carlo, I know you can run this business for me. We're leaving for a trip."

"I'm not sure I can do this as well as you."

"Do the best you can, that's all anyone can ask."

After explaining the inner workings of the store, Vincent handed over the keys with tears in his eyes. DeoMonte trusted no one. *Trust only family (Fidati solo della famiglia)!*

"I should be back in a week or two Carlo."

Vincent lived by a few but intensely strong values, he was steadfast in his loyalty to family and his faith, which now was being tested.

Later that evening Vincent unveiled the plan to Rosa. "We have to leave here."

Rosa again asked, "But why?'

He recounted the story of the mob insistence of the *shake down* payments to stay in business but not the degree of danger they were in now.

"Those strange men who came here are evil, part of La Cosa Nostra, very bad men. They threatened us."

"Can we not go to the police?"

"Rosa, my innocent Rosa, the police can't protect us. Some of them are even paid off and would look the other way. You know books; I know the world."

The chase scene she had witnessed previously now made sense. She wondered aloud if there were not another way. The tense silence that followed from her husband was all the answer she needed. Vincent subscribed to the *man of the house* mentality and felt no need to explain any more. The decision was final and required no more discussion.

Together they hatched a plan to gather up a few of their most necessary belongings as to not raise suspicions of their permanent departure.

"Listen to me Rosa, take only what you need."

"We have little, but there are things that I will not leave behind."

Basic clothing, a family Bible, and some small keepsakes were stashed in innocent looking sacks. It was a sobering exercise taking inventory of your most basic belongings. After all, they had work hard most of their lives.

The uncertainty of their future hit them as they assured each other that everything would work out.

As they embraced, Rosa spoke, "Vincent, I trust you with my life, I will follow you and be obedient to you."

"I will protect you as best I can. We can start over."

"We may even do better in America; we'll work hard and hang on to each other. It's a new world and a new start."

Another possible advantage was the availability of doctors and medical help. Rosa always seemed to be sick, her energy level low, and she spent days bedridden. She suffered silently, but her illness was evident. Maybe a change of location and this new land would offer a better life.

To avoid any more confrontation or confusion they both waited to tell their family members about their move to America.

Hand in hand Vincent and Rosa stood in the courtyard of her parents the DeNatali's and tried to explain their decision. "We're going to the United States for new opportunity," Rosa explained as Vincent stared at the ground.

"Why are you taking my daughter from her homeland," wondered Thomasino.

Vincent addressed his father-in-law, "We want to start a new life; do things we can't do here. Raise a family with chances for a better life."

After talking to Rosa's parents, it was determined that travel plans from the seaside city of Naples by steamship would be the safest, most logical escape. Informed by a citizen who had previously made the trip, he explained that the two could book passage aboard a ship for 44,397 lira each, leaving their life savings to about 662,000 lira or about $410 US dollars. If they were willing, they could travel in a method known as *steerage*. This standard of transportation could be booked for less money and would still get them to their destination.

"We will leave for Naples in the darkness, Rosa. We will be safer that way. We'll go by train to Naples."

"What will we do when we get to Naples?" asked Rosa.

"We will go by ship to the United States."

After dark the couple took a long last look at their store front, and loaded down by their belongings, they walked to the rail station. Neither could resist looking back. The last of the days light was showing through the bell tower of the church—the church where they had both been baptized and married. The cobblestone road they had traveled hand in hand and was the road to familiar places was now looking narrow and lit only by the rising full moon.

Rosa asked Vincent, "Are you afraid?"

"I'd be more afraid to stay than to go."

There was no joy in the hearts of this couple as they were overcome with a flood of memories and the uncertainty of what lay before them. The only place they had ever really known, memories of family and a simple life, and now they were being almost forced to leave. They were leaving the old world to start a new life. They felt more anxiety than adventure, and with a tearful goodbye, they bid farewell to their lifelong home.

Chapter II

The Transatlantic Escape

In Villa Cristo people worked hard, played, and prayed together. Sunday mass and holy days were observed with attendance by most everyone. The church consisted of an old stone structure with stained glass windows and was the scene of baptisms, weddings, and funerals. The little villa was less than perfect, but it was peaceful. Often the younger residents sought a better life by moving off in search of fortune and a more exiting life, much like Vincent's brothers. Family meals as well as holidays were festive and found families piled around tables full of food—traditional Italian dinners and deserts were always served. An Italian tradition that was strictly followed was that the male members of the family were seated and served by the women. After the men finished, the women ate and then started the cleanup while the men retired to shady spots to drink more wine, discuss the events of the day, or play cards or maybe bocce ball. The memories of such events brought smiles to the faces of Vincent and Rosa DeoMonte.

Vincent was a less than romantic partner. The two didn't always exchange "I love yous" before falling asleep each night. Rosa would proclaim her love, but even when Vincent didn't reciprocate, she knew deep down he loved her; he loved her in his own way.

After watching his father's work ethic, Vincent followed by working alongside him and spent time seasonally in Rosa's family's vineyard. Early on he decided formal schooling wasn't necessary because he would learn a trade and earn an honest living using his hands more than his head. He hid his embarrassment over his limited ability to read and write. As a boy and even young man he tried to avoid conflict, but if he felt threatened, he let his temper get the best of him and took his frustration out on the transgressor. Often feeling inadequate, he tried to be dependable and let his actions speak to his station in the community.

Any kindnesses toward Rosa were very much appreciated by her. While he rarely spoke any love language, he did occasionally compliment his wife.

"You look nice today."

"Thank you, Vincent. I try. I want you to be proud of me."

"You're a good wife, you cook, clean, and take care of our business and home."

The occasional compliment, a new dress, or the rare bouquet of wildflowers fueled the hope that he would become a bit more mellow. Their days were often almost robotic in nature, but they had become comfortable with their tedious routine. Rosa saw her husband as a hard worker and trusted him to make business decisions. She believed that their future, although slow, was a sure path to long term happiness. Their circle of family and friends was close knit, but there was an unspoken code of privacy in each family. The store occupied most of their time, though Sundays were reserved for rest and often visits with other members of the community. With little entertainment, laughs may have been infrequent, but most days ended with peaceful sleep and normal plans for the next day. Slowly they were building a good life and were hoping to start their own family with children to carry on their name and the business.

"We have to get up early and get ready for business tomorrow."

"Can't we stay up and talk?"

"We can talk while we work in the morning, time for sleep."

The time had arrived for the next part of their adventure. Vincent and Rosa sat side by side in a railroad car, the first rail travel experience for both. The hum and rhythmic thump of the rails was monotonous, and the ride left no view of the southern Italian countryside as it was hidden by a veil of darkness.

Rosa was emotionally drained. "I'm getting sleepy Vincent."

"Lay your head on my shoulder and sleep. I'll stay awake."

The moon was blocked by the cloudy night sky, and the couple remained silent for much of the ride. In his heart Vincent felt like they were being exiled, not leaving on a pleasure trip. He remained suspicious of everyone and felt that tingle in his neck from believing someone was staring at them from behind. Were they being followed? He dared not stare, but his eyes darted around the passenger car. Strangers, all these unfamiliar faces unnerved him. Who were these people? Why were they on the train?

Rosa commented, "This railroad car smells like smoke from cigarettes and cigars."

The seats were tattered and uncomfortable and Rosa noticed that the window she stared out of was cracked. She wondered silently what was to become of them. Her nervousness was punctuated by her queasy stomach which seemed to be her constant companion due to an undiagnosed illness. Many of the passengers chattered nervously as the train made its way through the countryside.

"This will give us some time for me to teach you more English, enough to make you comfortable in the United States." Vincent grunted a small sign of approval and uttered, "I'm Italian."

The time passed slowly until after what seemed like days but was only hours, lights could be seen in the distance—a blend of city lights and the rising sun.

"Are you tired Vincent?"

"A little, but I have to keep my eye's open all the time."

The train slowed as they pulled up to a wooden landing at the station, they were just outside the Naples city limits. Their luggage was retrieved from the overhead bins, and they waited in line to depart the train. They could smell the ocean air, a new scent for the couple who had rarely left the confines of Villa Cristo. They scanned the sky in search of the sight to match the sound of seagulls—also another foreign sight to them.

Rosa spoke first, "It all looks so different."

Vincent added, "Do you wonder what the United States looks like?"

"I saw pictures in schoolbooks. Some of it looks like Italy, but much of it looks very different."

There was so much going on around them, the conversation gave them temporary relief from their worries. The pre-trip jitters soon brought them back to reality. Rosa spotted several steamer trunks on the train landing and wondered if that was a necessity for their voyage.

"Vincent do we need something like this (*Vincent, abbiamo bisogno di qualcosa del genere*)"?

After surveying multiple sizes and shapes, it looked like a good idea to transport the only possessions they had rescued from their home. A small shop displayed the trunks, and the couple, toting their bags, entered and asked about the availability and price of a small black steamer trunk in the corner of the store. Vincent inquired, "How much (*Quanto*)?"

The shop keeper replied, "This trunk is used and is priced at 16,443 lire, $10 American."

Vincent agreed begrudgingly and paid. As Rosa began carefully loading their belongings into their new purchase, Vincent noticed a bank where he might be able convert his Italian currency to U.S. dollars. The couple carted their trunk to the building across the street, and Vincent entered to complete the transaction and soon wrapped the bills in his handkerchief and pushed all but $20 deep down into his pocket. The $20 bill was hidden in his right shoe.

As Rosa waited outside, a stranger approached her and tried to strike up a conversation. Vincent seeing this through a window bolted from the bank building and in a loud, angry voice began chastising the man and his wife. The stranger turned away making a quick exit, Vincent admonished his wife. "Don't talk to strangers!"

With tensions already high, she responded only with an icy stare.

Each grasped one of the side handles on the trunk and began walking clumsily toward their destination, the shipyard. They made their way slowly and silently, hauling the cumbersome trunk toward the docks visible in the distance maybe 100 yards away.

Rosa, exhausted and still a bit angry at Vincent's harsh words, had taken a seat on their luggage. Vincent approached a ticketing agent and inquired about booking passage to New York.

"How much for two people to travel on board to the United States? We want to go steerage." The look he got from the agent should have told him something. It was a combination of surprise with a side order of disdain.

"Have you traveled steerage before?"

Vincent merely replied, "No."

With no more conversation, tickets were stamped and put in a small envelope. As Vincent walked a way, the agent sarcastically called out, "Good Luck (*Buona fortuna*)."

Vincent walked to his wife holding the two tickets for the steamship *William Peirce*. They made their way after getting directions to the gigantic ship. They looked at each other almost to say, *Is this really happening?*

"No matter what happens, Vincent, I love you."

"Stay close to me Rosa, we do not know what lays before us."

Now the reality and magnitude of this quest hit them.

After showing his tickets to the boarding agent, he was given a luggage receipt.

"Don't lose this. It's the only way you can get your bags back when you arrive," advised the agent.

"I won't lose it."

Rosa asked, "Do you want me to hold onto the ticket?"

Vincent ignored her question.

After they retrieved a few items they might need on the journey, they locked their trunk and watched as their belongings were whisked away amid a wide variety and assortment of other passenger's travel luggage. They were ill prepared for what came next.

Other passengers, well dressed and looking very affluent, were being escorted to the top deck of the monstrous vessel. As they made their way up a creaky metal walkway, they were ushered into a cavernous area below deck.

The uniformed man called out, "Steerage travels this way."

As they made their way below deck into an area who's only light was from evenly spaced portholes eight feet up. They were greeted by a smell that was a curious combination of stale human waste and the bleach which they had been accustomed to using in sanitizing the store. More pervasive was an overwhelming odor of stale, foul air. As more people entered it became apparent why there was a discounted price to travel less stylishly. The portholes that allowed limited light offered no ventilation.

Instructions were barked out in several languages about the availability of meals and the restriction from the upper decks and other areas of the ship. In Italian, "*Non puoi andare sopra il ponte* (You can't go above deck)."

The cross section of nationalities on board became more evident as people began to converse and search for other passengers of their own native homelands. Nervous smiles were freely exchanged as the multiple dialects were discovered and groups of people with the same dream began to form. The next several days would be spent below the deck and in harsh, Spartan conditions.

"I feel like I'm going to throw up. I feel dizzy, Vincent."

"It's probably the smells and the food. There's not much we can do."

"I can hang on. I'll try to sleep."

Meals proved to be a mad dash—kind of a *come and get it*

affair. A hand bell was the signal that food was about to be served. People swarmed to giant metal pots of warm food that would be unceremoniously dipped and splattered into old metal bowls. Passengers who were smart enough to hide a fork or spoon could retrieve the unappetizing fare into their mouths conventionally. Others used their fingers to shovel food into their mouths. Meals were different every day and might consist of a stew, pasta, or soup. Often it was a combination of what the first-class passengers didn't eat the previous day.

Ocean going travel was tedious. The top speed of most of the steamship was 30 miles per hour. The 5,300 miles from Italy to New York took eight to ten days. Those who opted for steerage generally shared the hull of their particular vessel with over 2,000 more like-minded passengers.

Vincent and Rosa huddled together in the evenings. Sleep came slowly. One saving grace was the rolling of the ship which served to rock all the passengers to sleep.

The night whispers of the other passengers made for a strange blend of languages, and they were united in wishing that this trip was over.

"Vincent are you asleep?"

"No, I feel like I have to stay awake and watch over you."

"Oh Vincent, I have God for that. He will watch over both of us."

"I was trying to imagine our life in America, Rosa."

"We'll have years of happiness, and our hard work will pay off." Rosa voiced trailed off as she drifted into sleep.

Because of the minimal light, it was at times hard to determine the time. During the days they would take turns moving around in an attempt to break up the boredom. One would hold the spot they had staked out as their home territory while the other would walk amid the maze of strangers. They both avoided socializing.

"Try not to look at anyone as you walk, Rosa. We need to mind our own business. I'll watch you as you move around."

As the days passed, depression crept in. Rosa felt poorly but didn't complain. To attempt to lift their spirits they talked about what America must be like. Conversations centered around what their life might be like, but migrated often to memories of their lives in Italy.

Rosa spoke of her hopes and dreams, "It will be exciting to live in a bigger city. We'll make friends and learn about our new country. I'm excited but also a little afraid."

"I'll protect you and take care of you. We don't need a lot of friends. We need family, our own family."

Vincent and Rosa had childhoods that were intertwined because of the proximity of the residents in the small town. Now they were preparing for more people and a city.

"Remember the small stream that flowed just outside Villa Cristo? I always liked it when we would take off our shoes and wade the shallow, cool water. Do you think there will be a little stream near our American home?"

"I don't know. Were there pictures like that in the books you read in school?"

"I don't remember. I was daydreaming about you, our children ,and grandchildren most of the time. I'm sure there will be a place like that. I like to believe every place has streams, pastures, bright skies, and flocks of sheep with shepherds tending them, and grapes growing in the fields close by. I hope there's a nice church close by."

Throughout the days onboard the ship, they imagined life in the United States and shared hopes and simple dreams—home, family, and good jobs, most of all safety and peace. The nights seemed long—the summer heat was unbearable and the accompanying stench was repulsive. The simplest of pleasures were impossible—no way or place to bathe or washing clothes and changing into different clothing was impossible because most of their belongings were stowed in their trunk. The bathroom facilities available were anything but private and equally as disgusting as most other steerage activities.

"Surely we are getting close to the end of the voyage." Rosa hoped for them to dock soon and depart this terrible travel. "I've lost track of the days. It seems like they've all run together."

"We have to be getting close. Maybe we can ask one of the ship's crew."

Vincent periodically would check the pocket watch that he had been given by his father years ago. Time seemed to stand still, yet he remained vigilant, his eyes scoping out the area constantly. Their life savings was tucked into his front pocket which he constantly patted nervously to feel for the money and make sure it hadn't been lost or stolen.

Vincent had asked Carlo, who had years of schooling, to write out his and Rosa's name on a sheet of paper to use for identification. He had also memorized locations—New York City and more important St. Louis Missouri.

"Vincent, I talked to a few people who knew of this St. Louis. They said it was big and everything moved quickly. They say there is a place of mostly Italians, they all joined in to make a large neighborhood, something like our village."

"I hope we can find people who speak Italian, understand our customs, food, faith, and culture. I want to find work and settle down. I want to escape far from the threats and any danger."

Rosa followed along with little knowledge of this plan to join the colony of Italian Catholics.

"God will guide us," Rosa said. She often pulled out a weathered leather purse that contained her rosary and a few coins. The rosary beads had long ago surrendered the black lacquer that covered the individual beads from years and prayers. The cross on the rosary had worn to a smooth finish with the figure of the crucified Christ almost unrecognizable. Thousands of times the beads had passed between her fingers as she prayed the individual prayers. Particularly now she prayed feverishly for her husband, her health, and her future.

The days aboard the slow-moving ship passed imperceptibly, but finally on the eighth day there was a huge stir of excitement.

Fear and faith were served in equal amounts at that moment.

"What is it? Why is everyone excited, Vincent?"

"I don't know. It must be important."

Then for a moment the face of the Statue of Liberty appeared through the portholes of the ship.

Rosa recognized this as the entrance to the United States. "We're here!" she exclaimed though tears of joy.

New York Harbor. The United States greeted the DeoMonte's and all those seeking the new life, the American Dream. Now aware of what people were cheering about, they both smiled nervously, not even sure what it was they were smiling about.

"We're here, we've arrived in America (*Erano qui, Siamo arrivati, è l'America*)," being shouted out in their native Italian was music to their ears.

Vincent and Rosa hugged, and tears of joy escaped their eyes. In unison they said, "My love (*Amore mio*)." Rosa, beaming with joy, blurted out, "I want to start a family soon!"

Things often do *not* work out the way people hope. Little did they know.

Chapter III

A New Life

The procession of immigrants departing the ship was moving agonizingly slow. It had the look and the feel of cattle being herded, and everyone after days of the traveling ordeal was anxious to be back in the open air and on land. Vincent clutched Rosa's hand as they inched their way forward.

"Hold onto my hand so we don't get separated."

"I'm so glad we have arrived and are on land Vincent."

"Just hang on, we'll get through this together."

Other passengers climbing the ramp were craning their necks to get a first glimpse of this place called the United States. After hours of trying to disembark they began the search for their single piece of luggage. Seeing others retrieve their belongings the DeoMonte's again found themselves in what seemed an endless line.

A uniformed agent called out, "Luggage pick up here." He was holding up a suitcase to signal to those who weren't fluent in English.

Marching through the line with ticket stub in hand Vincent handed over the claim check and waited impatiently for the steamer trunk containing their precious few possessions. Repeating the scene from over a week ago, they each took a hold of a handle and started to the next stop to be identified, go through a medical check, and receive the next documents.

"Follow these travelers Rosa. They look like they know what to do."

Lines had formed that again were snaking through a massive processing center. Slowly each person answered questions about their name, country of origin, age, and more. The noise was deafening as multiple languages were trying to make themselves be understood over the din. Tiny steps, feet shuffling, the lines moved at an incredibly slow pace.

"Stay close to me," Vincent said loudly to Rosa.

She nodded her understanding. After several more hours they reached the front of their line. Exhausted, they strained to listen to the instructions they were given and prepared to answer the questions required to be allowed entrance to the streets of New York City.

A language and words familiar to them came from yet another man. He looked like many men from home, an Italian.

He asked, "*Come ti chiami* (What's your name)?"

Vincent smiled but was barely able to be hear. He replied, "Vincent DeoMonte, and this is my wife Rosa (*Vincent DeoMonte e questa è mia moglie Rosa*)."

Rosa remained silent as to not talk over her husband. No one was able to hear over the background noise and frustrated the clerk who repeated the question. Nervous, confused, and words being drowned out, Vincent was struggling to recall his early English lessons. The clerk looked angrily at the pair and shrugged his shoulders. Remembering the paper Carlo had written he pulled the rumpled piece of paper from his pocket and handed it to the clerk through the opening in a wire-screened partition.

The poorly written scrawled note was read out loud by the frazzled clerk. "Vincent LeoMorte?" Barely able to hear, the anxious, hopeful, and confused immigrant Vincent smiled then nodded yes.

The poor penmanship now made a permanent change in the lives of these Italian immigrants. Not uncommon during the process, names were erroneously changed to a different spelling and pronunciation. The name DeoMonte was now legally documented as LeoMorte! Not realizing the error, the couple took their paperwork and moved to yet another line for a quick physical checkpoint used to try to eliminate the entrance of sick passengers into the United States.

"Rosa, another line for us."

"I hope we're done soon; I'm not feeling well."

"Soon, Rosa, soon."

Physicians were manning a medical assembly line of a wave of human beings. Stethoscopes listened for the regularity of heartbeats, a look in the ears, eyes, and throats, and a visual check of the wellness of each potential new citizen was conducted.

The summer conditions were taking their toll on Rosa, and as she was about to be examined, she passed out hitting the floor with a sickening thump. Eyes rolled back, unresponsive, and pale she was carried into a room a few feet away.

"Rosa, Rosa," the panicked Vincent called out, but his wife couldn't hear him.

Vincent was told to wait outside. In the dimly lit hallway, he took a seat on their trunk. His nervousness wasn't very well concealed as his hands shook uncontrollably, sweat beads poured off his forehead, and his legs were in a constant twitch. After what seemed like hours but was only 15 minutes, Rosa appeared and exited the room with a doctor supporting one arm and a nurse the other. Some color had come back to her face, and the doctor leaned over with his diagnosis.

"Your wife is alright; she just pregnant (*Tua moglie sta bene, è solo incinta*)," the physician said.

"What?!"

Rosa's face was locked in a look of fear while Vincent appeared stunned by this announcement.

"Did you know?" Vincent asked Rosa.

"I had no idea."

A new land, home, job, and a new baby? The stunned Vincent instinctively reached for his pocket to check the presence of his life savings, his immediate thought being, *Can we afford this?*

Unnerved and panicked, his most sobering thoughts turned to his wife.

"I'm worried. Can you survive having a baby? Can we have a healthy baby?"

Rosa pulled her rosary from her pocket, saying, "Vincent, God will see us through any storm."

He wondered, *Will she be able to do this, survive the birth of a child?* He stood up and embraced her, hoping to reassure her even though he had doubts. Plans for two turned instantly to plans for three. His emotions were mixed, but he knew their faith would sustain them.

After gathering themselves, they started making their way to the roads of New York and soon realized the streets were not in reality paved with gold. They felt foolish, and the knots in their stomachs grew larger.

"This doesn't look like what I thought it would," a shocked Vincent said.

"Vincent, we will make it, as long as we're together."

But the biggest surprise was the enormity of the city itself. Villa Cristo boasted about 400 residents; New York City five and half million. The huge buildings in the heart of the city created a skyline that very few people of any nationality could imagine. The heat radiating from the pavement was stifling. In the shadows people of all descriptions were walking shoulder to shoulder with strangers. Cars, certainly a rare sight in southern Italy, were moving at scary speeds. Amidst the confusion the Italian immigrants took in every sight and sound.

Is this what our new home will look like? wondered Rosa. *What have we come to?*

The blaring of car horns, people stopping at corners watching odd, three-colored traffic signals, huge store windows with more clothes and housewares than they even knew existed. Policemen were riding horses in the streets. The smell of fresh air from their homeland was replaced with fumes from factories, businesses, and automobiles. Stores had displays of dead chickens and raw meat, an assortment of clothes, and in the windows a mannequin modeled ladies' underwear! Vincent and Rosa turned away in embarrassment.

"What kind of place was this Vincent?"

A flood of emotion had overcome both travelers. Hope and optimism had been replaced with confusion, fear, and a large dose of an unsure future. The nauseating feeling and jangled nerves would be their constant companions for several days to come.

"How are you feeling, any better?"

"I'll be fine; I'm just tired and feeling weak."

Vincent was now second guessing his decision while Rosa was relegated to just following along submissively. This was the man she trusted and loved, now in a foreign land she clung to him with a strength tempered by an equal amount of fear.

Almost immediately after this fantasy faded, they were greeted by the sweet smell of a street vendor's food cart. Strange looking meat—hot dogs! They resembled the Italian sausages (*salsiccia*) from home but looked and smelled much differently.

"Let's try this food, maybe if we eat, we'll both feel better."

"I have *mal di stomaco* (an upset stomach)."

"You need to eat something, something for you and the baby."

Ravenously hungry Vincent held up two fingers and handed the man the $20 he had retrieved from his shoe. The vendor stared at the bill and then Vincent, who stood in amazement as the vendor started returning several different looking bills and a few dull coins. His first transaction on U.S. soil was confusing. Still not comfortable with currency, a new learning experience, he couldn't be sure of how much he was getting back. The couple wolfed down the foreign food and used his handkerchief to wipe the saliva from the corners of their mouths.

"That's a train whistle. Let's start that way Rosa."

They followed the sounds of the bells, whistles and screaming steam release to their next mode of transportation. They were learning quickly.

Vincent hoisted the trunk onto his back. "I'll carry this from now on. I need to protect you from lifting and carrying the heavy things."

An exhausted Rosa said, "I'm tired I hope we can rest soon."

Vincent's mind was racing. He silently vowed to protect his wife and child from any harm. They soon arrived at the train station. Winded from the walk, they sat down on a bench and watched as people scurried about the station.

"Rosa, look how the people move like ants, they're all in a hurry."

"Quiet, Vincent, they'll hear you."

New and nervous they watched to see where travelers went and mimicked their actions to continue the next leg of their journey. After Vincent found an agent who could speak Italian, he inquired about the cost of the train trip from New York to St. Louis.

"A ticket is $32.00."

Vincent looked at his roll of money and thought how fast it would go.

The train trip was 950 miles. What choice did he have?

"I need two tickets."

After they exchanged money for the tickets, the man advised him, "The next train will be leaving in three hours, go to this track." He pointed to the left. "Good luck and have a safe trip. Do you understand?"

"Yes, thank you."

As they made their way to the waiting area for the train trip, the newly named LeoMortes, still unaware of the inadvertent name change, sighed a breath of relief as they anticipated the long trip to what they hoped would be their new home.

"Again, we wait Rosa. At least we can travel like people on the train, not like animals on a ship."

Again, a check of the time on his pocket watch, Vincent figured the 19-hour train trip would put them in St. Louis, Missouri, at around noon the next day.

Tickets tucked into his front pants pocket, Vincent asked Rosa,

"How are you feeling?" Before she could reply he asked further, "What do you think about bringing a baby into this world?"

"I'm tired and excited."

Vincent looked quizzically at his wife. "In Italiani."

Rosa replied, "*Sono stanco ed emozionato.*"

They took turns napping on the hard bench. On waking Vincent looked around to find a bathroom.

"Keep your eyes open. I'll be right back."

As he made his way into a men's room he was bumped by a man in the doorway. He immediately felt a tug on his pants where his watch was attached to the belt loop in his slacks. This crook was trying to steal his pocket watch! Vincent reacted immediately and followed with a violent, abrupt push of the criminal into the closest wall. *What kind of place is this?* he thought. He hurried back to Rosa. He could wait a while longer, and he wanted to make sure she was not the target of another lawbreaker.

"A man tried to steal my watch, we have to be on guard all the time."

No more sleep for him, but Rosa leaned over with her head resting on his shoulder. Despite the noise she was soon sleeping soundly, and Vincent realized how innocent and vulnerable she was in this place. He thought about how much he loved his wife in a new way he had never imagined. She was carrying a baby—his baby—and he vowed to make a better life for his growing family.

After sitting, and the occasional short walk to stretch their legs, they heard a booming voice announce, "Train leaving on track four for St. Louis, Missouri."

They understood enough to leap to their feet to prepare to board their second train in ten days. They stopped only to ask multiple other travelers until they found another couple from Italy who directed them to the correct spot to board for the long ride to their next destination.

"It's this way. That is the train you want," said the stranger.

Rosa leaned in close to Vincent. "I hope they're on the same train as us."

Their conversation was interrupted by the high pitch of train whistles announcing its arrival, the steam released from the locomotive also startled them each time they occurred. A maze of trains was all around them, now they just wanted to find their seats and begin the final part of their search for this mystery location—St. Louis.

"That's the one, that train right there," volunteered another conductor. There was a waiting train across the tracks. They watched as smoke billowed from the stack of a black, beastly-looking locomotive. This was the mode of transportation that took them from Villa Cristo to Naples, then the horrid experience on the steam ship, now another train would transport them to their final stop. This was lots of miles for people who had rarely left the safety of their ancestral homes.

Trunk in tow, they worked their way past the baggage car into an already crowded passenger car.

"Now we can go to the bathroom," announced Vincent.

They took turns going to the onboard lavatories to at least splash some water on their faces and unashamedly did a restricted cleanup of their bodies. They dabbed themselves dry with faded, off-white cloths from a pile of towels on the side of the sinks. Hardly a hot bath but some welcome temporary relief from the grit and grime of extended travel time.

"Rosa, do you want to sit by the window?"

"Yes, I want to see everything."

Rosa took a window seat while Vincent sat between her and a large man who sported a long beard and appeared to be a businessman by the way he was so neatly dressed. As he settled in, Vincent's relaxation turned to panic. His right-side front pocket was empty. Their money! He jumped up only to notice his balled-up handkerchief was sitting right beside him on the seat. He hoped the stranger next to him hadn't noticed, or he might try to lay claim to the secret stash. Vincent felt Rosa's hand searching for his, she needed the touch of reassurance that his grip would supply.

A loud announcement of, "All aboard!" startled them, and the train started to move, slowly at first and then gaining speed as it passed between many more identical-looking, long lines of coupled cars.

"Finally, on our way," an impatient Vincent said.

They felt relief at leaving the large, noisy, and perplexing look of such a mammoth city. As the train reached previously unexperienced speed of 50 miles an hour, Rosa peered out of her window and noticed the reflection of her husband in the glass. She smiled as his classic Roman profile was reflected in the window.

"You're very handsome."

Vincent smiled. "I know what I look like. We had mirrors."

After a short while the big city skyline turned into more of a rural landscape, and there were hints of the terrain of southern Italy. The sight of large rivers and deeply wooded places was intriguing to the travelers.

They poked each other often, spotting a new sight with the repeated phrase, "Look at that."

The motion of the train rocked many of the travelers to sleep. This created an assorted chorus of snores, breathing sounds, even giggles along with hushed conversations by those unable to doze.

A sharp shift in direction awakened Rosa in time for her to catch an intoxicating view of the sunset over a large field of tall corn with a large, red-roofed barn, and a plain, white farmhouse nestled between other fields. The view caused her to emit an audible sigh. She hesitated to wake Vincent to share the view—he was experiencing his first untroubled sleep in days. The golden sun slipped into the horizon and in minutes was just a memory. For the first time in a while she felt at peace, and she reached for her rosary, offering prayers of thanksgiving and hope for the baby inside her.

As night fell the passenger car fell silent, and most everyone had settled into a group sleep. Hours and miles passed, as a noticeable change in speed was the only indication that they were nearing the city of St. Louis.

"Wake up Vincent, the train is slowing down."

A garbled announcement was ended with the words, *St. Louis.* This was home. Various emotions erupted from the weary travelers, and people, tired of being confined to seats, almost simultaneously stood up.

"It feels good to stand up," Vincent said as he stretched and bumped the man next to him.

Rosa said, "I'm anxious to see the city, but I'm a little scared too."

"We can't let anyone see that we are scared. People prey on the weak," countered Vincent.

A large overhead sign with oversized red letters reading, **Union Station**, greeted the train. Now to explore this place and find the Italian ghetto hopefully located nearby. The immediate appearance was that of the metropolis they had just left but smaller in size. More tall buildings and swarms of people all seemingly in a hurry. After once again being reunited with their single piece of luggage, Vincent and Rosa stared at each other.

Now what? wondered Rosa.

After a short walk they fortuitously spotted a fruit stand with a lone figure, a short dark-haired man, standing in front of it with an apron snuggly tied around his waist. The stand had a small Italian flag on either end.

"Look Rosa, that's a good sign."

"Vincent, he looks like one of our countrymen, hopefully he can direct us to the Italian section of this city."

The stand owner beamed brightly as Vincent greeted him in his native tongue. "*Buon pomeriggio cugino* (Good afternoon cousin)."

Still a little hesitant to try his English he continued, "My name is Vincent."

In response the man said, "I'm Vito Pagano." After exchanging pleasantries Vincent picked out a few pieces of fruit, two apples and a half dozen peaches, Rosa's favorite.

"I want to buy these."

Vincent's intention was more to ingratiate himself to his new acquaintance rather than as a business transaction.

"We just arrived today, this moment from Italy. Can you tell me how to find the Italian part of town?"

Smiling the stand owner simply said, "Sure."

"I owned my own business, a grocery store in Villa Cristo."

Vito continued, "There's a community containing almost all Italians starting six blocks north."

He began describing the completeness contained in a large area, "There's a church, St. Francis of Assisi, several stores, and almost everything you could need located in that area."

Buses ran past the group as did these strange looking trolley cars traveling down the center of a familiar looking street constructed of cobble stone—it looked just like home in Italy only wider and longer.

Vito explained much about every aspect of navigating the streets, the living conditions, and how to stay safe.

"You should know many Americans (*Americani*) dislike many the Italians invading their city," he cautioned Vincent. "It's important that you try to speak English so as not to anger the old-time residents of this country."

Rosa, in the meantime, was listening closely but exhausted and ready to get unpacked and off her feet.

"Vincent, can we go now?" an impatient Rosa asked.

Vito mentioned, "There's an Italian grocery store—the Valenti brothers, Lorenzo and Sam, they own and operate it."

Vito who had learned enough English to get by offered to help Vincent and Rosa get aboard a bus rather than walk the six blocks.

"Let me show you my friend. You might get lost."

The prospect of getting lost sent Vincent into a paralyzing fear.

"If you can wait, I will show you the way and introduce you to some of the other Italians."

"Thank you, Vito. Is there some place to stay around there?"

Vincent was overjoyed at Vito's insistence they spend the night in his small apartment.

"When I first arrived, other Italians did the same for me. We have to stick together."

Vincent and Rosa accepted the kind gesture and for the first time in a while were feeling good about the decision to settle here.

This was good, maybe Rosa's prayers were being answered.

Chapter IV

Settling In St. Louis

After a short bus ride, Vito said, "Follow me," as he escorted Vincent and Rosa up a flight of steps to a small apartment. It was dimly light by one lamp and sparsely furnished. Vito lived there with his wife, Concetta, and two small children, both boys, one named Santo, the younger one Nino. Both boys had the look of the children from southern Italy with large, dark brown eyes and hair to match.

"This is my wife, Concetta." She was a short, stocky woman who looked like she enjoyed eating as much as cooking but had a kind face. Her garb was like Rosa's—plain and a faded black.

Typical Italian, she asked, "Are you hungry?" What a question.

Vincent responded, "We haven't eaten all day." Feeling awkward, he added, "We can pay you for your kindness."

Vito shook his head. He explained, "This is the same welcome I got when I first arrived. I appreciate the chance to do the same for another *Italiani* (Italian)."

Vito showed them to the room the boys occupied. "I'm sorry this small bed is all we have to offer." The room was furnished with only a bed and a small dresser that showed a lot of wear. Happy to have a real bed to sleep in, they returned to the kitchen from which eminated the smell of genuine Italian sauce from a deep pot resting on the eye of a stove.

"Oh, the smell! It reminds me of home, Italy," Rosa said.

"America, this is our home now, Rosa," replied Vincent.

Rosa noticed another pot was boiling and had a mound of

linguine noodles rolling in the boiling water. A loaf of hard-crusted bread was siting on a paper bag and had already been half sliced in preparation for the meal.

"Come, sit down," Vito said with a smile. Sitting down and sliding up the table, Vincent noticed the family had been Americanized as everyone sat at the table—not just the men, as was the old-world tradition. Mismatched plates were heaped with the linguine, and the smell of all the ingredients of the sauce caused Vincent and Rosa to embarrassingly salivate. Garlic, oregano, basil ,and the tomato smells made it seem like home, the home that they had fled.

Ready to start, Vito said, "Let's eat."

Simple fare but a feast to the weary family, they made plans for the next day while devouring the meal. Remembering his previous advice from Vito, Vincent responded, "Thank you," followed by a quizzical look as if to ask, *Is that correct?*

The men talked and planned to get further acquainted in the morning hours.

The DeoMonte's thanked their hosts, "We'd like to go to sleep now if that's all right." They excused themselves and adjourned to the bedroom to retire for the night. They carefully disrobed, folded their clothes, and laid hem on the floor, their underclothes served as their sleepwear.

As they tried to fit themselves into the small bed Rosa commented using one word about the close quarters. "Nice."

Vincent didn't share her sentiments knowing any night movement would wake the other because of the additional weight in the bed caused it to groan.

Nonetheless, Rosa took a deep breath and took the thumb on her left hand and felt for the tiny gold band on her ring finger, a ritual she performed each night to insure she hadn't lost her simple wedding ring. "They're very nice people, I think we can be happy in this city."

Vincent took her hand and kissed it gently as he rolled away almost slipping off the side of the bed. Rosa rolled with him to take her normal place, "spooning" with him as was their habit for many years. She whispered to Vincent who already was snoring, "I love you."

Finally, a good sleep.

The sunrise served as their alarm clock, and as was their custom, they dressed quietly with little conversation passing between the two. They were surprised to see Concetta already up and a small can of coffee sitting on the sink. A red, white, and green banner indicated that this was an Italian brew, but the familiar smell was enough to convince the pair. An old metal percolator sat on the stove and a small glass knob centered on the lid showed the coffee was almost ready.

They entered the room with a quiet, "Good morning."

With little more to offer, their host poured the hot coffee into three cups as Vito appeared through a hallway, coming in quietly. Steaming and stout, the strong coffee provided a caffeine jolt, and Rosa gasped as she burned her lips on the black beverage.

"Good coffee, strong and hot."

The children were laying on their parents' bedroom floor, concealed in a pile of quilts and still sleeping soundly.

"Hope you slept well," Vito said to break the silence.

Vincent responded, "Very well (*molto bene*)." As Rosa smiled and nodded in agreement, and at the same time, in hushed tones, not sure of her English, said softly, "Yes, thank you."

As they drained their cups, Vito announced, "Let's take a short walk and introduce you to the neighborhood."

Rosa asked, "Can we visit the church? I would like to pray."

"Sure," said Vito.

The three stepped out of the old brick building, down the stone steps, and out into the humid, morning air. Vito began taking on the role of tour guide walking briskly and pointing to various buildings and identifying their purpose and owners.

"This is the business district, all Italians!"

"It's nice to be around our own people," Vincent added.

"All families; we're safe here." Responded Vito.

In the distance a church steeple stood, the bell in the tower visible in the morning sky.

"There's the church, and down the street over there is the fish market, a pool hall, a shoemaker's shop, a barber, the tavern, a tailor store, and finally, at the end of the block, the grocery store I told you about yesterday. I can take you to the grocery store after we take your Rosa to the church."

As they walked toward the church, Vito began memorizing the layout and hoped that maybe he might get a job opportunity or place to stay close by.

After reaching the church, St. Francis of Assisi, they all climbed the steps, pulled open one of the large oak double doors, and stepped into a quiet vestibule leading to the main church.

"The church has been here a long time," whispered Vito reverently.

Every sound was magnified by the vaulted ceiling and stone walls; even their footfalls echoed off the walls. A giant crucified Christ was casting a shadow over the center aisle. It appeared to hang in midair from the ceiling and just above the cloth draped altar. A lone figure, a veiled lady, was kneeling on the left side in a pew halfway up to the communion railing. The stained-glass windows depicting the life of Christ were magnificently illuminated by the sun rising in the eastern sky. The colors were vivid, the entire scene silently demanded a reverence reserved for holy places.

"It's beautiful," Rosa said as she genuflected and took her place at the end of a pew in the rear of the massive church. Vincent whispered, "I'll be back in a little while to get you."

Exiting quickly Vincent caught up with his new friend, Vito, who suggested, "Let's go the Valenti brother's grocery store and let you meet them."

"Wonderful"

The men walked down the block and stopped at a store front hallway down the street. A circular sign read:

VALENTI BROTHERS GROCERIES

The pair stepped in; the squeak of a rusty hinge announced their entrance. The wood floor seemed to give slightly under the weight of the men. Behind the counter stood the proprietors—Lorenzo, the older of the Valentis, and Sam, the shorter brother, balding with thick, black-framed glasses.

"Good morning." Vito extended his hand to Lorenzo, "This is Vincent. He just arrived from the old country.

Vincent then joined in the conversation. "I owned a small grocery store in Villa Cristo."

Without hesitation Lorenzo glanced quickly at his brother and said to Vincent, "We've been looking for some help. Are you interested in a job?"

Stunned Vincent enthusiastically replied, "Yes!"

Overjoyed at the prospect of Vincent's good fortune Vito bade them farewell. "I'll see you later Vincent. Good luck!"

"*Scusaci* (Excuse us)," said Lorenzo as he and Sam stepped behind a curtain and conferred in a backroom. While they talked, Vincent surveyed the store and its contents. A wooden counter with separate compartments and glass front panes ran the length of the store. Every type of pasta noodle was there along with a large metal scoop to dip out contents to place on a nearby scale. Behind the counter, shelves held canned items and a few decorative pieces. Miniature Italian flags, small ceramic figurines of stylishly dressed Italian people, and a tiny model of a brightly colored horse-drawn cart used during festivals and holidays was the center piece. A refrigerated case—a recent acquisition—stood at the back of the store and held salami, cheese, olives, and more meat products. Sliding back doors offered access to the cold storage items.

While walking the store Vincent noticed a massive brick oven in the rear of the store. *Could it be?* He saw all the implements required to bake bread. The sight of all these things brought back memories. Distracted, Vincent hadn't noticed the presence of the Valentis, they were standing side by side and a few feet away from him. Sam asked, "What do you think of our store?

Vincent replied quickly, "I like it very much."

The brothers looked at each other, each waiting for approval from one another. "How would you like to work for us?" Not wanting to appear desperate Vincent inquired as to the pay. "*Quanto pagherai* (How much will you pay)?"

The brothers again stepped out of sight to determine an answer. "We can give you three dollars a day for six hours work. You would get Sunday off."

Vincent inquired, "Who bakes your bread?"

Sam responded, "I do."

Vincent countered with, "What if I baked it the night before (*E se l'avessi cotto la sera prima*)?"

The brothers were elated at the idea. "We could give you two more dollars and some groceries for the extra hours work."

Five dollars a day, and groceries! Bread for Monday would require him to work on Sunday night. At the time the average household earnings in the United States was just over $3200. Trying to figure on the fly, Vincent wondered aloud what rent was in the area.

Prepared to bargain even further Lorenzo added, "We have a two-room furnished apartment above the store; you can rent it for seven dollars a week."

Tears welled up in Vincent's eyes at his good fortune. They sealed the agreement with a handshake, and Vincent promised, "I'll be back at four o'clock this afternoon to begin baking tomorrow's bread."

Lorenzo asked one more question. "Can you speak more English? Our American customers, *Americani,* want to be addressed in English."

Vincent processed the question slowly, understanding a few words and answered back in a single word reply, "Sure." Silently he knew he would have to brush up quickly on his second language skills.

Trying to hide his excitement, he waited until he was out the door to run to the church to tell Rosa the good news. He almost fell trying to run full speed to the church building.

Yanking the massive oak door open, barely stopping to dip his finger in holy water and perform the sign of the cross, he scanned the church pews for Rosa. Almost out of breath he slid into the seat next to her and delivered the news excitedly.

"Yesterday—no job, no home. Today—job and home!"

She looked at him with great surprise at his message and the delivery in another language. "What's this (*Che cos'è questo*)?"

Vincent chided her, "In English, not Italian. We must use our English. I got a *lavoro*, eh…*job*…at the Valenti store."

A crudely stated, mixed message, but she deciphered the joyous words her husband had delivered. She looked at Vincent still trying to catch his breath and in a single word asked, "Home?"

"We stay in a room above the store."

Again, in a single word she wondered, "Above?" Rosa held up her rosary and despite his earlier command said in her native tongue, "*Ho pregato per un miracolo e ne ho ottenuti due* (I prayed for a miracle, and we got two)."

As the colors from the stained glass shown down on them, they took a place on the kneelers, held hands, and prayed in thanksgiving for their unexpected blessings.

They left the church, paused on the steps, look lovingly at each other, and Rosa spoke, "God is surely smiling down on us, we weathered the storms."

The couple began to make their way through the maze of buildings, inspecting the neighborhood in the morning light. In the distance on the next street over were high-rise tenement apartments. There were clotheslines across every balcony where recently washed clothes were drying naturally. The morning sounds of neighbors calling to each other from place to place, babies crying, dogs barking, and the occasional car horn blaring, which startled them both, made for a strange scene.

"In some ways this is a strange place," commented Rosa.

Pigeons circled overhead and landed on lines that ran from pole to pole, and people began to emerge from their homes strolling along the buildings and at times disappearing in the alleys that separated the structures. All the hustle and bustle made for quite a scene, much different than the sleepy village that was their home two weeks ago.

"It is strange, but now this is our home, our home for years to come. The home of our new baby," Vincent responded.

At a small café that had outside tables, the happy couple decided to celebrate with cups of genuine espresso. As they watched traffic flowed past, and familiar-looking people, very Italian, greeted them as they strolled by.

Spirits soaring, they decided to visit Valenti's for two reasons; so Rosa could meet the brothers and they could get a look at their new living quarters.

As they reached the door of the grocery, Vincent reminded his wife, "English please." They entered. Sam Valenti was at behind the display case wearing a tattered, stained, and wrinkled apron that had seen a lot of use. He greeted the couple.

"Good morning."

Rosa responded with a false sense of confidence, "Good morning!"

Sam smiled as Lorenzo made his appearance and walked around to shake the hand of his new employee and his wife.

"I imagine you would like to see the apartment?"

In unison they replied, "Yes." They went to the rear of the store and began the climb up a set of creaking steps, cautious to hold the rail that felt as loose as the boards on the stairway. A right turn at the top of the steps put them in front of a door that had a glass doorknob and faded wood as well as peeling black paint. As they tried to open the door, Lorenzo threw a knee into it to force the stubborn entry. Sunlight was the only available light until Lorenzo pulled the chain on a naked light bulb just above a large table. Three chairs were pushed under the unvarnished table, and a small stove was in the corner. A constant hum was coming from a refrigerator. They were ecstatic to see *ice box* as they called it, a relatively new invention.

Sam Valenti had been the last occupant of the room but had

since moved to a small home of his own. They could see through an arched door a brass, unmade bed. The linens were in disarray, and a woolen blanket was hanging off the bed onto the floor. A glance around the room gave credence to the John Howard Payne saying, *Be it ever so humble, there's no place like home.*

Peeling paint, cobwebs, a layer of dust that covered every flat surface—everything needed a good scrubbing. An old clawfoot bathtub was hidden from view behind a wall leading to the bathroom. A water stain on an otherwise white ceiling was evidence that the roof may have a slight leak. Nonetheless this place was heaven sent.

The DeoMonte couple was thrilled to have a place of their own. It was safe, dry, and shelter for them. Vincent thought how convenient it would be. Rosa's thoughts reflect that of a mother—her baby would be born here.

Vincent looked at his new employer and announced, "I'd like to fire up the wood burning oven and get started baking bread for tomorrow."

Lorenzo smiled in agreement. Moving cautiously down the steps the DeoMonte's made plans for moving their few possessions from the Pagano place to their own apartment. Rosa returned to the Pagano's to gather their clothes and their steamer trunk.

Vincent wrapped a white apron around his waist, anxious to get to work. Wood ignited, it might take an hour or better for the oven to reach baking temperature, so Vincent made his way to help his wife pack, tidy up their room, and haul their belongings back to the second story apartment they would call home.

By the time Vincent arrived, Concetta Pagano had laid out a small, midday meal.

"I hope this is enough," Concetta said.

"It's more than enough. Thank you for your kindness."

Vincent and Rosa ate quickly. There was work to be done. As Rosa said her goodbye to Concetta, Vincent slipped into the room they had occupied the previous night and unfolded a five-dollar bill, leaving it on the dresser as a token of appreciation for the kindnesses shown them. One more time the trunk was transported on Vincent's back as Rosa had armloads of clothes to lighten the load of the luggage.

"Rosa, don't try to carry too much. We'll get moved."

Rosa worried about their possessions. "I hope our things didn't get broken on the trip."

Entering the front of the grocery store, Vincent half-expected one of the Valenti brothers would offer to help get the load to the top of the steps. Both brothers stood by as Vincent struggled to make his way up to the second story. Puffing hard and pulling the trunk behind him with each step he climbed, the base of the trunk made a slamming thump on each step as he inched his way up one step at a time. Rosa waited at the base of the steps before beginning her climb with the folded clothes partially blocking her view. With all their worldly goods in the center of the floor Vincent brushed his wife's hair out of her eyes, "You look beautiful," then he started down the steps to check the progress of his oven. His words put a smile on her face that stayed there for hours.

The bread-baking spot had a large worn wooden table which clearly showed evidence of previous use. The center of this table had a depression indicating years of work—the edges of the wood top had a trail of black cigarette burns marking where earlier users had rested their smokes as they went about the business of baking bread. Excess flour was in all the cracks of the ancient workspace.

Who knew an old table could hold so many stories?

Vincent found a bucket and filled it with hot water to bring the table up to his standards as the brothers sneaked frequent peeks at their new employee. Every move calculated, Vincent went about the set up silently. Soon a giant bowl held a combination of flour, warm water, and yeast mix. Sam Valenti waited to see if Vincent added anything else to the recipe. Sure enough a teaspoon of sugar and two teaspoons of salt made their way into the bowl, and the hand-mixing began.

This would be a test batch for Vincent, producing a couple of full-size loaves. Kneading the dough with unmeasured hand-throws of flour went on for several minutes. Vincent allowed himself a smile as he realized he was being closely scrutinized; he welcomed the spying eyes as he did what he had done so many times before in his own store back in Italy. Letting the dough rise, he checked the oven to see if it *felt* like the 400 degrees it needed to be to bake the bread evenly. He scattered flour on the surface of an enormous wooden paddle used to slide the dough in and the finished bread out. The handle showed significant wear from what was likely decades of use and the production of thousands of loaves of *pane*, bread in Italian. Vincent always saved a small amount of dough to make *panini* (buns). He planned to surprise Rosa.

A few hours later, beautifully baked bread was laying on another table. Lorenzo and Sam walked over to inspect the freshly baked loaves.

They complimented Vincent. "This looks very good."

They tore a loaf open and sampled the warm, crusted bread and the perfectly cooked inside.

"Looks very good and tastes even better, you are a real Italian bread baker Vincent!"

Vincent, proud of himself proclaimed, "You see bread, I see my name. How many loaves would you like for tomorrow?"

"How about a dozen," responded Sam.

Hours later as Vincent climbed the steps with three buns, he called up to Rosa, and as he handed her the surprise allowed himself a celebration. "Today was a good day."

Rosa kissed him gently on the cheek. "I hope we have many more good days."

Chapter V

New Life

As weeks passed, Vincent and Rosa settled into a pattern. Vincent would be a few minutes early reporting to work, he could start restocking shelves and sweeping the floors, then prepping his bread-baking work area. The Valenti brothers arrived each morning finding cans stacked on the shelves with military precision, the counter was cleaned. Bread was displayed and was almost always sold out by 1 PM. They even had restaurants inquire as to the availability to get the bread that the store was becoming famous for offering. While Vincent had become a customer favorite as he waited on the clientele, suggested food, recipes, cut lunchmeats, and cheese, the brothers knew they couldn't keep up with the demand for the large increase in bread business. Pulling Vincent aside one day at closing time, they explained the need for him to bake bread full time.

"Larry and I can take care of the customers; we need you to bake more bread."

"I can do that, but what about the other things I do? Restocking before we, I mean *you* open, waiting on customers?"

"Vincent, we need more bread, the customers are asking for more ,and we run out early. We can sell to businesses and the public!"

"Just bake bread, the same bread you've been baking. We'll take care of the rest."

"I can do it. How about some specialty buns and loaves?"

"Just bake bread!"

Vincent saw this as job security and happily volunteered to do whatever was necessary. His new schedule would have him start the bread baking process around 6 PM and work until about 4 AM. Rosa would be right upstairs, and he could check on her periodically.

"Rosa admitted to Vincent, "Sometimes the smell of the bread baking wakes me up, and then I crave it."

"Every once in a while, when I have the time, I'll bring a fresh loaf upstairs."

"Can you *fix it up* for me."

"You mean cut it long ways, drizzle olive oil, grate some Romano cheese on it, sprinkle the salt, pepper, and oregano on it?"

"Yes, that's it. And bring me a few slices of salami and olives—it's like a feast to me."

Simple pleasures for simple people.

It was December of 1921. Rosa's physical shape was showing the signs of a baby on the way. Each week the couple managed to save a little of Vincent's pay. Hidden not too carefully on an upper shelf in a jar, the American currency was counted routinely as if they couldn't believe their good fortune. The second-story apartment was tidy and uncluttered and being modestly furnished including plans for the arrival of a new family member. Vincent had painted the rooms a light blue to cover the imperfections they found when they arrived. Small adornments were added, and of course the few items they carried across the Atlantic were carefully displayed and served as reminders of their years in the *Old Country*. But this was home now, and they had high hopes as they measured their progress. Rosa's health was always in question, good days were rare, but she remained optimistic. They had yet to find a doctor and certainly no answers to her constant fatigue.

"How are you feeling?"

"Some mornings not so good, I can't tell if it's the baby or just my usual not feeling well."

"You must take care of yourself. That baby is important. He will carry on our name."

"How do you know it's a boy?"

"I just know, I have a feeling."

Navigating the apartment steps was becoming a bit difficult for Rosa, but she almost daily made her way to the church a few blocks down the street. Even on the days she was feeling poorly, she found her way to the church pews to pray. Her rosary was a source of comfort as she prayed for every intention dealing with their future.

On a Sunday, while attending mass with Vincent, they met a young priest who had recently been assigned to the church—his first parish.

The priest was on the steps speaking to the parishioners as they exited the church.

"Good morning, Father," said the normally shy Rosa.

"I'm Father Angelo Parisi."

"This is my husband, Vincent DeoMonte."

Awkwardly Vincent blurted out, "You look awfully young to be a priest."

Recovering quickly, the priest responded, "I'm fresh out of the seminary, just been ordained."

The young priest continued, "Rosa, I see you often kneeling in the back pews by yourself."

"Yes, many times the church is empty, it allows me to talk to God privately."

"How long have you been in this parish?"

"Only a few months," Rosa said.

Vincent added, "We came from the old country, Villa Cristo."

Rosa unable to hide her joy added, "We're going to have a baby." The priest formed the sign of the cross over the couple, congratulated them, and excused himself leaving with a, "God bless you both *and* the baby."

They would see him often and eventually count him as a friend. Despite his youth, Father Parisi would become a big part of their lives and become like family.

Being Sunday, Vincent had no work responsibilities until that evening when he would be baking a large batch of bread for Monday's opening business. They both felt a sense of pride by their accomplishment at gradually assimilating to their new life in a new country.

"We're Italiani, but we are becoming good Americans," proclaimed Vincent.

In the cellar of the store Vincent had found an old winepress, musty smelling and covered in grime. He wondered about the history of this artifact and who it belonged to. He asked the brothers.

"I found an old press downstairs in the basement, who does it belong to?"

Sam and Larry Valenti looked at each other and gave a simultaneous shoulder shrug.

"I'd like to buy it."

"You can have it for, let's say, five dollars," offered Sam.

"Deal," said Vincent, mentally calculating that was a full day's pay.

That evening, in the catacomb of the building, Vincent planned to begin making wine to supplement his income. The winepress had been stored since the beginning of Prohibition in 1920. Vincent was unaware of the law but had heard of bootleggers marketing alcohol, a situation he didn't understand completely. There was no such regulation in Italy. Familiar with the process of winemaking from working with Rosa's family in their vineyard. Vincent understood it could be a matter of weeks and aging several more months before he had drinkable red wine. Much like baking the bread, he felt confident he could successfully produce wine from the local grapes. *Why not?*

In the dank secrecy of the cellar, he began his venture. After a few batches he began to store bottles of the red wine on a rack he fashioned from old scrap wood. The dark green, glass wine bottles were left over from the previous press owner and were scattered all over the cellar. A thorough clean up restored the bottles to like-new condition, and he found a case of wine corks buried under a pile of debris; he was in business. Once the wine was adequately aged, Vincent hid a bottle inside his coat and took the familiar walk down the block to give it to his good friend Vito Pagano as another thank you for his help months ago.

Vito continued to cement the friendship by frequently bringing fruit and vegetables to Rosa and Vincent. Vito asked Vincent where he had gotten the wine.

"I made it myself," Vincent innocently replied.

"It's against the law (*È contro la legge),*" warned Vito in hushed tones.

"I'm not selling it," countered Vincent, *and after all* he thought *there was sacramental wine used in the church.*

After a pause, Vito offered, "We could make some money selling this."

"How?" asked Vincent.

"Hidden at my fruit stand," replied Vito. "It would be hidden and offered only to trusted customers."

Hesitantly, Vincent agreed. "It must be kept a secret, and we'll split the money evenly."

Slowly and surreptitiously they started a small enterprise bringing both men a few extra dollars each week. There were lulls in the wine delivery as Vincent had to try to replenish the supply, but he managed to stash extra cash. Rosa was not aware of this illegal enterprise. Her health remained poor, but she managed to cook and clean and was fervent in her prayers along with her regular church visits. She often ran into Father Parisi who asked about her health and Vincent.

"So, how's is our little expectant mother today?"

"I'm a little shaky and ready to meet this baby."

"And Vincent—how is Vincent?"

"*Bene*, I mean good, Vincent is good. He works hard. I'm so glad we met you Father. I hope you'll baptize our baby. You're such a good young man, a devout man of God."

Rosa enjoyed attending Father Parisi's masses and receiving his frequent blessing. They gave her a sense of peace. Some days she struggled to escape the confines of her bed but hid her weakness and pain from Vincent.

"Rosa, you look tired today. Are you doing all right? You look pale, sit down."

"I get tried easily. Sometimes I stay I bed a little longer. I'll be fine."

Coupled with the pregnancy complications, her energy levels limited her physical activities. Vincent watched her closely and often thought of how tiny she looked except for her bulging *baby belly*.

Their first Christmas in the United States was celebrated with small gifts—she had made him a wool scarf for the cold Missouri winter mornings; he had found a carved nativity scene which they placed on a corner table.

"I made you a scarf, I know it's cold outside and even sometimes downstairs."

"*Buon Natale*, Rosa I got you this," Vincent said as he handed her the unwrapped wooden nativity scene.

"Vincent, in English. English! Merry Christmas," Rosa teased him.

"I bought you a can of peaches from downstairs."

"Vincent, I love the peaches. I even drink the syrup! But save the money. You work too hard for it."

"No fresh peaches now, and I know you like peaches. Every once in a while, it's all right. One can is seven cents. Early this morning, when no one else was there, I hit it on the side of the counter, dented cans are six cents."

Rosa laughed. That made Vincent smile, and they both had a look of love on their faces.

She cherished any kindness from Vincent, even a can of

peaches. He was an unemotional and stoic man, but she knew his love was manifested in his strength and was glad to have his rare attention and loving glances and longed for his verbal affirmation of love.

They spent many evenings, even though both of them were exhausted, talking about life during their early years in Italy.

"Remember when we were young and would see each other around town or in church? I knew I loved you then, Vincent."

"I imagined what it would be like when we could be together, get married, have children. I thought about when we could buy a nice, small house. I never thought we would live anywhere but Italy."

"I guess you never know what life will bring, Vincent."

In his private moments, Vincent wondered about the baby. Would it be a boy to carry on the name or a petite dark eyed girl like her mother? Being new to the country, a new father and provider, he was a bit overwhelmed at the responsibilities that already came with his new life.

Even in their most tender and open moments, Vincent held back some things. He didn't ever tell anyone and certainly not Rosa his vision of the encounter, and the fatal ending with the lion hung in his mind like a picture on a museum wall, fixed and closely guarded. Each time there was a negative occurrence, he had a flashback to the ominous sentence of Cent'Anni, one hundred years.

One Sunday in January, before mass, Vincent had requested Father Parisi hear his confession. As he entered the confessional, Vincent yearned to unburden himself of the dark secret he was carrying about his vision from months before.

"Bless me Father, it's been years since my last confession."

"Go on."

Not wanting to send a message of superstition, Vincent proceeded with sins. "I've been impatient, unkind, lost my temper ,and told a few lies."

"So, is that it?" asked Parisi

Then after taking a deep breath he decided to trust the young priest with the *curse* he had come to fear. He explained in detail. "I had a vision of killing a lion, and it brought a curse on me and my family for 100 years. After that there were threats from Italian mobsters, and we left from our home in Italy."

The priest paused and quietly addressed the confession and the revelation of the nightmare haunting this parishioner.

"First, for your penance say five Hail Mary's and three Our Fathers, I absolve you of your sins in the name of the Father, the Son, and the Holy Ghost. As for your concerns about the dream and curse of 100 years for slaying the lion, if this is what made you decide to flee your homeland, go home and read in the Gospel of Matthew chapter 2, verses 13-23. Now you are free to go and sin no more."

Ashamed to admit his illiteracy, Vincent agreed to reference the passage in their family bible. In the Bible verse Vincent was required to read it said, *An angel appeared to Joseph in a dream and telling him to flee Egypt with Mary and infant Jesus.* What was the priest's point? Was this blasphemy? Was this a foreshadowing of some kind? Vincent thought, *I went for comfort and to unburden myself, now I'm more convinced than ever that my future is doomed.* Vincent spent many hours while going about his daily routine thinking about the similarities *and* differences of his family and situation. His decisions sometimes troubled him but more often brought him peace.

Vincent and Rosa became comfortable in their *little nest* and ventured out occasionally to add to their furnishings. While they were in America, their home more resembled Italy. Simple pleasures like bed linens, a baby blanket, cookware, matching dishes, and silverware all added a touch of family and small doses of prosperity.

Rosa seemed happy and even made a few church friends who greeted her with nods of approval and waved as she exited the church and headed back to the safety of her tiny home.

Over the weeks, Vincent eventually calmed himself and

reflected on all the good things that had happened, the blessings bestowed on him in the last six months. *I have a job, a place to live, I've saved some money and we have a baby on the way. I'm on my way to the American Dream I was hoping for when I came here. For now, life is good.* Given a new lease on life, Vincent remembered many of the stories he heard as he sat in the church pews in Villa Cristo. Even if he couldn't *read* the Bible, more importantly, he could *live* the Bible.

Conversations Vincent and Rosa had lulled him into a sense security.

"Vincent are you happy?"

"Happy? I'm satisfied. I'm doing the best I can. I worry."

"Worry about what? We're doing well."

"Life is so fragile. I worry about the storms."

"Storms?"

"Not rain, wind, and snow—life storms."

"But everything is going so well."

"I guess you're right, we have been very fortunate. You're right, Rosa."

More optimistic, Vincent made plans for his future and that of his family. He felt better, surrounded by his countrymen and willing to do the work he, like many people, just wanted to do his job, protect his family, and find a way to be part of the community and the country. After all, he if he did good, he would receive good.

What could go wrong?

Chapter VI

A New Leaf on the Family Tree

Often as the winter evenings slipped into darkness and before Vincent went down the steps to begin work, the couple would talk about their hopes and dreams. The year 1921 was over, and the promise of a new year, 1922, was secondary to the reality of a new life coming soon.

"Our baby can be anything in America, Vincent."

"I just want a happy, healthy baby."

"I can feel the baby moving inside me, it will be fine."

Rosa was in full bloom; her bulging belly and the pregnancy was sapping her strength, but the joy of the baby moving inside her more than compensated for the discomfort she lived with daily. A trait shared by women of all nationalities, Rosa cradled her baby bulge with her hands as she moved. Cautious as she made her way awkwardly up and down the steps clutching the railing, she left only to make church visits, pray her rosary, and attend mass on Sunday.

St. Louis winters were certainly harsher than the winter months of southern Italy. The DeoMonte's were used to low temperatures in the 50s and highs in the 70s and rain. The snow was new to them and more tolerated than celebrated.

Travel in the snow was unusual for Rosa, and the slippery sidewalks had her taking tiny steps and bundled up in layers of warm clothes.

"Do you have to go to church when the weather is this bad?"

"I don't *have* to I go—I *want* to. It gives me peace."

"Please be careful. If I could, I'd walk you there, but I can't leave."

"I'll be fine."

Rosa looked like a child inhaling the cold air and then laughing as she exhaled steam. As the snow fell, she stuck her tongue out to catch a flake and almost slipped. As she made her way to the church, she noticed that the black wrought iron hand rails going up the steps of the church had icicles hanging from them and that they served as light prisms reflecting a rainbow of colors. She saw it as a sign from God.

Some mornings after services Father Parisi took the time to escort her home, offering his arm to ensure her ability to stay upright despite the frozen pavement.

"Rosa, how are you feeling?"

Rosa looked over at her friend

"I'm fine, a little tired but that's not unusual."

"Are you frightened about the baby coming?"

"Oh no, Father. I'm a child of God. He always protects me."

The priest smiled at the childlike faith expressed by the woman.

Vincent watched up the street to make sure Rosa was safe making her way back from the church.

"Thank you, Father. I have a loaf of fresh bread for you to take back to the church rectory."

Father Parisi feigned his reluctance to leave with a loaf of Vincent's very popular bread. "Oh no, that's not necessary."

Honestly, he could scarcely wait to get back and share his reward with the other priests and nuns.

The countdown had begun for the arrival of the baby, and as with any other couple the closer to the delivery time, they wondered more and more if it was a boy or girl. In the tradition of the Italians, the first names were predestined to be that of the parents.

If it was a boy, Anthony, the Americanized version of Vincent's father Antonino—if it was a girl, Gina Lucia after both grandmothers.

"Anthony is quiet today, and for the last few days. I haven't felt much movement," Rosa commented.

Vincent detected worry in her voice. "Are you sure everything is okay?"

"I'm sure. I prayed—it will be fine."

The dreary weather didn't dampen the spirits of the couple as they anticipated their life-changing events.

One day Vincent suggested to Larry that he might consider hanging salamis and pepperoni in the front store display window. "This is something I had done in my own store."

Larry, in a gruff voice, reminded Vincent "this is *not* your store, and this isn't Italy."

Larry was secretly envious of the popularity that Vincent had with the customers. Despite his reaction, after a week Valenti decided to try the attention-getting ploy. People traveling the sidewalk would stop, look, and enter the store, and it also didn't go unnoticed that the sales of the eye-catching items rose dramatically. Sam Valenti was keenly aware that the Italian bread had become the calling card of the store, and the Valenti brothers' grocery store flourished.

Vincent became popular and the patrons would routinely walk to the rear of the store in search of him. He could almost always be found near the brick oven and was visible to the visitors who called back to him. He would flash a smile and wipe his hands off on his apron. It was impossible not to notice the smile he was wearing and the ample amount of flour on him and his clothing. Wiping the sweat from his face and forehead, Vincent would step out to engage in brief conversations with many of the longtime customers.

"How's it going? How is Rosa?" The exchanges often migrated to the weather, life in America, and the arrival of the baby.

"It looks like the *Americani* (Americans) like the Italian bread."

These talks were a mix of broken English and Italian phrases that made many patrons, even if for only a moment feel more at home. Vincent would minimize the distractions as he spotted glances of disapproval from the Larry and Sam Valenti. Despite their agitation over the interruptions in his baking duties they admired Vincent's popularity. They knew he was good for business.

It soon became a custom to celebrate Saturday with Vincent paying seven cents for that can of peaches Rosa loved. She rarely left the apartment, he would call out to her as he ascended the steps, "I have surprise for you."

She would smile as he opened the can and brought a fork to help her retrieve the slippery peaches.

"I love the peaches, and I love you." They both laughed at the peach nectar that often made its way down her chin despite her efforts to be careful. Vincent loved her, too, but in his own way. His childhood was devoid of emotional expressions of love, and Vincent rarely vocalized his feelings, but Rosa cherished his occasional words of love and the hugs she wished would never end.

The heat from the mighty brick bread oven would rise and warm their apartment. Rosa spent hours staring out the single apartment window that offered a view of the bustling St. Louis streets. The corner of Seventh and Cole was almost non-stop with a variety of traffic. Cars, trucks, foot traffic, and the street-cars were of interest. Vehicles were inhabited by all types of people, and Rosa often wondered where they were all going.

A look around the apartment showed improvements, an old rag that had served as a window cover was now replaced with an inexpensive curtain. With no way to regulate the heat Rosa sometimes slid the window open slightly to allow some cooler air into the room. Cooking pots rarely left the stove top, and a lone drawer housed the plain silverware used at their mealtimes. Minimal closet space didn't pose a problem because they had a minimal amount of clothes and shoes. A recently acquired royal blue coat Vincent bought to shield Rosa from the cold hung by itself on hook in the small hallway. Religious statues were scattered around the apartment, and the wooden Nativity scene from Christmas had earned a permanent place on a small table.

"We have a comfortable place to live and all that we need," Rosa said with a satisfied tone in her voice.

"It's nice for now but we will need more room after the baby arrives."

"It will always be special to me."

Rosa's frailty was compounded by her condition during the later part of her pregnancy, and it worried Vincent.

"Are you sure you're felling well enough to cook or clean?"

"Other women do it; so can I. I just get dizzy and a little tired faster. I'm sure this is what every woman goes through."

She often could hear muffled conversations from downstairs, and she smiled each time Vincent's new friends inquired about the baby and how Rosa was feeling. She spent hours daydreaming about the life that was soon to be born into this place they now called home. The dollar-a-day rent of the apartment was deducted from Vincent's pay, and slowly the DeoMonte's savings grew.

In the early morning hours, Vincent would trudge up the stairs from the store to his little safe haven. Sometimes Rosa would have fallen asleep in a luxury item they had purchased, an oak rocking chair. They convinced themselves that it would come in handy to rock the new baby to sleep. Many times, Rosa would be laying in their bed clutching a pillow which she secretly pretended was Vincent. His absence was felt even though he was just feet away baking his signature bread.

"I'm ready for this baby to be here, Rosa."

"Not in our time, Vincent; in God's time."

The calendar had flipped to March weeks ago, another *no baby yet* month. Rosa's pain was evident in her face but not her words.

"Do you want to feel your baby moving inside me?" She would guide his hand to the location of the movement.

Vincent had felt the baby move often and believed Rosa placed his hand on her stomach often to assure him that there was a baby in there. As they neared the actual arrival, the plan was to use a midwife, a common practice for people who couldn't afford hospitals, to assist in delivering the baby. Again, the Pagano family was coming to the aid of the DeoMonte family. Concetta Pagano had experience as a midwife and was willing to help. Not being sure of the conception date Vincent and Rosa impatiently waited for the arrival of the newest member of the family. The days dragged on.

March in St. Louis can be cold and windy, and that was exactly what the day was like on the last day of the month and still no baby. Friday was always a busy day at the store because people got paid on Fridays. This day was no exception, groceries and bread were leaving the store quickly. Large paper shopping bags strained at the weight of sliced lunch meats, cheese, olives, and canned goods, and almost everyone left Valenti's with at least one loaf of bread.

Vincent was a lone figure moving about the store long since closed for the day. The oven was full of just finished bread as he slid the old paddle under the loaves to remove then and slide them off onto a table.

"Vincent, it's time," came the call from upstairs.

At the words Vincent bolted up the steps, that is until he missed a step and came back down to the landing followed by a string of Italian curse words. Gathering himself and ascending two steps at a time he found Rosa standing in the kitchen in a puddle. With no idea what was happening he blurted out.

"What am I supposed to do?"

Rosa just barely holding herself up was making her way to the bed where this child was about to be born.

"Go get Concetta," Rosa said as she collapsed onto the bed.

Vincent again almost tumbled down the stairs and struggled with the front door until he remembered it was locked. He turned the latch and without stopping to close the door found himself knocking on the Pagano's door.

"Rosa is having the baby," he said grabbing Concetta by the hand and whisking her out the door, down the steps, and into the street with the only light from the dim streetlight on the corner. They made their way into the grocery store, and Concetta, much calmer than Vincent, suggested he stay downstairs.

"Wait downstairs, there's nothing you can do up here except get in the way. I'll call you if I need you."

Ignoring Concetta's advice Vincent climbed back up the steps and assured Rosa, although he himself wasn't sure, that everything was going to be all right.

"You're going to be fine; I'm praying to God to take care of you and the baby." This proclamation of faith stunned Rosa who rarely heard Vincent speak this way. She smiled through the pain and found it a comfort.

Returning downstairs and pacing, Vincent's work ethic kicked in and he prepared the next batch of bread to go into the oven. After what seemed like hours but was just a matter of minutes, Vincent heard the cry of a baby. His immediate thought was of the well being of the baby and his overwhelming fear of losing his Rosa.

Was she strong enough to survive childbirth? Anxiously and fearfully he peaked through the bedroom doorway. Resting on Rosa's chest was baby wrapped in a small blanket. Rosa was pale and crying. Concetta's smile was reassurance that everything was okay. Then the next words rang in his ears.

"You have a son, a baby boy!"

He walked to Rosa's side and wiped the sweat off her face. "Are you okay?" She just nodded yes, looked at the baby, and her head dropped suddenly. She lay motionless.

Vincent panicked until Concetta consoled him saying, "She just fell sleep. She's weak."

A mixed tear of fear and joy trickled down Vincent cheek. There was his son, looking no bigger than the loaves of bread he baked. Concetta ushered him out of the room. "It's probably best if I stay until morning."

Vincent didn't hear anything she said. A thousand thoughts crossed hiss mind.

He felt that rush of fatherhood—his mission now was to

protect, love, and provide for his child. He realized what a tremendous sense of responsibility he now was faced with.

Vincent stopped to bow his head and prayed a prayer of thanksgiving and hope. His prayer was interrupted by the smell of burning bread.

Back to work. The next few hours became a blur as the enormity of what had just happened set in. The entire scene fell silent except for the occasional whimper of a newborn that Vincent would become familiar with in the coming months.

The sun rose on this the first day of April. Vincent had fallen asleep in the rocking chair, and as he awoke from what seemed like a dream, he saw Concetta sitting at the end of the bed holding Anthony. He could barely make out through the sparse sunlight Rosa reaching for her son ready to begin nursing the hours-old little boy. To the new parents it seemed miraculous, this little bundle was theirs.

Rosa, like new mothers of centuries past, would unwrap the baby to inspect him, counting in Italian the ten toes and all his fingers. Red and wrinkled, he looked like a miniature man.

Vincent called Concetta over after seeing the folds of his skin, red face, and unsightly umbilical cord and asked, "Is he supposed to look like that?" Concetta laughed at Vincent's inexperience and replied, "He looks like a healthy *bambino* (baby boy)."

Concetta returned home to tend to her own family with the promise of returning later that day. Being Saturday, Vincent would have no bread to bake today.

"I'll be right back; I'm going down into the store get a few things to make a pot of sauce," Vincent said in a low voice.

While down in the store he also announced to anyone within ear shot that there was a new baby in the DeoMonte family.

"I have a son, a baby boy, Anthony DeoMonte."

All the customers clapped and pounded on the back of the proud father celebrating his new arrival.

He peeked in on Rosa and found her motionless, eyes closed. Automatically concerned, he placed his hand on her chest to check her breathing which seemed shallow but was steady. The baby was sleeping peacefully complete with a tiny snore.

Vincent browned a little onion, some garlic in olive oil, and added some tomatoes along with a handful of sugar to neutralize the acid in the tomatoes. There was no meat to add to the sauce, but this would be enough to sustain his weary wife. Two hours later linguine pasta was boiling on another burner, and the simple meal was ready.

Rosa ate sparingly, more tired than hungry; Vincent held his son nervously. As soon a she finished, he hurriedly handed the baby back—he was a nervous new father.

"I don't want to do anything wrong."

"Vincent, he's healthy and strong, you aren't going to hurt him."

Days passed, and Concetta felt a little less needed, and her visits became more infrequent. The baby seemed to grow and change by the hour. As he moved and made the little squeaks and squeals, they looked at each other and just smiled. Rosa never tired of looking at his little fingers and could scarcely believe his tiny fingernails.

Mother, and eventually father, also became more comfortable with their parental responsibilities. Vincent marveled at how a baby who ate so little could poop so much and often. Rosa was tired most of the time and barely left the comfort of their bed. The bottom dresser drawer was the poor man's baby bed. The open drawer was lined with soft blankets. Little Anthony was satisfied with his makeshift sleeping arrangement.

Rosa was regaining some strength and was anxious to get her baby to Father Parisi to have him perform the baptism of this little gift from God. Vito and Concetta Pagano were asked and agreed to be godparents to the first United States citizen born to the DeoMonte family. Conceived in Italy but born in America made Anthony legally a United States citizen.

The future was looking bright for this family.

Chapter VII

Life Changes

As Tony, Anthony's nickname, grew he took on some of the features of both parents. His firm jawline and Italian nose were definitely his father's features; his dark brown hair and even darker brown eyes matched his mother's look.

On a Monday morning Vito agreed to accompany Vincent to City Hall to get a birth certificate for Tony. This would require the immigration papers Vincent received as they were processed through New York upon their arrival from Italy. Once in line, Vito helped introduce his friend.

"This is my friend Vincent DeoMonte. I'm Vito Pagano. He needs to get a birth certificate for his son."

Pagano presented the papers to the female clerk; she ran through the information needed to fill out the form.

"There's a charge of 25 cents to process the paperwork," the clerk informed them.

As she got to the name section, she opened the carefully folded immigration papers and asked about the full name. "It says here you're Vincent Antonino LeoMorte."

All the color left Vincent's face. LeoMorte translated meant *Dead Lion*. Vito was occupied and hadn't heard the exchange.

Vincent replied, "That's not right."

The clerk peering out over her thick bifocals responded, "That's what it says right here sir, this is a legal document!"

Not wanting to create any more of a problem, he sheepishly agreed. And so the family name was memorialized as *LeoMorte*.

All the way back home Vincent agonized over the revelation of the bad dream that seemed to resurface at the most unexpected time. *Would this curse ever end, or was it truly Cent'Anni?*

The men made their way quickly across the marble floor, large columns, and business offices to get back outside.

Vincent decided Rosa would not be told about this. Once home the immigration papers along with the birth certificate were stored in an envelope buried in the bottom of a dresser drawer.

The incident was eventually forgotten, and life continued.

Being an inexperienced father, Vincent was introduced to new things on a regular basis. He was surprised at how soft his sons' skin was. He would gently run his calloused hands down the baby's arm and couldn't help but smile when he got close enough to smell the sweet scent of his baby's breath. Baby Anthony would move his hands and feet simultaneously and then almost take on a look of seeking approval. Sudden stops in activity followed by a red face and grunting meant a diaper change was required. Each day was eventful. Learning to turn over, crawling, and grasping small objects were all celebrated. Rosa appeared to be happier than ever before, her maternal instincts were perfect. Vincent worked hard, smiled constantly, and saved money with the hopes of making a future for his family.

Months gave way to years, and in the winter of 1925, Rosa announced that she was going to have another baby.

"Vincent, our family is again going to grow."

"What do you mean?"

"We're going to have another baby."

"Are you sure?"

"Pretty sure."

Rosa's revelation took Vincent by surprise. He had wondered and had a hard time differentiating between Rosa's common morning nausea and her weakness. There were days when it was difficult to leave the bed they shared, and now it all made sense. This news was greeted with mixed emotions. Little Tony was soon to be three, and now there was another baby due in mid-summer.

A concerned Vincent asked, "How do you feel about having another baby?"

Rosa saw the fear in his face and said, "In the Our Father we pray, *Thy will be done*. If this is God's will, then so be it."

Vincent feared for his wife's well-being. The first baby took its toll on Rosa, but before long they both embraced the idea of adding a new life to their family. The optimism was tempered by Vincent's concern over the financial effect of their growing family and the reality that while his family was getting larger, the apartment would at least seem smaller. Between his wages and winemaking venture, the couple had managed to save just over $900. They ate meager meals; pasta was cheap and easy, and many things could be added to it to make it appear a different meal. The baby required very little, although he outgrew clothes regularly. Luckily the Pagano family had two boys and lots of hand-me-down items. New clothes for any of the three was a rare luxury. Neither Rosa nor Vincent minded the sacrifices.

If they traveled around town they usually walked, though they had learned some of the workings of the public bus system. An occasional mistake on directions or routes meant a longer bus ride and the need to find their way back home. This was a source of frustration for Vincent who felt embarrassed and endured the pain of illiteracy.

The average home in St. Louis was selling for $6,200. Vincent had only two products to offer his employers—bread and wine—and the price of homes seemed unrealistic. The wine was a perilous venture but was adding income and padding their savings. Approaching the Valenti brothers for a raise seemed out of the question. Another baby and a new home? Was this even a possibility?

Father Parisi had become a trusted confident and counselor. With Little Tony in tow, Vincent and Rosa ventured out to see if they could talk to him about the situation. Entering through the side entrance of the church, the couple stopped to pray—Rosa praying for guidance; Vincent praying for patience as Tony, who had escaped his grip, was weaving in and out of the maze of pews. After a few minutes, Father Parisi unexpectedly appeared at the front of the church, busying himself around the altar. He noticed the family and moved in their direction.

Vincent greeted him with a handshake and asked, "Can we talk to you outside for a moment?"

"Of course," answered the young priest. "But it's a little cold outside. Maybe you would be more comfortable in the rectory?"

Rosa, unable to contain her excitement, blurted out," We're expecting another baby!"

"So that's what this is about," the priest said, beaming a smile. "Another little parishioner."

"No, no Father, we have some questions." Vincent chimed in.

They followed the priest out of the church building and through the backdoor entrance of the rectory and made their way to a small parlor. Rosa held her son in her lap to avoid any disruptions.

"How can I help you?" asked Father Parisi.

Vincent started, "With another baby coming we may have to move and try to buy a house."

"Exciting, a baby and a home," the priest said with enthusiasm.

Vincent continued, "We don't know where to go, or how to buy a house."

Father Parisi leaned in. "I think I can help. Just on the edge of the city sits an Italian section known as *the Hill*. The residents want to keep the area all Italian. In order to do this any home for sale is sold to the church there, and the church acts as a real estate broker. Do you both understand this?"

Vincent and Rosa looked at each other and responded, "No."

"I'll help you," offered Father Parisi, who had a little news of his own. "In a few months I'm being assigned to St. Ambrose church. It's right there on *the Hill*."

God was surely shining down on the couple.

Silently Vincent vowed to save every penny he could in order to make their dream of home ownership come true.

In August of 1926, another son arrived. Paolo, who would be known as Paul, was a difficult delivery. Concetta did all she could, but finally declared, "We have to have a doctor. I can't do any more for her."

The delivery of this child convinced Vincent he would be satisfied with the two sons and his wife. He prayed fervently and all through the night stayed beside his wife.

Vincent prayed, "Please God, don't take my Rosa. I need her more than you do."

The doctor arrived and checked Rosa closely and checked the baby over. Vincent was concerned over the look on the doctor's face.

"She needs a lot of rest; the baby looks fine."

Rosa's recovery was long, and she seemed to never regain the physical condition she had previously. Vincent realized he had almost lost his Rosa. The second-time father juggled work and taking care of his family, but he was wearing down. Slowly they both regained a renewed spirit and strength. The boys grew and the once-cozy apartment seemed to close in on the family.

In January, their friend Father Parisi returned for a visit and to say mass at St. Francis Assisi. After mass he was greeting people in the rear of the church and stopped Vincent and Rosa to admire the children and give them some news.

"Good morning, it's nice to see this beautiful family."

Rosa had Little Tony by the hand and Vincent was proudly carrying the baby, they made a nice-looking family. The priest had been vigilant in watching for homes on the Hill. "There's a small, older home at the corner of Shaw and Marconi that will be available in the spring."

Overjoyed but apprehensive, Vincent immediately asked, "How much does this house cost?"

Father Parisi replied, "I think because it's small, a little bungalow, and older you could get it for around $4300."

Rosa looked at Vincent and said, "God has once again blessed us."

Vincent began to try to compute the numbers in his head. As near as he could figure they would owe the astronomical amount of another $3,000 to make the home theirs. *Old school* Vincent didn't like to owe anyone. He also had the 100-year curse on his mind. What of something went wrong?

In March, Little Tony would be four, and the news came that the house was available. Father Parisi would meet the family at the store and guide them on the bus trip to the Hill to preview the little house.

"You should take some cash to make a down payment and secure it," Father Parisi advised Vincent. Vincent went to the stash of cash he stored and slowly counted out $500 and then recounted it out loud with Father Parisi's help.

He looked at the priest and asked, "Is that enough?"

Parisi nodded yes.

In fact, behind the scenes Father Parisi had interceded on the part of his friends to get them a better price. They were quite a sight as the five people boarded the bus that would require a transfer to a second bus in about 20 minutes. The priest dropped the 60 cents in change into the bus box, and they searched for seats close to the front to facilitate the change to the second vehicle. Bus number two would bring them right to the front of the church, St. Ambrose, where the family would be introduced to the pastor, Monsignor Palazollo.

A brief formal introduction was followed by details about the potential purchase.

"Can we see the house please?" pleaded Vincent.

"Of course," the elderly clergyman responded. "It's just two houses down. Father Parisi has the key."

Trying hard to control their excitement, the DeoMontes giggled as they made the short walk and saw the little gray house with a black roof for the first time. A *postage-stamp* front yard was bisected by a set of concrete steps that led to a wooden door that featured a small four pane window.

Rosa, beaming, said, "It looks perfect!"

Turning the key in the door, it was obvious as they entered that the previous owners had kept the little place immaculate.

"Look Vincent, a real house, a dream house. Our families in Italy would be impressed."

With hardwood floors all through the house, a small living room led to the kitchen. Before they made their way there, inexplicably Vincent's eyes were drawn to a stain glass window in the hallway on the west side of the house. He nudged Rosa and pointed to the image, they looked at each other and smiled. Sunlight streamed through the brightly colored panes which showed a single rose and a leafy stem. Was this a sign that this little place was meant for them?

The kitchen was equipped with some older appliances—an electric stove and small refrigerator.

"Rosa, I can imagine you cooking here and us taking our meals around the table."

A rear window allowed a view to the backyard. A sharp turn lead into a hallway then to a single bathroom. The light green tiled bathroom featured a small tub, a large beveled mirror, and one small sink, nothing flashy, but it was all they needed. The bathroom separated two bedrooms, one to either side at the end of the hall.

"Look Vincent, we can have our own room and a room for your sons."

Father Parisi held back a chuckle at the simple joy the young family found in the tiny house.

Each room had small windows with rollout cranks used to open the screened windows for fair weather ventilation. Vincent noticed the bathroom faucet had a slow drip and a small crack was near the ceiling of the hallway. No matter this was like a palace to the couple.

Another door which appeared to go nowhere revealed a set of steps leading down to a small cellar that contained a coal-burning furnace for the heating system. A few more details got the attention of the DeoMontes—a closet still had the smell of moth balls, and linoleum in the kitchen had a burn spot, probably from an errant cigarette. Looking out the window from the kitchen to the fenced backyard, incredibly Vincent saw wooden framework for a grape growing arbor! The grape vines took up most of the backyard and appeared healthy but were in winter hibernation. The winemaking operation could continue. This humble home looked perfect to Vincent and Rosa.

"Oh Vincent, I love it."

The group hurried back toward the church, partly to escape the cold and more importantly to try to close the deal.

Monsignor Palazollo was puffing on a pipe and inquired, "What do you think?"

Vincent without speaking extended his hand with the cash as if to answer.

"I'll prepare the paperwork. You'll make your payment directly to the church."

To reassure the Monsignor, Vincent said, "I have more money for you. I can bring it to you this week."

The elder clergy pulled out a pencil and piece of paper. Seeing this, Vincent worried that he would be asked to review the figures and contract. Father Parisi, recognizing Vincent's plight, put his hand on his shoulder and said, "We'll go over this together."

The look on Vincent's face was pure relief at dodging any embarrassment.

"Fourteen dollars a month will be your payment," said Monsignor Palazollo. Later Vincent would realize that was only double what his weekly rent had been.

After a quick visit to the church to say a prayer of thanksgiving, they bade Father Parisi goodbye and boarded the bus for downtown St. Louis. Vincent concerned himself with memorizing the route the bus was taking in order to plan his daily trips to and from the grocery store. Watching landmarks and making mental notes he clutched Rosa's hand as his other hand was occupied trying to hold on to his squirming four-year-old son. Committing every detail to memory Vincent felt his stomach churning. *So many details.* Was he making the right move? Would he be able to pay for this house? Would his family be safe and happy in this location?

"Are you happy, Rosa?"

"Yes, we will have many years of happiness in that house."

Vincent allowed himself a smile as he realized from listening to gospel readings in church that there was a parallel in the stories of bread and wine, the two gifts he was dependent on for his livelihood. He had even in secrecy asked Father Parisi about his view of the illegal winemaking.

"Vincent, the Lord provided bread and wine to his flock in order to save the world. I think He would see it as you trying to save your family."

It seemed that God always provided him with all he needed. The road ahead looked wonderful! It almost seemed too good to be true.

Maybe it was.

Chapter VIII

Tough Times

The house had a bare look because of the lack of furnishings. "Rosa, I talked to the Valentis, they said we could have some of the old furniture from the apartment."

"Vincent, I talked to one of our neighbors, they have an old cradle and secondhand bed we could use for the boys."

Rosa busied herself trying to make the house more of a home for her family.

Also transported was the ancient winepress rescued from the basement of the store, this was essential to bringing in additional income. Prohibition was still in place, and even though the winemaking operation was risky business, Vincent was willing to take the chance. Rosa recognized Vincent's intentions but dutifully remained silent.

"We could use more furniture Vincent; it would be nice."

"We can save money and then buy more."

For now, they were comfortably nestled in, warm, and hopefully safe.

The next few years were truly transitional.

Rosa started a Sunday afternoon conversation. "We go to Sunday mass and never mix with the other people."

"We have our family, that's enough for me. More people means more trouble."

"We could make friends."

"I don't need many friends. For me, family is everything. I trust family only."

Vincent spent time commuting and constantly worrying about the future and welfare of his family. As the weather warmed, he began to nurture the grapes which looked to be mature and hoped for a harvest that would turn from grapes into wine and ultimately into money.

Sam Valenti approached Vincent one day. "Vincent we know you have a growing family, we're going to give you a five cent an hour raise."

"*Grazie*, thank you," an ecstatic Vincent replied.

"The customers love the bread and you."

This meant he would realize an additional three dollars on completion of his 60-hour work week. Some of the extra money would go toward bus fare and some would be a church contribution in appreciation for his abundant blessings. Whatever was left, if any would go to savings, but with two small children, it wasn't likely there would be any money left over.

The family found comfort in routine; Vincent had mastered the daily transportation schedule. Rosa was a good mother but wasexhausted by day's end. Her spirit was stronger than her body. She prayed often and made a home for her family. At six years old Tony would attend school just down the street at St. Ambrose.

"You need to do well in school, it's important," Rosa told her son.

"Papa didn't have to go to school to bake bread."

"You want to be able to work with your brains instead of your back."

It was a struggle for the high energy little boy to sit still and listen to the lessons. Even though education wasn't stressed at home, Rosa realized in this new world schooling was more necessary than in their native Italy. They both had shared dreams for their children beyond working with their hands and backs.

It was 1928, and life on the Hill was generally monotonous.

Rosa made it a habit to visit the church each day as she walked her older son to school. Father Parisi had become a fixture in the church and in the Italian community.

The influx of immigrants continued as people who had heard of the land of opportunity flooded the country. Many stayed in the East where they landed, but often new arrivals headed to cities that had established ethnic strongholds. There was feeling of familiarity and safety when the population was comprised of mostly the same nationality. St. Louis was no exception.

The true ghettos were collections of the same nationalities, compact areas and crowded homes, multi-family structures known as flats frequently housed several families, mostly relatives. Inside the homes there were cheap meals, generations became part of the fabric of this area and many other metropolitan areas.

All this was good for the grocery business, and the Valenti grocery benefited from the swarms of Italians seeking familiar foods. Being able to eat as they had in the past was a form of comfort.

"We have loyal customers; some even shop twice a day like the genuine Italians," Sam Valenti explained to Vincent.

"In Italy meals are a celebration," Vincent added.

"We celebrate money my friend," was Valenti's reply. "Your concern is that they all leave with a loaf of bread."

Vito Pagano would stop in often for food and to renew the friendship he had with Vincent, both benefited from the relationship. Vincent strayed from his stance of trusting only family.

"Vito, you are more like a brother than a friend."

"You are the same to me Vincent," responded Vito. "We have to stick together to make it in this country."

Vito and his wife certainly had proven themselves and had earned the title of family. When the families got together their discussions were centered around family, food, and the state of the world—at least their small section of the world. Conversations punctuated with the most recent births, deaths, and marriages kept them both up to date on local information.

On Saturdays many of the local "Italiani" would drag chairs out to the store fronts and hang out. The neighborhood businesses became meeting places where residents felt safe and comfortable from the larger world where they were at most accepted for their work ethic. The Italians were cautious around the "*Americani*" knowing the obvious disdain some held for the "invaders."

Disaster knows no ethnicity. In 1929 The Great Depression struck. Vincent's world was small. He certainly didn't read newspapers, but word spread about this financial failing.

As always Father Parisi was there as a calming voice but also to explain the plight of the American citizens of all nationalities.

He put it in the most basic of terms. "People are losing their jobs, and this is becoming a time of suffering for many."

Vincent felt panic and compassion for those waiting in what had been named *soup lines*. "What can those people do, Father?"

"Band together. People in this neighborhood have pride in taking care of their own."

"I'm grateful to have job. I would like to help, but my family comes first."

The sight of people roaming the streets with looks of despair required little further explanation to the DeoMontes, immigrants thought they had found prosperity in the United States. These people feared what they didn't understand. The St. Louis Italians banded together out of necessity and struggled mightily to eek out any living and found strength in their faith and family. Meals were rationed and hope for better days kept people of all nationalities and denominations going.

"We have a hundred ways to make pasta," boasted Larry Valenti.

Vincent added, "People will always need food."

Valenti's stayed open, but many items weren't available and even the others were limited. The Depression worried Vincent, after all Sam Valenti had made the bread before, what if the brothers relieved Vincent of his duties? Just as he had anticipated the Valenti's announced that they needed to talk to Vincent.

The grave looks on their faces signaled the seriousness of the situation. "Vincent you know times are tough, to stay in business we have to cut your pay." The words were a relief for the baker who feared being fired."

"We can only afford to pay you twelve dollars a week. It's either that or we have to let you go."

"I need the work and the money; I'll stay on and work hard."

"You keep baking bread, and we'll take care of you."

Vincent smiled and shook hands with the brothers, but he didn't trust them.

This was a large pay cut, but he would still have a job. His thoughts instantly went to how he could provide for his family and survive this major life-changing event. His mind went to his other business venture, wine making, which was bringing in an extra five dollars a week. This would be even more important now.

The bus ride home that day was a jumble of emotions. With an ailing wife and two small sons did he dare tell Rosa of the financial fall? He also lived with the danger of the wine production and sales being discovered, he needed the money but feared the price he would pay for this infraction of the Prohibition laws. As the bus rounded the last corner toward home Vincent decided to withhold the bad news from Rosa. He could still make his house payment and they already lived frugally; they could ramp back a little more. They would hang on to each other tightly and weather yet another storm. Their love, though not extremely romantic, was still strong. *Family is everything.*

Life became a daily struggle. The pressure of the times took a toll on many residents regardless of nationality or geographic location. Rosa, as always, found strength in her rosary and daily prayer.

Clutching her ever-present rosary, Rosa said, "My faith is strong, God will see us through. We'll be tested, but He will provide."

Vincent's faith wasn't as strong as Rosa's. "I've been tested all my life, this is just another storm to be weathered."

"We have to be able to count on each other, we must stay strong. I'll say extra prayers."

"You always do."

Vincent worked long hours late into the night and needed to sleep during the day. Rosa's energy level varied—often she was weak almost to total exhaustion and caring for the children was a challenge. Little Tony showed limited interest in school, and his grades reflected it. Despite his father's threats and his mothers urging, he seemed destined to struggle academically.

"I need you to work hard in school—right now that's your job my son," Rosa pleaded.

"Your only way is through school; all these people are suffering now because they are out of work," Vincent explained.

Little Tony looked at his father and replied, "Papa you still have work. You didn't go to school."

"I'm lucky, and we want better for you. You go and work hard now, so you won't have to work hard later and worry."

"I'll try."

Vincent worked extra hours for no pay and continued to press grapes and bottle wine. Long days for short pay became common but at least he had a job.

The bus rides gave him time to think and try to plan for his family's future. He never second-guessed his immigration into America.

In a difficult time, he certainly wasn't thriving, but he was surviving, and that was enough for now. At the store, Vincent retrieved a cardboard cigar box from the trash. It was his version of a safe. The box with fancy gold lettering on it had a small brass nail to keep it closed, and the Italian flag was prominently displayed on the front. He didn't trust the banks with his money—after all, they went broke.

Occasionally he had to tap into his meager savings, but he

guarded that cash in his cigar box as it insulated him and his family from homelessness.

He also was aware the very thing that sent him scurrying to his new home had also made its way to the United States—the mob. Hard times brought out the worst in some people, and these certainly were hard times. Much worse than his bootlegging wine was the gambling, prostitution, and criminal activities that produced income for the most nefarious of the neighborhood.

Many days the notorious men would visit the grocery store, sometimes just as customers but often to plot and plan their next caper.

"Hey, bread-baker."

Vincent barely acknowledge their presence and busied himself with his duties.

"I'm talking to you!"

"I just want to do my work; I don't want trouble."

"You be respectful, and there won't be any trouble."

Now the conversation caught the attention of Larry Valenti, "He just bakes bread for us. Vincent mind your own business!"

"We work hard for our money, and you let these crooks come in and steal."

A frightened Valenti said, "Don't pay attention to him. He doesn't speak for us."

The thug angrily proclaimed, "You make sure we get our payment and keep this fool quiet—or else!"

Vincent hated the underworld characters and often remembered the fear he experienced in Italy. No matter what happened, he would not cross that line and join their ranks. His hatred was kept in check by fear for what these gangsters were capable of doing.

On one of those days, Vincent asked Sam Valenti, "Why do you give these guys payment?"

"They come to collect money for *protection*," Valenti said with disgust.

Vincent didn't comment further.

Valenti continued, "I'm afraid of what they might do if I don't pay."

"I thought I left that behind in the Old Country."

"No Vincent, the riches in this country made it even more inviting for them."

"When does it stop?"

With a roll of his eyes Valenti turned away and said, "Never. It will never stop."

As many couples were falling apart because of the Depression, Vincent and Rosa seemed to draw closer together. They depended on each other to make a life for themselves, and their sons, Tony and Paolo. Although the world around them seemed unceasingly bleak, they found joy in simple pleasures—their children, a good meal, taking their usual place in the church pews, even their garden and certainly old-fashioned life as a family.

"We're doing well Vincent; God has continued to bless us."

"God has blessed me with a lot of hard work and worry," came the sarcastic reply from Vincent.

"You shouldn't say that; it could always be worse."

"I don't see how."

In early 1933 the Great Depression was ending. It had taken a toll on every resident and everyone welcomed back the slow growth and prosperity that America had once known. The repeal of Prohibition followed in December; America again had reasons to celebrate. That day the Valenti brothers surprised Vincent with a raise to get him back to his previous pay level and even added some additional because of the upturn in the economy and his hard work.

"Thank you for working hard and helping us through a rough time, Vincent. We're increasing your pay. Merry Christmas."

"I don't know what to say." *Maybe Rosa's prayers helped after all.*

Now there would even be enough for a few modest Christmas gifts.

It was mid-December, and the DeoMonte family was preparing for what would be a joyous Christmas. They had managed to survive the most historically difficult economic times experienced by the United States.

A fresh snow covered the streets of St. Louis, and Rosa stared out the frosted front window anxious to see Vincent step off the bus after his last workday for the week. She looked at the parked cars wearing a three-inch blanket of snow and watched as the flurries floated under the streetlights and looked like flakes of diamonds. The bang of the duct work as the heat was rising from the cellar startled her and brought her back to reality.

It was Rosa's custom to pray with her sons right before they were covered and kissed.

"Tony, Paolo, do you want to pray the rosary with me before you go to sleep?"

"Pray for what, Mama?" Tony asked.

"Everything—our family, our health, for others."

"Maybe tomorrow, I want to go to sleep. How about tomorrow?"

In a matter of minutes, the boys, now eleven and seven, were sleeping soundly.

The approach of Christmas had for the first time in a long time created excitement in the house. They had even put up a Christmas tree; their old treasured wooden Nativity scene sat under it. The tree was for the most part bare but still generated a feel of an American Christmas.

Vincent was in sight. He had his hands in his coat pockets and was hurrying to the house lit by a single lamp in the front window. He was beaming an unusually large smile as Rosa swung the door open to greet him. They shared a simple quick kiss, and she inquired, "Such a big smile. What brings you this much joy?"

"I've got great news. I got a raise today, we're going to be okay," Vincent said.

Rosa replied, "Once again God has seen us through a dark time."

It was 3:30 AM, Vincent stood behind his wife and hugged

her tightly. Still dark, they stared out the window at the snow which reflected a sparkle from the streetlight. This was true peace on earth.

Eventually, hand in hand, they made their way to the bedroom, anxious for a good sleep. They were greeted by the groan of the joints from their weight settling down on the wooden bed. In an unusual gesture, Vincent kissed Rosa passionately and declared his love.

"My dear Rosa, you have my love. You stood by my side during the darkest times, gave me two sons, and take such good care of our family. I love you!" He leaned in and kissed her forehead gently.

She gazed at him and proclaimed, "This is the happiest I've ever been!"

They were hand in hand, neither able to sleep. They stared at the ceiling, minds flooded with thoughts of the future. He pulled her in closely, and they drifted off to sleep.

"Truly God is good. I love you," whispered Rosa.

Slowly Vincent was awakened by the stirring of the boys. Normally Rosa would have been up to start breakfast for her family. He thought how the winter stillness created an unnatural quiet. Barely awake Vincent rolled over, and Rosa was still sleeping. The only light in the room emerged from an open crease in the curtains.

She looked peaceful in the pale light and had a faint smile on her face. He reached over to her and touched her hand. It was cold.

In a surge of emotion Vincent leaped from the bed screaming, "Oh my God. No!" He fell to his knees stunned and speechless by the thought that Rosa was dead. His hands shaking, he struggled to get back to his feet and even breathe. He hesitated to reach for her fearing the final confirmation of what he feared. He instinctively slid his hands under her back and neck trying to raise her, the earlier jolt of adrenaline robbed him of any strength as she fell out of his arms back onto the bed, limp and lifeless.

Thirty-five years old and gone? Instinctively he hoped this was only another bad dream and repeatedly tried to wake her. He gazed at her. She was pale and cold to the touch. She had passed peacefully and quietly in the early morning hours.

Shocked, he looked at her and pushed a wisp of her hair aside.

He found himself studying the contours of her face, he looked at her like he was seeing her for the first time, knowing he was seeing her for what might be the last time.

The true depth of his love was revealed as for the first time in a long time, Vincent wept. Vincent had heard people speak of a broken heart, now he clearly knew what a broken heart was. Through his tears, Vincent hoped Rosa knew how much he loved her and recounted what was his last kiss and his expression of love. He felt the moist warm tears on her face and suddenly thought maybe she was just sleeping, but he realized those were his tears on her face.

The only woman he had ever or would ever love was gone.

With eyes closed, he ran his calloused fingers over her forehead, to her eyes, along her nose, and gently caressed her lips—it was as if he was memorizing her face with his fingers.

She was gone.

Chapter IX

Growing Older and Growing Up

The tragic loss of his wife left Vincent a mere shell of man. He numbly walked through his obligations as a father and employee. Neighbors, realizing his plight, would often bring food for the boys who otherwise could only count on a school lunch for a meal. The Italian community especially on the Hill watched out for each other but also kept their distance with limited contact with Vincent. Father Parisi took on a guardian role for the boys but noticed only sporadic school attendance by either Tony or Paul. Somehow Tony managed to graduate the eighth grade. In 1936 many children didn't continue their education past grade school. Paul, now ten years old, mimicked his brother in his reluctance to apply himself in the classroom.

Vincent seemed to age rapidly in the eyes of his few friends. The life-altering loss of Rosa drained Vincent, he agonized over his situation, struggling with a reason to live. A pattern developed of arriving home in the wee hours of the morning and sleeping until noon, and his sons for the most part we were left to their own care. Any interaction between the three was emotionless, and minimal conversations took place.

"Papa do you want to me to try to make food for our supper?"

"I don't care, do what you want."

"Mama was a great cook!"

Vincent didn't even acknowledge his sons' comments.

Beds were never made; most meals were like a scavenger hunt, and the house, dusty, cluttered, and dirty showed a lack of attention. An enormous inner conflict emerged. Vincent could see Rosa in the faces of his sons—especially Tony—and this became a painful reminder of his loss but was also his only remaining connection of his beloved Rosa.

"Papa, I don't see any sense in going back to school next year."

"Then you need to find someplace to work. Working is more important that any school. The real school is that world out there, that's where you learn."

With no value placed on education by Vincent ,Tony dismissed the idea of returning to school. Paul soon joined him in the disdain for education, and they spent their days roaming the neighborhood streets. Confronted about the attendance deficiency by a truant officer and Father Angelo Parisi, Vincent shrugged off the importance of a formal education.

"Those boys need to be in school," Father Parisi insisted. "They have a bleak future running the streets. They'll end up in trouble. So that's your idea of an education? Do you think that's what Rosa would want for her sons? Let God guide you in your thinking."

Vincent angrily replied, "Your God took my Rosa. I'm left to raise my sons. God has nothing to do with it! They'll get a better education in the streets then they could ever get in a school." His frustration boiled over at the accusation that he wasn't a good parent.

Vincent was enraged, and he turned sharply away. "We have nothing to say to each other."

Parisi called out to Vincent, "God still loves you."

"He abandoned me. I have no God."

The mean streets of St. Louis were a cruel teacher, but surviving meant you could make it anywhere. Becoming street-wise would prepare the boys for all life's challenges. After all, hadn't Vincent proven education wasn't needed?

Rosa's cousins, the Catanzaros, decided to move from St. Louis to join other family in California. They suggested maybe the boys would be better off there.

"Let us take the boys to California and give them the life they can't have here."

Bristling at the idea of his sons moving, Vincent unleashed his anger with a tirade of Italian curse words leaving no doubt that he resented the idea. "My boys stay here!"

Young Paul was convinced this new adventure would be fun and pleaded with his father for the freedom to join the cousins on the relocation to California. "Let me go, Papa. If it doesn't work out, I can always come back."

Already reeling from the loss of Rosa, Vincent barked back at the boy, "If you go don't come back, ever!"

After constant badgering from the Catanzaros, Vincent reluctantly agreed to allow his youngest son to go. "He'll be better off in California. He'll have chances he wouldn't get here in St. Louis."

"Take him and go. It'll be one less person to worry about."

Tony never wavered and advised his father that he wanted to stay. "I want to stay her with you, Papa. I can help take care of you."

"I don't need anyone to take care of me."

Vincent cautioned Tony, "Little is required of you, but know this, if you get yourself in trouble, you're own your own. This is a tough world—if you want to be a man then you'll be treated like a man."

Vincent's world seemed to be in a constant free fall.

What Tony lacked in formal education he more than made up for with being quick witted, and he depended heavily on his survival instincts. He ran the streets and would often hitch a ride into the city, less than a mile away. He learned street skills. With a small piece of heavy wire, he learned when bent properly he could open the coin box of a pay phone. This didn't yield a gigantic score but often two or three dollars in coins were the payoff for his *work*.

If he was out very early in the morning, he had learned that the trucks that distributed the local newspapers, the *Post-Dispatch* and *Globe Democrat,* would toss bundles out along the street in front of the newsstands. He could dash up grab a bundle of newspapers, find a city street corner, and sell the papers for two cents each and literally make a quick buck on the ill-gotten 50 papers.

Along the way he also learned dressing poorly, shivering in cold weather or making a sad face often earned him tips from the occupants of the passing cars or pedestrian's walking by in search of the day's news.

Tony felt comfortable in the downtown neighborhood. He had gained a reputation for being tough and quick to fight—word spread, and most people avoided him. Some of the other older boys tested him only to find out he fought like a man twice his age. Tony gained respect and even fear from those who knew of him and his reputation.

As he worked his way through the metropolitan maze of downtown St. Louis, he heard the whispers.

"That's Tony DeoMonte, he's bad news!"

"Don't cross him, he's tough and mean."

Tony wore the reputation as a badge of honor. Others saw him as a bad egg who would end up in jail or dead.

He got to know almost everyone in the neighborhood, and his father generally was already home and wouldn't be back to start work until around six o'clock. Tony turned on the charm and found ways to ingratiate himself to many of the residents and the merchants. One morning hanging out in front of the popular Little Italy restaurant, he was passed by a tall, well-dressed man entering the building. The man, wearing an expensive looking topcoat, sharply creased pants, a starched white shirt, and the shiniest shoes Tony had ever seen, exchanged pleasantries.

"Hello."

Tony looked up and replied, "Good day, sir."

Later the man looked out the door and called to Tony, "Hey son, can you come over here?"

Tony looked up saying, "Who me?"

"Yes."

Tony, fearing he was about to be called down for some recent infraction, tried to decide whether to run or respond further. He moved toward the man.

"Do you know where Valenti's grocery store is just down the street?" asked the man.

Tony answered, "Sure, my father works there."

"Really? Who's your father?" asked the man.

"Vincent DeoMonte"

"The baker?"

"Yes sir."

"He seems like a good man. We get our bread for the restaurant there, and I need you go to the store and bring back a half gallon of olive oil for the restaurant. Here's a dollar."

Tony looked at the dollar and wondered why the man would trust him with the money. He ran quickly to the store and was back in a few minutes. He walked into the restaurant and was surprised by all the activity; people were moving about with precision, and each smiled as they passed him. Tony spotted the man who had sent him on the errand.

"Here's your olive oil and you change."

The man smiled widely and handed the change back to the boy saying, "This is for your help. By the way, my name is Tommy Russo. This is my restaurant."

"I'm Tony DeoMonte. Thank you very much, and thanks for trusting me."

"Sometimes you're tested, if you can trust people with small things often you can trust them with bigger things. No school today, Tony?"

"Nah, I don't go to school anymore."

Mr. Russo then asked, "I think you mean, *No, sir*, and in that case how would you like to work for me?"

Tony answered quickly, and recognizing his verbal indiscretion replied, "Yes sir!"

"Come back tomorrow at 10 AM," said Russo.

Tony was already taller than his father and his frame was filling out, he also inherited his father's values of hard work, loyalty, and hot temper—from his mother he carried the ability to *read* people, also her had kind side, if you gained his trust. This combination made him likable but also a bit of a con man.

Tommy Russo saw a bit of himself in the boy.

"You remind me of me when I was a kid."

"Is that why you gave me a job?"

"I try to give the local Italian boys a break. I keep one working here to help them and their families."

Russo and his wife, Esther, were childless, and she was now passed her childbearing years. They lived in a home just at the edge of the city and had opened the restaurant ten years ago.

The authentic Italian recipes, excellent food, and top-notch customer service made Little Italy a favorite dining spot, drawing patrons from all over the St. Louis area. Tommy Russo was a demanding owner but paid his staff well. The restaurant was known for its meat, chicken, and pasta dishes. Homemade spaghetti and ravioli were popular, and the sauces had people begging for the recipe.

The atmosphere was pure, old country Italy. At the entrance there was a rack for customers to hang their coats and a mat to kick of the snow and rain. Each table featured a red checked tablecloth, and in the center of each table was an empty Chianti bottle with a candle. A mural depicting the Italian countryside covered the entire wall, and the aroma from the kitchen caused mouths to water.

Before the meal was served, a complimentary basket of warm bread was brought out with a small bowl of olive oil for dipping. The oil was blended with oregano and lots of garlic and was anxiously anticipated by the restaurant's loyal customers. An ample supply of wine was available and enjoyed along with the true Italian meals and was an additional incentive for the customers many of who came every week. At the checkout there was a toothpick dispenser, a basket of mints, and a fishbowl contain red, white, and green matchbooks advertising *Little Italy*. The place was a gold mine.

That weekend Tony told his father about his new job. "Papa, I've got a job." Vincent accepted the news quietly and merely nodded his approval.

Tony continued seeking his father's approval. "I'm working at Little Italy, the restaurant up the street from Valenti's—a real job, not street hustling!"

Vincent had become aware of his son's activities and inside was glad to see he was going to work a more traditional job than the resume of misdemeanors he had been involved in most recently.

Working to not show his pride, he said, "So you got a job, doing what? Are you getting paid? I hope you don't do something stupid and get fired."

Despite the size and age differences, Tony feared his father. Secretly he craved his father's attention and wanted him to be proud, but they were both incapable of a healthy relationship. Their's was clumsy at best, soon they found themselves just sharing a house and barely even crossing paths.

Rosa' death made a normally unemotional man even more of a hollow man. He stopped attending church which became evident to Father Parisi, but he wanted to give Vincent time to heal.

"I don't see you in church anymore Vincent."

"Church? My home is empty and quiet, my wife is gone, one son moved away. I work, I come home. This is my life."

"God loves you, I love you, your family loves you."

"That's your God. my world is dark; don't speak to me of love. Everything I loved is gone. You go back to your church and leave me alone."

"I am always here if you need me."

Mr. Russo took an interest in Tony and watched over him. Tony slowly came to admire and trust Russo who was teaching the young boy all about the business. He enjoyed his new employee's eagerness and attention to detail. Russo noticed the positive response to the praise he heaped on the boy and imagined that it was new to him. As Tony showed more interest, he was given more responsibility. He went from menial tasks like errands, clean up, taking trash into the alley to busing tables and even assisting in the kitchen.

"You're doing very well, Tony! I'm proud of you."

"Thank you, sir. I like it here. I like you."

"You're going to do well. Work hard, keep your nose clean, and always do a little more that is expected. That's a big key to success, it will set you apart from everyone else."

Tony watched as he passed the cash register and noticed the drawers brimming with all denominations of bills. At the end of the week, Mr. Russo made it a point to pay all the restaurant workers personally and thank each for the work they had done.

"I watch you, Mr. Russo, so I can learn likes and dislikes."

Tony took pride in attending to something before being asked. The smile that Mr. Russo gave him was worth more than the pay at times, the bond between the boy and this man was being firmly established.

It wasn't uncommon for Tony to be the last one paid, and Mr. Russo often slipped a folded dollar bill into Tony's shirt pocket saying, "You did a good job this week. I see potential in you, but I'm always on high alert, I know about your reputation in the neighborhood."

At times when customers had a little too much wine, and they became loud and unruly, Tony rushed to the aid of his employer.

One such time Mr. Russo reprimanded Tony saying, "I appreciate your concern, but I can take care of myself and this business."

Tony asked around the neighborhood, "Do any of you know anything about Tommy Russo?"

One of the group responded, "He's the toughest guy downtown; everyone fears him that's why no one tests him."

His huge hands and broad shoulders gave a few clues as to

his ability to handle himself. This was a side of Mr. Russo Tony had never seen. Tony always saw him as a kind man, but he always seemed in control of every situation.

Occasionally Esther Russo would come into the restaurant. She always found Tony and made a point to tell him how much her husband thought of his young apprentice.

"You know, Tony, my husband thinks the world of you. He speaks of you often at home and how you remind him of him when he was your age."

The flattered Tony responded, "He's more like a father to me than my own father."

Tony found in Mr. Russo what he had yearned for from his father—acceptance and love. As the months went, by the two unlikely Italiani became closer and closer.

The economy continued to grow, and the restaurant was booming. Time passed, and Tony was ready to celebrate his 18th birthday. As a surprise for the young man who was more like family, Mr. Russo ushered Tony out to the front of the store to show him a 1932 Ford coupe and handed him the keys to his first car.

"This is s a special birthday, so you should get a special gift."

Tony's only reply, "For me?"

Faded black paint, a gray cloth interior and whitewall tires all were indication that the car had seen some wear, but to Tony it was like a limousine.

Tommy Russo beamed as he said, "No more bus. Gas is 11 cents a gallon, and now you can get around on your own."

Tony hugged Mr. Russo so tight the car keys fell to the ground. Tears welled up in the boy's eyes, and for the first time in his life he was without words.

He had become a great employee, trusted friend, and now the relationship had taken on more of a father-son feel.

Vincent was lost in his own world, more like a personal prison, and barely noticed the absence of his oldest son. He had fallen into a robotic trance—climb aboard the bus, march into the store—sometimes without speaking a word—bake his bread, barely stopping to eat or interact with the customers. His single day off was usually spent on the porch of the house sitting in an old green metal chair. Sometimes he drifted off into sleep and dreamed of his childhood days and his early life with Rosa. He cherished those dreams as a chance to again see her face and relive pleasant times. But the terror of one reoccurring dream affected him most—the young boy spotting the lion and fatally wounding it accompanied by the haunting words dooming him to a century of bad luck…Cent'Anni.

The old haunting vision hung in his mind like a picture nailed to a wall.

Chapter X

It's Not a Small World

While Vincent's world remained stuck in sadness, Tony was flourishing. Both had jobs—for one the repetitive drudgery of baking bread and the other a youthful enthusiasm for what the world was delivering to him. Tony was becoming almost an adopted son of Tommy and Esther Russo. He spent a few holidays with them and even accepted an invitation to a small farm they had *in the country.*

Tommy Russo always took the role of a teacher, every move calculated. "See Tony this is what you can have if you work hard." A small comfortable farmhouse, a small pond and a pasture that served to feed a horse who roamed freely between the field, and a barn. Tony was wide eyed at the calm and peace that came with the setting.

"This is wonderful. Do you ever ride the horse?"

Russo responded, "Sure he's pretty tame. Would you like to ride him?"

"I've never been on a horse." In a matter of a few minutes, Buster was saddled, and Tony nervously was sitting in the saddle.

"Just trust him, Tony. If he senses you're uneasy it'll make him nervous."

Slowly the horse moved in circles around the corral. This was a new world for Tony; he felt far away from the city.

It was just before Christmas, 1940. Esther came to the restaurant and found Tony.

"If you have no plans for Christmas Eve, Tommy and I would

like to invite you to our home to join us for our traditional Christmas Eve supper."

Tony was completely taken by surprise. "I'll check with my father to see what he is doing, but I'm sure he will just go to sleep early. He doesn't celebrate anything since my mother died."

True to his word when he arrived home Tony found Vincent sitting at the kitchen table with a strange drink. There was a tall glass of wine with what looked like sliced peaches in the bottom. Vincent didn't even acknowledge the presence of his son. He drank the wine and then took a fork to retrieve the peaches from the bottom of the glass.

Unaware of the significance of the peaches, Tony asked, "Papa the Russo's have invited me to their house for Christmas Eve supper. Do you mind if I go?"

"Do what you want," was the reply.

The restaurant closed early on Christmas Eve. The last of the customers were ushered out at 7 PM.

Russo suggested, "Follow me to the house."

It was cold and quiet as the pair turned the lock on the door and climbed into their cars. Tony was nervous about going to the Russo home. He followed closely and smiled at the reflection of the full moon in the rear window of Tommy Russo's shiny black Cadillac. As they pulled up the driveway, Tony was impressed with the size of this mansion. It looked like a dozen people could live there. The soft glow of candlelight from the front windows made the house look warm, welcoming, and like a real home.

As Tony entered Esther said, "Welcome to our home," and took his coat and hung it on a coat tree in the entry way. At the end of the hallway was a wooden bench with a ribbon on it. Tony thought to himself, *That's strange.*

Tommy Russo was waiting by the well-worn wooden bench seat. "Merry Christmas, Tony."

Tony looked at the bench, four feet long and out of place in this grand house. "Thanks."

"Does it look familiar?"

"No, sir. Sorry. What is it?"

"Father Parisi called me to ask for a donation to help renovate the neighborhood church, St. Francis of Assisi. I asked what they were doing, and he told me they were putting in new kneelers and benches."

Tony smiled faintly, still perplexed by the intended connection.

Russo explained further, "One of Father Parisi's favorite memories was seeing your mother take her traditional place in the last pew and at the far right—closest to the outside aisle, closest to the statue of the Sacred Heart of Jesus. I promised a large donation if he would save that section of the bench seat." When they were removing the seats, I had a carpenter friend of mine pick up that seat and make this bench out of it. Merry Christmas!"

Tony, tears streaming down his face, almost in a whisper said, "I love it!"

"Time for supper," Esther announced. A long, fully placed table greeted the three as they entered the formal dining room. Real silverware, linen napkins, crystal glassware, and silver candlestick holders made the table look fit for royalty. As the men took their seats, Esther left and returned quickly carrying three plates. On each plate there was bologna, bread, and green beans. From a silver coffee service, black coffee was dispensed into the fine china cups.

Esther was the first to speak. "Before we pray you should know this was what we had for our first Christmas together. It was all we could afford, and since then every Christmas Eve we traditionally have this for supper."

Tony was stunned at the love of these people and their reverence for tradition. The scene could have been the subject of a Norman Rockwell painting.

Tony looked up to Russo and aspired to be like him, but beneath the surface larceny always lurked in his heart.

"Gosh, I want to be so much to be like you someday, sir!"

"My young friend, like so many people you see what you want to see. My life is difficult, packed with pressure, lots of responsibility for myself and many others. It's dangerous life, sometimes exciting, but this life—our life—doesn't tolerate foolish behavior. There's always somebody waiting to take you down."

Russo noticed that Tony had been associating with some questionable characters, small time hoodlums. After closing time one evening Russo announced to tony that he wanted to talk to him. The serious tone of voice was like nothing he had ever heard before.

"I've seen you hanging around with people that I know are not the kind you should have anything to do with."

Tony's first instinct was to try to deny his involvement with the mobsters. "I'm just friends with a few of them—they're harmless."

Russo snapped back, "They're not harmless, they're worthless. They'll bring nothing but trouble."

"I can handle them; they wouldn't do anything to me."

"Tony, never forget this, people like that don't come after you, they go after what you love the most. It can be a wicked world. Let's take a ride."

Tommy Russo and his young friend stepped out into the street. "First thing is always look around you as you enter a new place—the street, a building and alley, anywhere—danger is all around for people like us."

This took Tony by surprise. "I always felt safe in the neighborhood."

"That could be a fatal mistake. Danger strikes when you least suspect it. You don't have to be afraid, but you do have to be aware."

They climbed into the front seat of Tommy's black Cadillac. The seats felt like an easy chair and had a sort of groaning sound as the leather stretched to accommodate the weight of the riders. The inside of this luxury car was immaculate.

"This car is cleaner than my house, but I smell smoke."

"Good, you were aware of something different, but it's a mistake to say everything your thinking out loud."

Tommy reached into the glove box where there was a red, white, and green box of cigars and removed one. "When I was about 11 my father caught me one smoking these," he said as he pushed in the cigarette lighter in the dashboard of the Cadillac. When it reached heat, the lighter popped out. As Tommy reached for lighter Tony noticed the red/orange glow of the lighter and the smell that accompanied the lit cigar.

Tommy continued, "My father said, *Do you like those?* And I said, *Yes*, not knowing what was coming next. My father said, *Good. Start eating!*"

"You had to eat the cigars?"

"The whole box. It's very unforgiving world out here, it doesn't tolerate foolishness. I learned that lesson quickly and vowed not to ever make the same mistake twice. I made decisions as if my father was watching, and it saved me a lot of grief. I respected my father, but I feared him more, that's why I hid what I was doing."

"Did you think that was fair?"

"The world is cruel and certainly not always fair."

"Is that why people fear you, because it's a cruel world?"

"Tony, people *fearing* you isn't a good thing—that makes them dangerous. You want people to *respect* you. A little fear is okay, but genuine respect is so much more important. Remember, to survive the storms of life, you must be ready all the time."

They made a turn around the corner, and Tommy spotted a young boy selling newspapers. Tommy called the boy over to the car.

"I'd like a paper," Tommy said to the young paperboy.

"Here you go Mr. Russo, Sir. I know who you are—no charge."

Tommy handed the boy a dollar for the five-cent paper, "Here you are son, keep the change."

As they pulled away, Tommy said, "That kid wanted to give me the newspaper because he feared me. I turned that around by being kind. It cost me a dollar, but now he respects me. The next thing is knowing who to trust."

"My father says trust no one but family."

"Your father is partly right, but you wouldn't have gotten in this car if you didn't trust me."

"I think I understand—trust is like respect, you have to earn it over time."

"Good, you're learning, but understand no one will take better care of you than you. Understand too, make every move you make count."

"I don't understand what you mean?"

"Did you ever play chess?"

"No."

"A great chess player anticipates his opponent's moves and knows ahead of time what his next six moves are going to be. In life, the life I live, I need to know what my next six moves are going to be."

Tony couldn't help but notice as Tommy's car made its way around downtown everyone smiled and waved. They all seemed to know Tommy. Tony dreamed of being like Tommy—nice car, beautiful home, dressed well, and seemingly worry free. The car seats were so comfortable he was almost falling asleep. He looked around and noticed all the accessories, a clock and even a radio in the dash. He also noticed a gun sticking out from under Tommy's seat.

"Why the gun?"

"Remember when I said, *nobody will take better care of you than you*? Well I've never been afraid to mix it up when I had to. I don't want to fight, but I will. Do you know the rules of street fighting?"

"I think so."

"By your answer I'd say, no. *There are no rules.* You always know who the winner is—he's still standing. Your enemy won't always come after you, they go after what you cherish, love the most. The price of great love is great grief at the loss of love."

The big black car wheeled back around to the front of the restaurant. They sat in silence until Tony, almost choking on the words, unfamiliar to him said, "I love you, Mr. Russo. Thank you."

Tommy Russo was bringing him along slowly and had big plans for the boy. Tony, now 19, was adjusting to a new lifestyle. He looked upon his birth father with a great deal of sadness and struggled with their relationship.

Thoughts beyond the neighborhood and the next day were lost in the moment. Then the world, everyone's world shook. News of the Japanese attack on Pearl Harbor created chaos, fear, and a sense of instability. Tommy Russo was grateful for what this country had given him and that translated into patriotism, something Tony didn't understand but accepted because of his relationship with Russo.

It was decision time.

Chapter XI

WAR!

The request was made for men to answer the call of their county and join in the fight for freedom. *Go off and fight who and for what,* Tony wondered.

He sought advice from the two men he trusted the most—Tommy Russo and Father Parisi. Each in their own way tried to explain the world crisis.

"Mr. Russo, I'm not sure what to do?"

"About what?"

"Lot's of people my age are joining the army, should I join?"

"Would you join because they are or because you want to?"

"I love this country and I don't want anyone destroying what it is."

"If you have the power to protect what you love then you do that. The more powerful you are the more you can protect that which you love. Do you understand?"

"I think so."

"When I was young, I wanted money, a good woman, and power. I have all three. Now I use my power to protect what I cherish."

It was clear to Tony now he wanted to protect the life he had found and the people important to him. He made the decision to join the army. This was quite an impulsive decision for a young man that had never been out of the neighborhood.

Tony ran into Father Parisi and asked, "Father, how does the church see me if I go to war."

"You should do everything for the glory of God and serve Him and your country. Joining the military is honorable but it's a decision you have to make."

"I love my family, my friends, my country, and my God."

In January Tony found himself standing in front of a recruiter explaining his decision to join the Army. He had helped his father search for his birth certificate and had made up his mind to defend his country against an unknown enemy. Vincent had long forgotten the name change that came on his son's birth certificate.

As Tony was signing in and being instructed as to what was expected prior to induction the recruiter was filling out the appropriate forms. The recruiter asked, "First on the list is your name, are you Anthony LeoMorte?"

Tony looked up and immediately said, "What?"

The recruiter repeated, "LeoMorte, that's what it says right here."

"That can't be right. My family name is DeoMonte"

"Son, are you questioning whether I can read or not?"

"No, I just think there is a mistake."

"There is, and you made it! First lesson in the United States Army—you follow orders without question. Do I make myself clear?"

"Yes."

Much as his father had done almost 20 years previous, Tony just accepted the surprise. From here on he would be Tony LeoMorte.

After completing the paperwork, the recruiter said sarcastically, "Be back here in 48 hours, Mr. LeoMorte."

Two days later, right hand raised, Tony and hundreds of other men had their formal swearing in and induction into the United States Army. As he left the army office, Tony was still in shock about the magnitude of his two major life changes. How could this be his legal name, and he was just finding out? So many questions about what his service would require of him. He didn't dare ask his papa.

Walking several blocks back to the restaurant he sought

the comfort, reassurance, and wisdom of his surrogate father Tommy Russo.

"Can we talk for a couple of minutes?"

"Sure."

"Did I do the right thing? These army people seem awfully mad."

"If you believe in your heart you did the right thing, then it is. Sooner or later you'll hear one of them say, *We have to break you before we can make you.* Your patience will be tested. Another of their favorites sayings is, *Your soul belongs to God, but your ass belongs to me.* Just listen and follow directions."

"What about my job, my car, my father, and our house?" wondered Tony.

"They'll all be here when you get back."

Tony felt a sense of relief at the counsel of his dearest friend. Now he had to break the news to Vincent. Tony worried about telling his father of his decision on the short drive home.

He found his father sitting on the porch in his favorite chair.

"Papa I decided to join the army."

"You did what? Why?"

"I want to defend the way of life the United States has offered us. I want to protect you, my friends and our family. I'll be leaving soon."

Vincent left the room feeling once more a sense of loss but in a different way.

On Monday Tony reported back to the army center having said his goodbyes; the most difficult to Tommy Russo.

"I'm leaving and want you to know how much you mean to me Mr. Russo!"

"You're not my biological son but as close as I'll ever come to having a son. Listen to what you're told, and when the time comes, you fight like your life depends on it, because it does. Do everything 100 percent."

"I understand. If I don't come back…"

"You'll be back, work hard, pray hard. and fight hard. I love you boy."

Long lines of men—young and older—were being given physicals followed by the distribution of army green issue clothing and more instructions. The line, to Tony, resembled a line of cattle being herded along. Orders being barked out, confusion reigned with multiple boisterous conversations occurring at the same time. People moving in all directions, each person wide-eyed and wondering what they had gotten themselves into.

After a fast five-minute physical, Tony was direct to another room with a half dozen barber chairs. No fancy haircuts here. Tony stared at the floor as his dark thick hair dropped.

Going from room to room, boys about to become men all smiled nervously as they all chuckled about their new look.

"Hey baldy."

"Yeah skin-head."

Seated in a room with 100 other new recruits they were being given directions as to expectations and tomorrow's travel.

"Listen up," screamed a burly man with the three sergeant stripes on his arm. "You're headed to your racks, get your equipment and then chow…go, go, go."

The raw recruits were herded to rooms with bare metal bunks, drab furnishings, and identical equipment. A bland, barely warm evening meal served on metal trays was preceded by the command that they had five minutes to eat and move to the next training session.

"No time for talking, eat and get the hell out of here."

Soon after they were quickly and clumsily marched back to the barracks where a nervous night of whispers in the dark followed.

"What did we get ourselves into?"

"Are you scared?"

"Shut up, you're going to get us all into trouble."

He was awakened by a screaming voice. "It's 5 AM ladies, time for chow in the dining hall. Be ready to go and out front in ten minutes."

A scene that minutes ago was silent now was a gigantic jumble of newly inducted soldiers awkwardly trying to prepare for their day. Looking at the clock on the wall, they were all shoveling in some mixed-up unidentifiable food mess from those same trays in order to insure they were able to comply with the order to be out front in a seemingly impossible ten minutes.

What looked like an endless line of buses spewing fumes lined Broadway. At each open bus door were uniformed officers screaming out instructions to board the buses. A trip from downtown St. Louis to Fort Leonard Wood would take about three hours with more instructions and weeks of basic training to follow.

The tall, skinny, blond-haired boy sitting in the next seat introduced himself to Tony. "Hi partner, I'm Arnie Alford, but everyone calls me Arkie."

"Arkie?"

"Yeah, my whole family lives in Arkansas, none of us ever been out of state until now."

"I'm Tony LeoMorte."

"Nice to meet you. Is that name I-talian?"

"Yes, it is but we don't pronounce it *I-talian*."

"Are you scared, Tony?"

"Scared of what?"

"These people always screaming at ya, the war, being on a boat, people you don't even know shootin' at ya."

"I guess, now that you put it that way. But I'm going to follow instructions, keep my head down, and my mouth shut. Maybe the war will only last a few months."

"I'm as shakey as a 50-cent ladder."

Tony looked over a minute later, and Arkie had fallen asleep.

The mile after mile, the new soldiers looked anxiously out the bus windows barely noticing the landscape, more worried about what was to come than anything else. The ride was eerily quiet.

Filing off the bus, the men were greeted with the introduction, "I'm Sergeant Sanders. So much for formality." He screamed out, "We break you before we make you."

Tony smiled remembering Tommy's reference to that statement.

"I'm not here to babysit you. You've come here raw recruits, and I will make men out of you, fighting machines. You will think and act as one. You will follow orders or else. Now go with Corporal Davenport. Move it!"

Tony wondered how all this was going to help defend America. He often felt disrespected and didn't understand the gruff treatment meted out by the officers. He also believed he was being singled out for criticism, something that never sat well with him. As the days passed the tension built up and when confronted by the sergeant about the condition of his bunk, Tony responded with indifference.

"Your bunk is a mess. You were taught weeks ago how to properly make it." Sanders then ripped the bunk apart throwing pillow, sheets, and blanket to the floor. "Now get it right."

Tony first just stared at his sergeant and then refused to pick up the remnants of his previously made rack.

"It was right!"

"What did you say? Are you arguing with me, soldier? Refusing to follow orders? I always heard you *whops* weren't worth a thing." The other men in the barracks watched in horror waiting to see what was going to happen to their comrade.

"That's not true, sir. And we're *Italian*, not *whops* or *dagos*."

"Sir? Did you call me, Sir?! You will call me sergeant! Is that clear, boy?"

"No, Sir. But my bunk was made, and you threw my stuff on the floor. I don't see why I should have to pick it up."

The Sanders rushed Tony, grabbing him by the arm. Tony's immediate response was to pull away, which further infuriated the sergeant. He left hastily only to return with a pair of military police. "Remove this man from the barracks."

One on each arm, the MPs dragged the soldier out as a hush fell over the building.

Tony was escorted to a large fenced area where soon Sanders came in through the eight-foot-high fence and locked the gate behind him. Having walked in with a shovel Sanders, lit up a cigarette. Moving up to Tony, almost nose to nose he handed the boy the shovel.

"Start digging."

Tony took the shovel and began to dig, never even glancing at any of the men in the compound with him. The midday Missouri heat and the accompanying humidity had sweat pouring off the angry boy soon. One foot deep, two, and then three. After a couple of hours, he looked up as if to say, *how much more.* The look was ignored by the men. Periodically Sanders would fire up another smoke and go back to watching the progress of his subordinate. Tired but unwilling to give in to the fatigue, Tony dug faster and deeper. He had almost disappeared into the hole as shovel after shovel of dirt flew out.

The first words spoken by the sergeant were, "Here's is a tape measure, let me know when the hole is exactly six feet deep, and I mean *exactly.*"

Tony took the tape. The depth showed was 5 ½ feet. More digging. After about fifteen minutes another depth check showed six feet. Peeking up out of the hole ,Tony announced, "Okay it's six feet deep, Sir. "

"Come over here."

A grimy, sweaty Tony climbed up and out of the spot and walked over to his commander. "Yes, Sir."

Take these cigarette butts, throw them in the hole, then cover them up and fill the hole completely. Do you understand, soldier?"

In a loud voice tony responded," Yes, Sir." The thought briefly passed through his mind to slam the shovel into the sergeant's head.

"Do you *really* understand?"

"Yes, Sergeant!"

Almost dusk, lesson learned, Tony was dismissed to return to the barracks and go to chow. As he entered the mess hall, no one spoke. He grabbed the now familiar tray and ate quickly, anxious to get back to a shower and that troublesome bunk.

The next day the recruits were hustled over to the rifle range.

Tony showed an aptitude for target shooting. An almost imperceptible smile showed up on Sergeant Sanders face.

"Not bad, where did you learn to shoot?"

"This is my first time, Sergeant."

Sanders also noted that Tony's friend Arkie seemed more than proficient with firearms.

"And what about you, Private Arnie Alford. Your initials are AA, right? Are you an alcoholic?"

"Well, my family made a lot of moonshine, and I did drink my share, or more than my share of that."

"That's your new name, boy. Moonshine. So Moonshine, how did you learn to shoot that well?"

"Heck, Sarge, if you don't know how to shoot in Arkansas you don't eat. I bet I killed 500 squirrels."

"Sarge? Did you call me Sarge?!"

"Yes, Sir."

"Sir? Did you call me Sir?!"

"LeoMorte. School your friend here."

Tony jumped in hoping to save his friend from the wrath of Sanders. Remembering his previous experience, at the top of his lungs Tony screamed, "It's Sergeant Sanders."

"Good boy, you may make it yet."

After eight weeks of rigorous training the platoon was set for maneuvers—their destination, Camp Beauregard in Louisiana. Back on the buses and equipped with full gear, the soldiers were going to be tested soon. Late summer in the Louisiana swamps was no step-up from the conditions at their first stop. Hot, snake-infested, and loaded with mosquitoes these conditions alone were challenging. Slogging through the swamp in full field gear and being constantly soaked from sweat and swamp water was miserable. The repetitious drills and physical demands tested the men mentally and physically. Tony excelled at the challenges and was excited at the promise of a week's leave upon completion of the maneuvers.

With very little place to spend his pay, Tony discovered poker and dice. After hours a group of like-minded gamblers met up to try their luck. Tony, *bitten by the bug*, was careless with his pay and soon found himself penniless, not even enough left for bus fare back to St. Louis for leave.

"Maybe you could ask your folks for the money," one of his buddies suggested. "Send them a telegram to see if they could send you some money to come visit home."

A few days later an envelope with $15 dollars arrived. A regular part of Tony's attire was a pair of dice and deck of cards.

"Okay boys, who's ready to roll the dice? Or maybe a little poker?" He found several bunkies eager for a game of chance. Tony now figured he was staked for the after-hours gaming but soon was broke again. Another telegram to Vincent this time went unanswered.

With hard work Tony finally found favor with Sergeant Sanders. Word came that this platoon was being sent overseas. Ships loaded with soldiers were bound for Europe. Tony's outfit landed in North Africa and almost immediately were bound for front line duty.

Prior to going into battle, Sergeant Sanders gave his troops some last-minute instruction.

"Always remember this—that man across the line from you is your enemy. Don't hesitate. I think about Psalm number 156 when confronted with any enemy."

Thrust into heavy fighting Tony was made for combat. Brave, tough, and almost reckless he volunteered for the most dangerous duties. Feeling invincible almost got him killed. In the middle of a fierce battle Tony, feeling bulletproof, volunteered to try to knock out a German machine gun nest.

"I'll go Sergeant, I think I can do it."

"These are real bullets boy. Are you sure?"

"This is what I trained for; I can do it."

The sights, sounds, and smells of war were all around him. His senses heightened, the smell of burning gunpowder, the terrible sounds of suffering from the wounded and dying pierced the air.

Hardly able to see through the smoke, he went charging up a hill into rapid fire. Bullets buzzed past him, and he tried to stay low. Dodging bullets, stepping over fallen soldiers from both sides, Tony moved into the face of the fire. He felt a searing pain as he was hit in the right leg and then felt a powerful hit to his chest. For a moment he thought he was dying. The bullet wound to the leg was bad; the shot to the chest had been absorbed by the pocket-size Bible given to him by Father Parisi. The pages of the Bible were shredded but his life had surely been saved by the thick little book. He thought about how he had meant to check Psalm 156, but the now mangled pages of his Bible would not allow for that.

Mission accomplished, Sanders himself hurried to the aid of his charge. "Good job son, we'll get you out of here. You're going to be okay."

Badly wounded he was sent to the rear and eventually on to Marseilles, France for R and R, rest and recuperation. His personality won over the captain in charge of the R and R center, who requested Tony be transferred to him. *Request denied.* Tony was ordered to return to his outfit. Tony took off and decided to *take a break from the war.* With his ever-present playing cards, dice, and a woman in tow Tony was like a tourist.

Eventually he returned and was rewarded for his transgression with a transfer to the front lines as a machine gunner. Tony's training and natural survival instincts kicked in. He spent the remainder of the war doing his duty on the front lines but longed for home. His wish was granted in early 1945. After he was again wounded, he was headed home—his duty done.

Now 23 and a bit tamer, Tony was welcomed back by Vincent, whom he had barely communicated with, Father Parisi, his downtown friends, and most by an anxious Tommy Russo.

Life was looking up.

Chapter XII

Love and Loss

As Tony reentered the world he had known before the war, he was changed, now a bit wiser and ready to take on the world. His relationship with his father still somewhat distant, with Father Parisi their friendship renewed and with Tommy Russo stronger than ever.

He resumed his duties at the restaurant and was getting back into the swing of things when it happened. Totally unexpected, out of the blue, he met a girl. Not just a girl, but someone special. Escorted by her parents, they had come to the restaurant to celebrate her eighteenth birthday. Maria Farantello was petite, dark brown hair, and big brown eyes—she was an Italian beauty. Tony felt that sensation of first love and excitedly begged Tommy to introduce him to the parents and the young lady.

"Who is that?" Tony asked.

"That is the Farantello family. Why do you ask?" responded Russo.

"Is that their daughter?"

"Yes, it is. Do you want to meet them *or* her," laughed Tommy.

Tony blushed as he nodded in agreement.

He hoped Russo's being familiar with the family might offer him a chance to get to know Maria better. Tony had dated a few girls, but he was busy working most of the time and then the war called him away. Now he had more time and interest in the ladies.

As the pair approached the table, Tony tripped and almost fell into the table where the family was now seated. His face went from blushing to blood red.

In a most charming voice Tommy Russo, bowing slightly said, "Mr. and Mrs. Frank Farantello this is my dear friend, Tony LeoMorte."

Tony thrust his hand out to shake with Mr. Farantello, but his eyes betrayed his intent as he stared at young Maria.

Russo suggested to Tony, "Why don't you get menus for the Farantellos."

As Tony moved away Russo looked at the parents and said, "He's a great young man, a war hero. I think he's infatuated with your daughter."

Mr. Farantello gruffly asked, "How old is he?"

"Twenty-three, but a gentleman and a young man with a bright future. I've known him for years."

Tony returned with the menus, and soon he disappeared but went just far enough away to be able to peek at the family behind a large potted plant.

Through a chorus of conversations he could hear the collateral sounds of the diners, the clinking of ice hitting glasses as water was poured, the silverware in use, and the occasional thud of the kitchen door being kicked to allow for the entrance and exit to the main floor. *Now what?*

Later, as the Farantellos finished their meal, Tommy slipped a plate to Tony with a cannoli and candle to bringto the birthday girl's celebration. As Russo began a hushed version of happy birthday, he elbowed Tony in an effort to get him to join him in the song. Tony almost dumped the Italian dessert into the lap of Maria, their eyes met, and they shared a laugh. *Boom!*

Tony made sure to be up front when the Farantello family was paying their bill, preparing to leave so he could help the ladies with their coats. Tommy bid them farewell and thanked them for coming in. Then Tony blurted out, "Can I call you?"

Mrs. Farantello quickly responded, "I'm spoken for, but maybe Maria would welcome your call." Laughter erupted from everyone but Tony. Mr. Farantello just stared at Tony over the top of his glasses with a mild disapproval.

"Yes, you may," said Mrs. Farantello breaking the tension.

Maria chimed in, "I'll look forward to hearing from you." Music to Tony's ears.

A week later after the young coupled talked, Tony was invited to the Farantello home for a visit and chaperoned supper. Russo's endorsement had done the trick, and so the romance began.

Maria had other suitors, and Mr. Farantello wasn't convinced that his daughter was ready for a serious relationship.

"You better never disrespect my daughter."

"Oh, no, I would never do that, sir."

"The only reason I'm allowing you to see her is that you're Italian and that Tommy Russo speaks highly of you."

"My intentions are honorable, sir."

"Talk is cheap, you have to show me. I'm inviting you to go to church with us. Don't be late."

Tony often attended church with the Farantello family, that and the glowing praise of Tommy Russo eventually won over Maria's parents.

The post-war era was marked with economic growth—people had jobs, money, and hope, the country was on the comeback, and people were thriving.

Meanwhile Vincent continued his monotonous routine and heard little from Paolo, still in California. Tony had also become even more distant and was occupied with growing his position in the restaurant. The father and son communicated infrequently and even then, their conversations lacked substance or any emotional connection. They had mutually taken on an indifference—no anger; just indifference. They shared a house but little else. In Tony's mind Tommy Russo was more like a father to him. And Russo and his wife had come to love Tony as much as if he were their own child.

As time passed Tony and Maria fell deeply in love. Life seemed brighter, and all the world appeared to approve of their budding relationship. They spent many hours together under the watchful eye of her parents.

The year now 1946. It was a Monday mid-morning when Tony arrived at the restaurant. The door was still locked, Tony used his key to get in, but it seemed eerily quiet inside. No prep work being done, no other employees busying about tables and booths. There were place settings, folded napkins, and on a long table inverted glasses sat in neat rows like a platoon of soldiers. It certainly didn't look like Little Italy would be ready to open for the lunch crowd. Johnny Manzo the head chef, a short stocky man who looked like he enjoyed his own cooking way too much, wandered in moving slowly toward the kitchen.

"What's going on? Is the restaurant not going to be open today?"

Johnny replied, "Oh, you haven't heard. Tommy died last night."

Tony fell to his knees in shock. "What happened?"

"He had a heart attack; he was dead when he hit the floor."

Tony was completely stunned and didn't try to fight back the tears. He wasn't ready for this. This man had in a sense adopted him. He and his wife treated him as if he was their own son.

"I can't believe it. What do we do now?"

Manzo explained, "I'm making a sign to put in the front window that the restaurant is closed until further notice."

Tony, for the first time in a long time, felt totally lost, dazed, and confused. His first thought was to go to Esther Russo, comfort her, and find out what he could to help. He arrived at the Russo home not remembering anything about the trip there, still in disbelief. He tried to compose himself as he knocked on the door.

Esther opened the door slowly, and before Tony could even speak, she tearfully said, "I don't know what I'm going to do." They embraced each other and sobbed grieving the loss of a man they both loved. Their tears flowed and mingled as they mourned this tragedy. Both Esther and Tony suddenly felt frightened and alone.

On Wednesday a viewing and burial was held. A long procession of cars made their way to Resurrection Cemetery, hundreds of people who knew Russo attended as a show of respect for the man who was a central figure in the community. Tommy was a confidant, a protector, and the person everyone in the neighborhood turned to in time of need. He could take care of anything.

The restaurant reopened as Esther took charge. People flocked to Little Italy to eat but more to share their stories about Tommy. Tony stayed by Esther's side every minute. Saturday at closing Esther asked Tony to follow her home, she needed to talk to him. As he drove toward the house, Tony wondered what Esther wanted.

They were seated in the living room, and Esther took Tony's hand. "We, Tommy and I, made a decision a long time ago that if anything happened to us, we wanted you to run the restaurant and eventually sell it to you."

Shocked at the news Tony didn't know how to respond.

"I can't afford to pay what the restaurant is worth."

"I'm set for life, and it was the plan to sell Little Italy to you for just a thousand dollars. You can pay it slowly over time from the profits of the restaurant."

Tony, still reeling from the loss of his friend, was feeling an incredible contrast, an enormous emotional gap—there was joy at this news and at the same time a deep sorrow for not only himself but for Esther and all the people who admired Tommy Russo.

After a few minutes he regained his composure. He thanked Esther and asked if there was anything he could do before he left. She responded, "No, I'll be fine," and he then started the fifteen-minute drive towards the Hill and his father's home.

Vincent didn't attend the funeral. He had mixed feelings toward the Mr. and Mrs. Russo and their relationship with his son. Besides ,he had bread to bake and wine to make.

Tony walked in slowly, loosening his tie, deep in thought. Being Saturday, Vincent was home but in his usual spot and his usual mood.

"Papa I have incredible news!" Vincent cast a sideways glance at Tony waiting for his announcement. "Tommy Russo willed me the restaurant."

"What means this *willed*?" asked Vincent.

"It's mine. I'll own it soon." Vincent's only reaction, a blank stare.

Tony had planned to meet Maria and her family at St. Ambrose for Sunday mass, then he could tell them and Father Parisi the big news. Tony now could ask Frank Farantello for permission to marry his daughter. The next morning Tony was on the steps of the church ready for the nine o'clock mass and waiting for the Farantello family to arrive.

Following protocol Tony approached Mr. Farantello. "Sir, can I speak to you for a moment?"

"As long as you don't make me late to mass."

"I'm going to be the new owner of Little Italy, and I'd like to marry Maria."

"Congratulations, but as far as marrying my daughter, I'll discuss it with her mother and let you know."

Tony knew not to ask the question of when. They made their way into the church and took seats halfway up.

As they were waiting for mass to begin Tony leaned into Maria and whispered, "Mr. Russo willed me the restaurant. Now we can get married." Maria squealed so loud the sound of excitement echoed off the stone walls of the old church and was loud enough to draw a look of disapproval from both her parents. Tony and Maria had already talked of marriage, but old-school Italian parents made the ultimate decision on such matters.

Right after mass Tony asked if he could introduce Maria to his father and drive her home immediately afterwards. Frank Farantello gave his permission. Tony tried to prepare Maria for what she would find behind the front door of his father's house.

"It's a little messy, and my father is very reserved; just be ready."

As they entered Tony called out, "Papa, I want you to meet Maria." Vincent entered wearing his work pants and a T-shirt, took one look and dropped his wine glass. His eyes welled up in tears, something Tony had never seen.

"My God, she look a just'a like'a you mama," Vincent said, lips trembling. He ran to hug her as if he was having a heavenly reunion with his dead wife. This hug was uncomfortably long, but Maria allowed it.

"Papa, I asked Maria's father if I could marry her. I hope he says yes. We don't have much time now; we have to go." Vincent couldn't take his eyes off this beautiful reminder of his Rosa. Vincent watched from the front window until Tony's' car was out of sight. The lonely man stared out for several more minutes lost in a mix of joy from the ghostly reunion and sadness.

Word had spread, and when the restaurant opened Monday Esther was there to give the news of the change in ownership and her blessing to Tony in front of the employees.

"Tony is now the owner of Little Italy; this is what Tommy and I wanted. Please respect him and give him your cooperation. I will be around for a while if you have any questions."

With no questions she asked everyone to go about their normal duties and again reaffirmed that she would like everyone to give Tony their full support and cooperation. The staff pledged to help Tony as a tribute to Tommy and in order to keep the restaurant open and maintain their jobs. Tony planned to follow Russo's lead as to doing business down to the smallest detail.

Some changes were on the horizon.

Chapter XIII

La Nostra Famiglia—Our Family

In September of 1947 Frank Farantello walked his daughter down the aisle, and Maria became Mrs. LeoMorte. Father Parisi officiated, and a large Italian reception followed complete with tables full of food and bottles of wine at every table.

Vincent came and sat in the back of the church, attended the reception, and drank too much wine. Things still weren't good between Vincent and Father Parisi, but they nodded to each other and called an unspoken peace treaty on this day. As the reception ran late into the next morning, Vincent left quietly.

Around 10 PM Esther Russo took the couple aside, "as my gift, and in memory of Tommy, I'm forgiving the remainder of the restaurant debt." Tony now owned Little Italy the business and the building free and clear!

The plan for now was to stay in the house on the Hill. Vincent was gone from about 4 PM until 3 AM. Tony and Maria were running the restaurant from mid-morning until closing at 9 PM. While Little Italy was doing well, Tony had visions of growth. He took out a loan to buy the building next door with some very specific plans. He brought in a construction crew and cut an arched doorway in the connecting wall. Knowing there was money in liquor, he added a bar, plus a lounge area and even added a small bandstand to bring in local entertainment. People would be able to drink and listen to music while waiting for their tables. Business took off and was booming. Tony took advantage of his status and became the patriarch of the whole downtown area. Having made connections all over he could get anything done. He endeared himself to the powerful and rich residents in all of St. Louis.

While Tony had planned for this growth there was some growth he hadn't planned on, Maria announced, "We're going to have a baby!"

Tony was ecstatic. "Family is everything!" In September of 1949 a son arrived and true to tradition the baby boy was named after Vincent carrying on the tradition of naming the first boy after your father, this was the case as far back as it could be traced. Vincent knew his father while reserved, was proud. After a brief hospital stay Maria was ready to come home.

It was a Sunday so Vincent would be home until 3 o'clock before taking the bus downtown to bake Monday's bread. As they pulled up to the door, they spotted Vincent perched in his chair. He stood up to meet them.

"Well, Papa, this is little Vince." Tony offered his father the chance to hold his first grandchild. Vincent, hesitant to take the child, held the baby as if he was a bomb about to go off.

"It's okay papa, he won't break."

Right before their eye's Tony and Maria could see the heart hardened by loss and self-imposed isolation was softening. A tear trickled from the corner of Vincent's eye onto the baby's forehead almost like a family baptism.

"He's a'beautiful," Vincent whispered in his broken English. "Here, take him," he said as he brushed away his tears fighting his feelings. After decades of being buried finally some emotion.

It would take some getting used to having a baby in the house, but Maria was good at adjusting to life.

Little Vince was the pride and joy of the LeoMorte family.

"I want you to just stay home and take care of the baby. I can run the restaurant."

"Tony, you're so traditional!"

"And what's wrong with that?"

"Nothing, I like it. I hope running the business by yourself isn't too much."

"I can handle it. It'll be busy, and I'll miss you, but it will be good to come home to my family."

With the addition of a child, Tony became serious about business in and out of the restaurant. His mind was constantly occupied with making money—lots of money. Little Italy was becoming a St. Louis institution, a place to see and be seen. Tony maintained his status as the person to go to with any problem. He added to his reputation of being able to *take care of anything*.

"Got a problem come to me." Tony had city hall wired. "If you needed anything, a business permit, or just to take care of a speeding ticket, any kind of favor, I have a solution."

He gained power and prestige as a friend to all. He was also feared. For a while he drew the line on violence but eventually found intimidation an ally. Tony began to travel with his own entourage—a huge man posing as his driver, Bill Belacino, known affectionately as *Bull* and additional muscle in a fearsome giant named Hugo DiCaro. Just the sight of the three men entering any place was frightening.

"I've heard it said, *power perceived is power achieved*." One man, Ronald, decided to test the trio. He had borrowed $500 with a promise to pay it back at the end of the month. When the payment was passed due by a week Tony and the boys called on him.

"I lent you $500 dollars and out of the goodness of my heart didn't even charge you interest because I knew your father. You promised to pay the loan back a week ago. It's due in full now."

The debtor responded with, "What's $500 to you? You don't need it."

"I want my money, and I want it now."

"You'll get when I decide to give it to you."

"Wrong answer." Tony looked at Hugo. "This *Americani*, he doesn't understand, no honor."

Hugo asked, "Do you want me to break his thumbs?"

Tony answered, "No, then he wouldn't be able to work and

pay me back." The disrespectful debtor had his car parked just outside the door. Tony suggested to Hugo that he should hand Ronald the steering wheel of his new car. Hugo snatched the car door open and with a mighty pull broke the steering wheel into two pieces and handed it to Ronald.

"Would you like another piece of your car removed or would you like to pay the $500?" Tony asked.

Ronald, weighing his options, decided for the sake of his vehicle and his own well-being it might be beneficial to ante up the $500.

"I'll come by the restaurant with your money."

At five o'clock sharp he stepped off the bus with five $100 bills and a humble apology.

"I'm sorry I was late; I didn't mean any disrespect."

"You were disrespectful, don't ever do it again."

Tony was in for another shock. Little Vince was scheduled for a twelve-week doctor's appointment, as was Maria. Vince got a clean bill of health, but Maria was due for a surprise. After her examination the doctor left the room and didn't reappear for fifteen minutes.

"Maybe you should sit down," he advised. "You're pregnant."

"Are you sure?" wondered Maria.

"Pretty sure."

Maria realized Tony took anything to do with family seriously. What would he think of another baby?

When Tony came home, she cautiously approached him and asked, "How do you feel about more children?"

"I'd love it, someday."

"How about now?"

"Now?"

"The doctor says I'm pregnant again."

Tony moved toward her, kissed her gently, and scooped up Little Vince announcing, "Another baby, family is everything!"

Meanwhile Vincent had been hearing stories periodically about Tony and his success but also about his dabbling in criminal activities. Vincent feared Tony was turning into what he despised most. Recalling the thugs in Italy that made him come to the decision to abandon everything he knew and come across the ocean. He bristled at the thought that his son Tony was becoming what he hated.

"Tony, what's wrong with you? You want to be a gangster?"

"No, Pop, I want to be successful and safe."

"You better be careful. Don't do bad things!"

"Bad things? Pop, you make it sound like I'm in the eighth grade."

Tony watched his business and prided himself on having plans to improve his status and to find ways to advance himself financially. Maria was satisfied to take care of the small home and her family. She didn't question Tony about business matters. Business was good, and money was rolling in.

People came to visit Tony at the restaurant and even occasionally at home. He had tried to discourage people from stopping in at the house, because he sensed his father didn't approve of people setting up appointments to see Tony, and Maria was becoming inquisitive but didn't ask why all the activity was taking place.

"Why do all these people come here asking you for favors?"

"They need help, and usually I can solve their problems."

"Let them solve their own problems."

"What good are connections and power if I don't use them?"

"You're going to get yourself in a lot of trouble. There's bad people out there."

Vincent continued to watch but kept an uneasy feeling about the life his son was falling into.

At the restaurant politicians and police were becoming regular customers. Everyone knew Tony and frequented Little Italy where they found food, friendship, and a mysteriously secret atmosphere. Back booths were often reserved for conducting private conferences. Groups of men seeking an audience with Tony spoke in low tones, doling out respect to this man who seemed to know everyone that was worth knowing.

"Hey Tony, you got a minute?"

"Why sure, what can I do for you?"

Often speaking in hushed tones, the business meeting often closed with the exchange of sealed envelopes. Tony was almost as busy with outside business as he was with the restaurant business.

The wait for baby number two ended in August of 1949 when Mary Rose made her appearance. Now there was a boy and a girl and a house that was becoming crowded. Tony tiptoed around Vincent but knew soon it would be time to leave this nest.

With two babies Maria stayed busy and Tony focused on building an empire for his family. He grew impatient with the daily routine of the restaurant business and wanted to expand his business holdings. The money was good, but he felt temptation tapping him on the shoulder. Tony was assembling a small army of employees—some with regular jobs; others who waited for their assignments from *Big Tony* as he was now being called.

Each day started with assignments for his *soldiers*, specific duties along with stern warnings.

"No need to be excessive, if there's a problem come to me."

Duties ranged from settling disputes among the neighborhood residents to collecting debts for business owners. After the reputation of Tony's helpers spread, it was a rare occurrence when they had to resort to violence.

The steady stream of friends took routine restaurant business and made it seem like a corporation. Juggling everyday duties was requiring Tony to spend twelve to fourteen hours a day overseeing operations. He developed a sharp eye for sizing up people, and the street smarts he developed made up for the traditional education he turned his back on as a young boy. It seemed that Father Parisi's worry over Tony's well-being was unfounded—by monetary measures he was becoming very successful. He looked upon the everyday workers and simple, straight-arrow citizens as what he referred to as *square Johns*, street lingo for the customers of prostitutes.

Tony had gone from a street hustler to a boss. He was being

chauffeured around in his own Cadillac now, wearing expensive suits, and carrying what the mobsters called *a roll*. To further define his personal style, he visited a downtown jeweler he referred to as *Julius the Jeweler*. Tony found it amusing to assign nicknames to many people.

Tony inquired about the possibility of getting a custom-made ring. "Can you do that?"

"Of course, sir." The jeweler showed him a catalog of rings.

"I want a ring that looks like a lion's head. I want it in gold of course," Tony advised the jeweler.

"Oh, yes sir, nothing but the best."

Tony said, "I'd like red stones for the eyes of the lion, to make the lion look fearsome."

"I can easily place rubies in the eye sockets. I'll give it to you at my cost. I can have it ready in a few weeks if that's acceptable Mr. LeoMorte?"

"That will be fine."

It wasn't uncommon for him to have $1,000 in his pocket bound tightly by the red rubber bands used by grocery stores to hold celery stalks together.

He had long since abandoned the practice of keeping a small roll of *mugging money* in his left pocket. It was a common practice for many to give a mugger a small roll with a twenty-dollar bill on top of two dozen dollar bills. No one would dare to steal from Tony LeoMorte. When necessary to pay for something Tony unashamedly flashed the cash but often out of reverence and respect for the powerful man, he was given almost everything and paed for nothing.

With his ability to take on any challenge, he now exuded confidence bordering on arrogance. He was getting ready to make his move.

Tony began to lay out big plans for his family and the future.

Chapter XIV

The Family Home

Tony, Maria, and the children had certainly outgrown the home on the Hill. Besides, it really belonged to Vincent. He often checked on Esther Russo and had admired the house she had shared with Tommy.

"Maria, I started looking for a house for us. I want something that fits us and our place in the community."

"Where are you looking?"

"I don't want to be far from the restaurant, and I want a place that gives us room to grow our family."

A large, beautiful, Victorian home built in 1910 came available, and Tony, Maria, and the two children went on a Sunday drive to visit the house. As they pulled up to the home it looked perfect, painted white, with a gray shingle roof, a large yard, fenced for security, three stories, five bedrooms, a detached garage, large trees, and all the amenities that signaled success. The wrap-around porches seemed ideal for summer sitting in wicker furniture, enjoying the southerly breeze the porch offered.

Maria was first to speak. "This place looks ideal for us. It's certainly big enough. Do you think it's too big?"

"No, we'll fill it with children and love."

"There's a man on the porch, he must be the real-estate agent."

They toured the home with a real estate agent who Tony found annoying, but Maria listened closely for all the details.

"This lovely home is perfect for your family, and in real-estate we say location, location, location. This is a great neighborhood."

Tony asked, "Is the house sound? Good electrical wiring, plumbing?"

"Oh, yes sir. Of course you can have it inspected. Trust me, sir, with a man of your importance I would never try to fool you."

"I trust family, and family only!"

"Well I didn't mean…"

"I know what you meant."

The agent was small in stature looked like an accountant, or as Tony called them, *bean counters,* and mentally nicknamed him *Mr. Milk Toast.* The little man in the blue wool suit and bad shoes was bland and plain and carried a folder with details about the home.

Maria continued to walk the inside inspecting everything from floorboards to ceilings. "I like the vaulted ceilings, they give a feeling of roominess. The large chandelier in the entry hall looked classy too."

Tony asked, "Maria, will it be hard to keep it clean?"

Maria was busy imagining beautiful tropical plants in the hallway and entertaining guests in the living room.

Tony looked at the large fireplace and said, "What about an oil portrait of the family above the mantle?"

"Yes, I can see that."

They wandered farther and entered an arched door leading to a big, tiled kitchen suitable for preparing meals of any size or just an informal gathering place for Italian-style family meals. Natural light entered every window, and there were several stained-glass windows scattered around to add a look of class and accent formal rooms.

"I can cook anything for a bunch of people in this kitchen. Isn't it perfect?"

"Maria, I can see you moving around in this kitchen, pans all over the stove, kids playing on the floor, and the smell of Italian food in every corner of the house."

A wide, winding, oak staircase leading to the second floor had well-worn steps, and a bannister shined from years of hands gliding along the wood while going up and down the stairs. A third-floor steeple would supply a panoramic view of the surrounding area and would add a feeling of living in a castle.

Tony commented, "Look at this back yard, those trees must be a hundred years old! Wow, a double door garage. We could fit two cars in there. Hey, look at that, it even has a brick barbeque pit."

Tony joined Maria as she continued to stroll from room to room and floor to floor. She imagined out loud what each room was best suited for and which child would sleep where.

"We could put Vince in this room, and Mary Rose could have a canopy bed and pink walls. Is that all right with you?"

"Whatever you want, this is your house."

"*Our* house, maybe?" Maria continued," I would change the paint in the master bedroom, and probably in the kitchen. I'd like a cheerier color, maybe yellow. We don't have near enough furniture to fill such a large house."

Tony smiled at her vision for the home and laughed as he reassured her, "We have money for enough furniture to fill any house."

Tony revisited the yard several times. With an eye for detail, he did everything with purpose. In his life—business and personal—he made every move count.

"What are they asking for this house?" he asked.

"$17,900, sir, but the price is negotiable."

Maria was considering taxes, insurance, utilities, and upkeep when she heard Tony say, "We'll take it."

Wide-eyed and surprised at his comment, Maria grabbed Tony's hand and escorted him to the next room. "Don't you want to know more about the house?"

"Don't you like it Maria?"

"I do, but shouldn't we try to negotiate the price, we paid $3000 for the car and didn't try to negotiate the price. Shouldn't we look around more, think about it?"

"We've seen every room, if you like it, I'll buy it."

"Just like that?"

"Yes, just like that. We'll call it Villa Cristo, just like the city in Italy where my parents are from."

"If you're sure, I can certainly see us in it. And there's room for more kids."

"And a dog. I want a dog. One of those *police dogs*, a German shepherd."

Tony informed the agent that they would take the house.

He asked, "Can you qualify for a bank loan?"

Tony laughed at the little man. "Call St. Louis Federal Bank and ask them if I can qualify for a loan. Tell them it's for Tony LeoMorte."

"I'm so sorry, Mr. LeoMorte, I wasn't sure that's who you were. I'll get started on the paperwork right away. The seller would like a 20% down payment. You should be able to move in in four weeks—if the bank okays your loan."

Doing the computation in his head, Tony took the roll from his front right pocket, counted out $3,850 and handed it to the agent. He nonchalantly said, "There's your 20% down payment. We're moving in next week. Do you understand?"

"Well. I don't know."

"I do! Next week."

Tony asked Maria, "What else would you like done to fit the house to your taste? Let's look around."

"I'd like the entry to make people feel welcome. Maybe some green, potted plants, a hall tree, a mirror for a last-minute check on how we look before we go out the door. How about fresh paint in the bedrooms, a new stove for the kitchen, and drapes for the windows."

"What about furniture?"

"We'll need a sofa, an easy chair for you, and a rocking chair for me to rock the babies to sleep. I would like their rooms to be brightly colored with shutters on the windows so we can keep it quiet and dark for nap times. Can we get a king-size bed for us, and a table and chairs for informal dining in the kitchen area, and oh, I know, a formal dining room set?"

Tony, taking mental notes, said, "Is that all? Done! I'll set up a handyman and a remodeling crew to take care of all that."

"We'll have to tell Papa that we are moving."

The next day a construction crew was there to start painting. Tony had sent Maria, armed with a checkbook, out shopping for furniture and accessories.

Tony nicknamed the head of the crew, *Handy Andy*. He approached the crew boss. "Here's a list of inside work, but I also have some outside projects for you. I want you to pour a six-by- six foot concrete slab with a four-by-two foot hole, dig the hole three feet deep in the center of the slab and then surround the whole thing with a seven foot chain link fence, install a gate to match the ten-by-ten foot enclosed fenced area. I also want you to build a doghouse measuring five and a half feet by three feet. Make it sturdy."

"Sir, you can buy a doghouse a lot cheaper than if you have me build one."

"Just build it and put it on a set of rails."

"A doghouse on a set of rails?" Handy Andy asked.

"On a set of rails so I can slide the doghouse back. Do you understand?

"Yes Sir, Mr. LeoMorte."

"Also, do you have someone who can make a wooden sign to put at the entrance that says, "VILLA CRISTO?"

"I have someone who will do you a good job. Did I hear you correctly—a doghouse on a set of rails?

"Yes!"

Soon the five-man crew had painted every room, installed a new electric stove, checked all electrical outlets and light fixtures ,and tested all the plumbing. Flood lights were installed on each side of the house to illuminate every inch of the property. Finally, a wrought iron gate was added to the front driveway entrance. Tony was fortifying the house with his family's safety first in mind.

By Friday the house was move-in ready, and delivery vehicles were lined up to deliver furniture and household accessories. Uniformed workers were moving past each other like five o'clock traffic on Broadway. The sound of furniture assembly was coming from every room. Some workers assemble beds, dressers, two sets of dining room tables and chairs while others were busy hanging draperies. A new washer and dryer set was placed side by side and hooked up to water and electric in a small basement, and the new stove was placed and plugged up in the kitchen as Maria requested.

Peering out the back window, Maria wondered, "Is that a doghouse and a fence around it?" Knowing full well it was, she was hinting at the reasons for the kennel set up since they didn't yet have a dog.

"Yes, I called a friend at the police department to find out about getting a dog and training it. We'll soon have what everyone calls a *police dog,* or as the cops refer to it, a German shepherd."

Tony spent some time inspecting the kennel construction—everything passed. The tall fence would secure the dog when it wasn't roaming the property. When necessary the canine security system would be comfortably housed in his custom-built home.

The house almost seemed like a dream. The Farantello family was financially comfortable but in no way wealthy. This house, Villa Cristo, was beautiful outside as well as inside and gave a distinct visual appearance of money, position, and power.

Maria felt safe and comfortable there. It took a while to get used to the size of the place and the maze of rooms. Five bedrooms for four people seemed a little much, but Tony wanted his family together always.

This house had room for the family to grow, and grow it would. In 1952 another son arrived. Dominic was a perfect addition at a perfect time. The children were stair-stepped; Vince was now four, Mary Rose was three, and now *Dom* was here.

Tony spoiled his children; Vince because he had high hopes for him, and he was his father's namesake, his little doll, Mary Rose ,because she had turned into a daddy's girl, and now

Dominic. The baby boy who looked one hundred percent Italian. Dominic, unlike the other children, was fussy and demanding. Maria hoped it was a stage he would grow out.

This was one beautiful family; Tony was protective, and Maria was nurturing. Tony not only thought family was everything but the only people you could trust.

Chapter XV

Doing Business

Tony kept a focus on finances and never seemed to be satisfied. More money meant more power. The addition of the bar and lounge area with the expansion of the building next door had money flowing in. He saw opportunity everywhere. Running a restaurant business gave him access to lots of potential income, normal profits were good, but he had a plan for increases in revenue.

He studied other operations, made it his mission to become familiar with how his vendors and suppliers ran their businesses. He avoided conversations with the owners but secretly befriended low-level managers, dock workers, and especially delivery drivers.

Tony himself visited food vendors and found the managers, introducing himself—as if he needed an introduction—and told him what he wanted: for $50 a week, his request was loaded on a separate truck and delivered to the back door of Little Italy. At the end of the week the driver was also given $20.

"Hello friend, I'm Tony LeoMorte," was generally the line he used. "How would you like some money on the side?"

Many of the targets would express concern. The meat packing house manager, Phil, asked, "What if I get caught?"

Tony's response, "Are you kidding me? I'll take care of you. It's been said, *one thing you can give and still keep is your word.* I keep my word."

"Yeah, but I need this job."

"*Cugino* (cousin), would you rather have me as an ally or an adversary? In this world your enemies are like wine grapes, they're much better when they're stomped flat."

"That's easy, an ally. I'm in."

"I'll take care of everything."

Vito Pagano noticed that Tony stopped buying produce and fruit from him for his use in the restaurant.

Vito asked Tony, "Did I do something to make you mad? You no longer buy from me."

"No, my friend I just found a better way to get vegetables."

"Is it the quality of what I have? I give you nothing but the best."

"No, I have a friend at the warehouse, first thing in the morning he loads the truck with everything I need free for the restaurant before the owner takes inventory. I slip him $10."

"I have to say, I'm surprised and disappointed. I didn't think you would be drawn into that way of doing business," Vito said, shaking his head.

"Remember who you're talking to. As you say Vito, it's all about business, and more importantly,m the money. I'll do anything… *anything…* to make a better future for my family."

Tony had a similar set up for almost everything he bought and those who serviced the restaurant.

When this deal started Tony always met the drivers. "Keep your mouth shut, do what your told, you make some extra money, and nothing bad happens. In Italian it's *Dire niente*, say nothing."

Tony was good to his employees. He felt that he was paying for their loyalty. One of the busboys who also helped receive the stolen goods found out about the arrangements and had a guilty conscience. After weeks of overlooking the shady business arrangement the boy went to neighborhood confidant, Father Parisi, and explained his feelings of guilt.

"Father I feel dirty. I'm part of a scheme to rob vendors doing business with Little Italy and Tony LeoMorte. I don't know what to do. I'm afraid of Mr. LeoMorte. Am I guilty too? Am I going to go to hell?"

Parisi promised to investigate. "I'll take care of it."

Father Parisi pondered how to carefully approach Tony about the breaking of the seventh commandment, *Thou Shalt Not Steal.*

The priest set up a way to *accidentally* run into Tony.

Since Tuesdays weren't the busiest day at the restaurant, he went to Little Italy for lunch. As he entered the restaurant he was warmly greeted by Tony. "Father great to see you! Have a seat, I'll get them to make you something special for lunch."

"That's not necessary."

In a voice as smooth as olive oil, Tony said, "I insist. Nothing is too good for my friend Father Angelo Parisi. Besides I need the prayers and heavenly protection."

The longtime friend moved to the back of the restaurant and sat at a booth for privacy. He sat facing the door, a long time Italian security tradition, even for a priest. This made it possible to see who came in. Tony disappeared into the kitchen and soon came out with a wine glass and a bottle of red wine.

"This is an unexpected pleasure. To what do I owe the honor of your visit?" Tony's radar was up knowing this was a radical change of routine for the priest.

His suspicions were confirmed when Parisi said, "Nothing special, I just wanted to come see you for lunch."

Tony broached the obvious falsehood immediately. "Priests don't make good liars. Part of street smarts is spotting when people are lying—you're lying now. Understand this; I live in a different world than you."

Parisi's face already told the story of his attempted deception.

"Okay, let's just get right to it. I had someone come to me and tell some very disturbing things about how you run your business. And before you ask, I would never divulge who came to me, it's just as confidential as confession. I'm bound by the law of the church as to secrecy."

They were interrupted by a waiter with a small antipasto plate. The smell arrived before the food did. Freshly sliced salami, pro-sciutto ham, wedges of provolone cheese, sliced bread, and a small bowl of warm garlic-laced olive oil with small bits of oregano floating in it.

"Here you are, Father," said the waiter, who departed hastily sensing the tenseness of the situation.

"Father Parisi, I love you. My mother did too. My father loves you in his own way, but I don't discuss my business affairs even with my wife. *Comprendere* (Understand)?"

"I do, but remember, your soul and your family suffers if you sin."

Tony mentally began going through the list of people who might have betrayed him. Surely not Vito Pagano! Maybe one of his co-conspirators. Quickly Tony formulated a plan.

Lots of the business that transpired were cash transactions. Tony weekly emptied his safe and carried cash home. To avoid any messy transport, he tightly wrapped most of it in clear plastic wrap and some was added to his eye-popping cash roll which was maintained in the thousands of dollars. To keep up appearances Tony had an accountant on his staff who kept the books but had limited access to all the financial information and was told to follow instructions and not ask a lot of questions. Only an Italian would do, but John LaRocca wasn't completely trusted. He was Italian but not family. Along with that, Tony paid a regular house payment and a car payment to keep appearances of every aspect of his life legitimate.

As he continued his normal routine, Tony scoped out everyone in his circle wondering who the snitch might be. The *rat* would probably exhibit a nervous behavior, and if he could discover who it was, they had to go. No one was going to jeopardize the LeoMorte family future.

Tony went as far as to set up a phony company, Metro Financial Management. He had LaRocca, the accountant, rent an apartment to serve as a business and mailing address. Any payments made could be converted to cash and with a checking account money could be distributed to again give an appearance of legitimacy.

Cash was piling up!

After weeks of unsuccessfully trying to spot the traitor Tony contacted Father Parisi by phone.

"Hello Father? Tony LeoMorte. Can I come to the church and see you?"

"Of course, when would you like to come by?"

"How about tomorrow afternoon around two, the lunch rush will be over then."

"That'll be fine, see you then." The priest felt a sense of relief. Perhaps this would save him from having to go to the law and to stop Tony's illegal activities. He had decided for Tony's own good he would expose his schemes—now he could be relieved of this burden.

Tony always prided himself on being punctual, something he learned from his father Vincent and from Tommy Russo. The next day at 1:45 Tony's freshly washed and waxed car pulled up to St. Ambrose church.

Time to confess his indiscretions.

He was greeted at the church door by Father Parisi.

"How are you today, Tony?"

"I'm good, thank you. And yourself?"

"I'm so glad to see you. I knew you'd be here. You want to clear your conscience, don't you?"

"I do. Can you hear my confession?"

"I can, let's go right over here to the confessional so we won't be disturbed."

They each entered the confessional; the place people go to confess their sins and seek forgiveness.

Father Parisi slid the small door open separated by a curtain and started, "Okay my son, go ahead."

Tony paused, wondering if he's doing the right thing, then broke a silence by saying, "Bless me Father for I have sinned; it's been about seven years since my last confession."

The priest was surprised by the length of Tony's absence from the confessional, but said, "Continue."

"Other than the normal minor transgressions I have sinned against several commandments—I've missed mass because of my laziness, I've looked at women lustfully and I've stolen…I've stolen a lot."

"I'm glad you've admitted to your mistakes. Is there anything else?"

"No Father"

Making the sign of the cross over the draped opening in the confessional toward Tony, he continued, "I absolve you of your sins."

"Is that it Father?"

"It is unless you have anything else."

"Just one thing, I know with your sense of righteousness it was probably a struggle for you to not reveal what you had learned about me and my business."

The priest, breathing an audible sigh of relief said, "To be honest I was going to turn you in for your own good."

Now the bombshell, "Well now since I confessed, you're bound by church law to silence. Remember that confidentiality of confession you told me about? Well, I'm invoking that right now."

The enraged priest screamed, "Get out."

Tony left but couldn't hide the smile at his clever manipulation of his priest friend. Problem solved.

Trust family only.

Chapter XVI

The Family Grows

Tony was gaining a reputation; word was spreading, and he noticed the stares from the people in the downtown area and on the Hill. To boost his income, he enlisted some out-of-town muscle to approach Louie Lamantia, owner of another restaurant, La Roma Ristorante, and pressure him to pay protection money. Three thugs were hired and brought in to threaten Lamantia and his family and put the fear of God in him.

Coming in unannounced, they boldly confronted Lamantia, "We'll make it easy for you—if you want to stay in business and be able to walk without a limp, you'll pay us every other week."

"Pay you protection money?"

"We prefer to call it insurance."

"I have friends, if you know what I mean."

"Well, you call on your friends and we'll call on our friends."

"Give me time to think about it."

"There's nothing to think about."

"How much do you want?"

"Let's start with a $50 token of your cooperation. Consider it a down payment on your insurance."

Lamantia reached into his pocket a peeled off a fifty from his bank roll.

The leader of the goons remarked, "Look at that you've got lots of money. We'll be back—don't do anything stupid!"

After being paid off by Tony, they were to return to Kansas City. The psychology was to create fear and for the victim to look for the most logical solution. Tony believed Lou Lamantia would approach him for protection against the thugs, and it worked!

Lamantia set up a meeting with Tony. The two met after hours at Little Italy while the restaurant was closed. All the employees were gone when the men sat down over a bottle of wine.

"The reason I asked to see you is that I was approached by three gangsters who are trying to extort money from me. They said that if I didn't pay part of my profits, they would run me out of business, harm me or my family. I didn't know what to do or who else to turn to. I thought immediately of you. I said to myself, *Tony LeoMorte can help me.*"

A sly grin came over Tony's face. "Who were these pigs?"

"I don't know, I've never seen them before. They're probably not local."

"Did you go to the police?"

"The police can't protect me; they don't care about the Italiani."

"What would you like me to do, my friend?"

"Can you protect me, my family, and my business?"

The mouse had taken the bait! "I can, but it would require a lot of time and manpower."

Car headlights flashed into windows of the restaurant, and Lamantia jumped fearing he had been followed.

"I don't care what it takes, I'd rather pay you than give into these thugs. Will you have to kill them?"

"I can't do that, but I can have a few of my men watch over your family, your business, and you."

"How do I repay you for that?"

"They were trying to steal a percent of your profit. What if you gave me just enough to cover my costs and to make them fear you? Make me your business partner. They would never bother you again. Think about it and let me know."

At that moment someone rattled the locked door. Lamantia's face was frozen in fear.

"I don't have to think about it, I trust you and know you will use all your power to protect us."

"Then that's what we'll do. You get the paperwork drawn up making me your partner with no mention of money or conditions, and I'll have one of my best men one assigned to your family and the another to your business. You'll never notice them, but they'll be around."

Tony knowing the threat wasn't real wouldn't have to do anything but collect money and eventually leverage the partnership—a perfect plan.

In 1953 I was born, the fourth of five children. I'm Tony. Most people know me as *Little Tony*.

I've been telling much of this story as it was told to me by my grandfather, Vincent, my mother, and by my father, Big Tony.

I was named Tony also. People constantly remarked how Little Tony looked identical to his father which only endeared me to him that much more. Big Tony had big plans for this little guy.

My mother, Maria, was the ideal mother. The house was always inspection ready as Big Tony was a stickler for order, detail, and cleanliness at home and at work. All the children clean, dressed well, gourmet meals on the table, and each family member treated with love.

Big Tony offered a maid and housekeeper, to which Maria responded, "I won't have strangers taking care of my family or our home."

Maria loved being a mother and got involved in school and church functions. St. Ambrose had a school next door, and a Catholic education was important to this high-profile family.

Yard work was taken care of by a gardener, *Butch*, who had explicit instructions. Tony explained, "You're to cut and trim carefully around the grotto dedicated to the Blessed Mother. Be careful around the flowers. My wife planted those roses around the feet of the statue and placed the stones around the base. Don't disturb them. I want the entire yard manicured. Do you understand?"

"I do, it will done be just how you asked."

"I didn't ask, I ordered. There's a difference!"

"Yes sir."

The other specific instructions given Butch involved cutting around the dog kennel. Big Tony had gotten his German shepherd, *Rocky,* and had him trained professionally. The 120-pound dog was a fierce protector of the property.

Tony's instructions were specific, "The dog must be in the kennel when anyone was in the backyard, no exceptions. Do not go inside the fence if Rocky isn't in his pen."

It seemed odd to Butch, but he was making good money for his work.

Rocky patrolled the perimeter of the fenced yard and would alert if anyone was even close to the property line. Even when in his doghouse in the ten-by-ten foot enclosure he would snarl and bark menacingly.

Big Tony knew someday it was coming.

It was an early Sunday morning when three black cars rolled up to the front of the LeoMorte mansion. Banging on the doors was followed by screams of, "FBI, open up."

Big Tony calmly asked, "What can I do for you gentlemen?"

Agents stormed into the house past Tony. "We're here to search your home." Their guns were in shoulder holsters but intentionally visible.

"Do you have a search warrant?"

"We do."

"May I see it?"

A frightened and confused Maria asked, "Do you want me to call our attorney?"

"No, it's fine."

Tony turned to the lead agent, a square jawed, broad shouldered man who identified himself as Kevin O'Rourke, and asked, "Can I put my dog up? He's a large German shepherd and doesn't like strangers. It's for the safety of you and your men."

"Go ahead. One of my men will accompany you."

"Rocky, get in your house!"

The big guard dog immediately responded by obediently going into the enclosure and laying down. Tony closed the gate to the kennel and motioned to the agent that it was now safe to come out.

As soon as the agent stepped into the yard the dog went into full attack mode jumping into the fence and growling his displeasure at the invasion by this intruder. Tony followed the agent around the yard as the FBI men inside went through the house in a room by room search. The dog never stopping its relentless display of anger.

Inside Maria turned into mama bear as the small children cried at the disruption to their Sunday morning. "You're scaring my children!"

"We're just doing our job, ma'am."

Tony and the other agent came back in the backdoor.

"If you don't mind me asking, just what is it you're looking for?" Tony asked sarcastically

His question was answered with a glare and silence. The Leo-Morte family stood by and watched quietly for an hour and a half as the room by room search continued. After an exhaustive search the FBI team left without apology and pulled slowly away from the house.

Tony sat down expressionless but was laughing on the inside. He had outsmarted the FBI!

The doghouse had been built on runners so Big Tony could slide it back and place the clear wrapped bricks of cash inside a secure safe under the doghouse. His stash of cash was safe, no one would enter the fenced kennel with that canine monster on duty. Each week the clear plastic wrapped bricks of cash were deposited into the concrete enclosed safe under the doghouse.

Not satisfied with his weekly payment from Louie Lamantia, Big Tony hatched a plan. Early on a Sunday a fire mysteriously broke out and destroyed La Rome Ristorante. Six months previously Tony had insisted that the restaurant insurance be doubled. Being a partner, now he would cash in on the destruction.

At home the LeoMorte children were growing physically and mentally. Vince and Mary Rose were thriving in grade school. Mary Rose is showing brilliance in arithmetic and was reading at an advanced level. Meanwhile Dominic, at four, was showing an unexplainable mean streak.

"I'm proud of the children Maria, you're doing a great job with them."

"They have their father's brains. Vince and Mary Rose will both be good at anything they try."

"How about Dominic, do you think he's normal?"

"Well he seems short tempered and bossy for a four-year-old. Maybe Catholic school will help him."

"I'm worried about that kid, but inside every boy is buried a man, we'll just hope he changes."

In 1956 Tony and Maria welcome little Angelina. Tiny tykes to toddlers were roaming Villa Cristo. For Big Tony business, legal and otherwise, was booming.

Infrequent visits to see Vincent, now in his 60s and more and more withdrawn, were painful reminders for the father that his son was part of the Cent'Anni prediction of a *tempesta segreta*, a secret storm. Vincent yearned quietly to see his grandchildren, but his schedule and his disdain for any sign of Tony's ill-gotten success kept him from taking advantage of going to his son's house.

"Pop, I could come and get you and bring you to the house."

"No! Your house was bought with dirty money."

"Maria and the kids would love to see you."

Vincent had been through so much he was emotionally bankrupt. "Maybe someday. Not now."

Tony's normal activities included collecting money at every turn. He descended deeper and deeper into dark, underworld activities.

Maria quietly questioned the financial success that appeared to come from the restaurant. In some ways she wanted to know, but was fearful of what she might discover if she dug into the reality of the separate world Big Tony lived in.

Time ticked away. In 1962 while Tony seemed distant the children monopolized Maria's time and attention. Vince at fourteen started accompanying Big Tony to the restaurant to help with menial tasks and learn the business. Mary Rose was at that awkward age—thirteen—loving school and is a big help with the smaller children. Dominic's behavior was a major concern to Maria, though Tony liked the boy's boldness that in reality masked a bully.

"Tony do you think there's something wrong with Dominic?"

In denial Tony said, "Maria, he's a boy; a ten-year-old typical Italian boy."

"But he's mean to other children and even our own. He picks on Angelina until she cries. She's only six and can't defend herself against him. He can't seem to get along with anyone, and his schoolteachers are constantly sending notes home about his behavior."

"I'll talk to him."

"I love you and the children, our whole family, I just want what's best for them."

"Maria, relax. Are you happy? Look at our life—it's perfect. We have a big, beautiful house, we are admired by the community, we're getting rich, and thank God we're all healthy. What more could you ask for?"

"I'm just scared. I don't know why but I am."

"Everything is going to be fine. I promise, trust me"

Chapter XVII

The Revelation and a Complication

In my small world all seemed fine, being *Little Tony* was a good life. For some reason when we met people, they always wanted to give me something, a half dollar, buy me candy or ice cream or a small toy.

It might be, "Hey kid, here ya go," as they tossed a coin, or some candy my way.

My father would respond, "He's a good boy."

In private he would tell me, "Don't let people make you feel like you owe them. You want them to owe you!"

I didn't understand at the time, but as I grew older it would make sense to me.

I wasn't very smart in school, but I also didn't work hard at it. Being thirteen in 1966 was difficult because I was at that awkward stage—not a child and certainly not a man. Grandpa Vincent was retired now and at 74 lead a pretty quiet, dull life.

I had asked permission to visit Grandpa Vincent after school; it was just a short walk from St. Ambrose to Grandpa's house, and I could stay until my father picked me up. After the last bell rang signaling the end of the school day, out the double doors I went dressed in my school uniform of navy-blue pants and white oxford shirt.

I was knocking on the screen door, then after a few seconds the wooden door. Grandpa must have forgotten I was coming over because he called out, "Yeah, who is it?"

"It's me Grandpa, Little Tony."

"Oh, yeah, sure come in."

I noticed on the kitchen table a half glass of wine. An almost empty gallon bottle of what people called *dago red* was next to the glass with a small knife and the remnants of a fresh peach, a little peeling, and the pit. As Grandpa made his way back to the table, I noticed that some of the wine had dribbled down the front of his sweat-stained t-shirt. He also looked a little unsteady on his feet, most evident by a wobble in his walk. He laughed, which was unusual, and convinced me he had a little too much wine as he said, "You want a some a vino?"

"No Grandpa, mom and dad don't let me drink wine yet."

"Is okay, I no tell."

"No thanks."

"Let's go in here," he said as he weaved through the hallway touching each wall as he did the *wine walk.*

We moved to what we called the *front room.* Grandpa, wearing old wrinkled khaki pants that looked like he'd slept in them, plopped into his faded, big, brown chair, and I sat at the end of the old worn couch closest to him. As we talked, I noticed his head nodding slowly forward. Tired or drunk he was drifting into sleep. I sat wondering what to do next, wake him or just watch the Friday afternoon car traffic passing the front window. A small snore confirmed he was now fully asleep when suddenly and unexpectedly he cried out.

"Grandpa, are you okay?"

With tears welling up in his eyes, in a whisper he said, "I'm a okay." But he was trembling.

"What's wrong?" Tears were now streaming down his face and now seemed to be highlighted by the afternoon sun setting from the big window.

"I'm a'tell you something I never tell anyone else in our family!"

I wondered what that could be and whether I ready to hear this big secret?

"Okay." I sat in the floor in front of him and took his hand.

"Many years ago, I had a dream, a very bad, scary dream. I was in Italy walking the edge of the mountains close to my village, then I spotted a lion in the trees. You understand what I'm a'say to you?

"Yes Grandpa, so far."

"I had a bow; you know what's a bow?"

"Yes, like a bow and arrow."

"Si, a bow and arrows, a bow. I shoot the arrow out of the bow and hit the lion. The lion fall a'down, and he die. I walk up to the lion, and he say, he curse our family. I ask for how long? He say, for 100 hundred years. Cent'Anni! You understand what I say, what I tell you?"

"All except Cent'Anni."

"This is the Italian for 100 year. You understand?"

"Yes, Grandpa but that's just a dream, it wasn't real, there's no curse."

Through his drying tears he says, "Little Tony, Little Tony LeoMorte, one day you understand."

Our stair-stepped family now consists of Vince—18 and the oldest, Mary Rose, the brain of the family—17, Dominic, the bully—14, me, at a socially clumsy age of 13, and finally daddy's *little angel* as he called her—Angelina, who was ten.

Vince had become a fixture at the restaurant and split his time between college at Washington University and Little Italy. His classic Italian charm makes him popular with the patrons and especially the ladies.

After high school graduation Big Tony returned to Julius the Jeweler and had an identical lion's head ring made for Vince to celebrate. The gold ring had diamonds for the eyes instead of the rubies Big Tony chose for his own ring. Big Tony saw to it Vince had a nice car, a red Ford Mustang, flashy clothes, and of course the lion's head ring. Vince was his pride and joy. Both could be found standing in the front of the restaurant and greeting customers, visiting tables, and often they sent complimentary bottles of wine or desserts to loyal patrons.

"Welcome to Little Italy. It's so nice to see you."

The men were given a hearty handshake, the women often got the *innocent* kiss on the cheek.

"If there's anything we can do for you let us know. Enjoy your meal with us."

The customers loved it! Little Italy became the *in place* to visit.

Often the elite of downtown would come in for lunch. It was a great business atmosphere and being catered to by the powerful, charming Tony LeoMorte made corporate executives and the rising stars feel special.

One Friday as the lunch crowd was arriving, in walked a group of well-dressed women, all drop-dead gorgeous. Big Tony spotted the group and made his way quickly to greet them.

"Hello ladies, I'm Tony LeoMorte." A few giggled at the thought that someone wouldn't recognize the now famous St. Louis figure.

The lady at the front of the group said in a low, sultry, Irish brogue, "I'm Bonnie Dempsey."

Tony was trying to turn on the charm but her accent confused him. "Did you say, *Bunny?*"

The amused women laughed in unison.

"Bonnie, Bonnie Dempsey," she corrected him.

Tony was taken by the beauty of each of these women, but especially Bunny.

Along with that accent, she had flaming red hair and the greenest eyes he had ever seen. Her figure and her smile all made her look like she should grace the cover of a magazine. He figured her to be about 30 years old.

"Do you ladies work here downtown?"

"I run a modeling agency here," Bonnie replied

"First time here to Little Italy? I can assure you, I would have remembered a woman of your beauty and obvious good taste in choosing to dine with us."

"Yes, my first time, but I'd heard of this place and of course of you, Mr. LeoMorte."

Now they were both blushing after the verbal volley of compliments.

"Let me show you to our best table reserved for the most elite customers."

As he led them to a table, he poured on the charm. "This table will give you some privacy and a great view of downtown." He quickly pulled the chairs out for each of the women, then motioned for a waiter to come over.

"These lovely ladies are my special guests, take good care of them."

"Thank you, sir."

"Tony, it's Tony. Let me know if there's anything you need, anything at all."

As other customers entered, Big Tony gave them standard greetings, but he couldn't take his eyes off the group of women—especially *Bunny*. He remembered this feeling from when he was a teenager. She returned his glances with a subtle wink and the 44-year-old felt butterflies in his stomach, something he hadn't felt for years. He noticed she was wearing a wedding ring and the realization hit him that he too was married. Tony really loved his Maria.

Their meal done, the ladies thanked Tony for the great food and excellent service.

"Most of us are from out of town, but whenever we return to St. Louis, we'll be back."

"How about you Bunny, are you from out of town?"

"No sir, I'm a St. Louis girl by way of Dublin, Ireland."

"I hope to see you again."

"Well sir, you just might. Thank you for everything."

"My pleasure, seriously my pleasure!"

Tony got back to business but secretly hoped he would see the stunningly beautiful woman again.

About two weeks later, on a Saturday night, Tony got his wish. In walked Bunny with a muscular looking, red-haired man.

Vince walked up and took Bunny's hand and kissed it, which infuriated her companion.

"Hey boy, get away from my wife."

"Tony, sensing big trouble, stepped in and said, "That's my son Vince. He doesn't mean any disrespect."

From behind the counter bodyguard Bull Belacino rushed forward.

"It's okay Bull, just a little misunderstanding." Tony extended his hand to the man.

"I'm Tony LeoMorte, owner of Little Italy. Welcome."

The man grabbed Tony's hand and tried to crush it with his grip disguised as a handshake.

"I'm Sean Dempsey. This is my wife, Bonnie."

"Can we get you a complimentary drink from the bar, or would you like to be seated immediately?"

Bunny answered, "Can we get a table?"

"Of course, right away. Vince, show them to table six."

The couple were seated, but Sean Dempsey continued to glare at Vince.

Tony always knew what he would do under any circumstances and wasn't intimidated by the Irishman.

After a few minutes, Tony visited the Dempsey table, barely making eye contact with Bunny not wanting to further escalate the already tense situation.

"I hope everything was satisfactory, Mr. Dempsey. We're glad you came in."

"It was fine," Dempsey curtly replied.

Bonnie added, "It was fabulous."

"We hope to see you again soon."

Sean's only response, "Ha, I bet you do."

Tony wouldn't let that fit of anger directed at his son be forgotten.

Family is everything!

The next Monday, just after the restaurant opened, Tony was surprised to see Bunny coming in…alone.

"All alone today?"

"Yes, I was hoping to talk to you."

"Sure, come sit down."

As Tony escorted Bunny to a booth in the back he again noticed her perfectly proportioned body.

"A booth in the back for privacy. Is this okay?"

"Perfect. First, I want to apologize for the scene Sean made here Saturday night. He's very jealous. He's insecure because I make more money with my modeling agency that he does as a carpenter."

"Excuse me, would you like a glass of wine?"

"It's a bit early, but okay."

Tony called out to a waiter, "Gino, two glasses of the house special wine please."

"If you don't mind me asking why are you running a modeling agency when you're obviously beautiful enough to be a model?"

As the wine arrived at the table Bunny replied, "I started ten years ago as a model at 17—modeling is a young woman's game."

"So, you're 27, and that's too old to model?"

Bunny picked up her wine glass, her wedding ring made a clear *clang* against the glass, a subtle audible reminder that she was married.

After a sip of wine, she said, "No, but I'm not as in demand as the teens and early twenties. My agency allows me to stay in the industry, make good money, and eliminates travel."

The limited sunlight coming through the windows illuminated Bunny's face, and Tony noticed that her high, prominent cheek bones and the downward lines to her rounded chin made what looked like a perfectly symmetrical, heart-shaped face.

"Pardon me for saying so but you look beautiful and certainly suited to grace the cover of any magazine or walk any runway as a model."

"Why Mr. LeoMorte, are you flirting with me?" she asked playfully.

"And if I was?"

"Well then I would find your company as intoxicating as this wine!"

Tony felt temptation rising.

"I can understand why your husband is jealous."

Breaking the sexual tension, Bunny said," I couldn't help but notice your ring. Why the lion head?"

"My name LeoMorte means *Dead Lion*. My son Vince has one just like it only the eyes on his are diamonds. I chose rubies for mine because it looks fearless."

"Are you fearless?"

"Right now I'm a little afraid of you," he said through a laugh.

"You needn't be afraid. Well, I have to be going."

"Will you be coming back?"

"Would you like me to come back?"

"Very much.

"Then I will."

A tidal wave of guilt came over Tony. With all the evil things he was doing would this become another transgression against Maria—and God?

Returning home that evening the inner conflict became more evident as my father's unrest manifested itself in his interactions with our family. I remember that night having brought home my report card. Vince and Mary Rose were excellent students, Dominic's poor grades were attributed to his obvious personality disorder, but my poor grades became the topic of conversation. I remember getting called into the living room. My father was seated on the couch, my report card in his hand. This couldn't be good.

"What's this? Why can't you get the grades Vince and Mary Rose got? I know you're not very smart, but this is unacceptable for a son of mine. You know if this keeps going, you'll never amount to anything. You'll end up like those Square Johns, being nothing more than a common laborer or truck driver."

I was afraid to speak. His words hurt worse than any physical punishment I could receive. I thought it wise to keep quiet rather than risk anymore harsh comments.

"This is constructive criticism," my father said in a booming voice.

To a twelve-year-old there is no such thing as *constructive criticism*—there's just criticism! It takes a toll on a young mind and changes you forever.

I learned over the years while I knew my father loved me in his own way, if he had a bad day it was likely that we would all have a bad day. When I was older, I also realized that he sought love, especially from women, because he had lost his mother at such an early age. I'm not sure he ever filled that gap.

When I could go to Little Italy with him, I watched as this gruff man turned into a gentleman. He handled everything with ease and had a charm, even if it was phony, that calmed even the most irate customer. At home I observed everything he did. I sought his approval and mimicked many things he did hoping he would notice and go easier on me.

I remember when I was little, I would sit in his bathroom and watch him shave—that's such a manly thing, shaving.

"Hey Dad, when do I get to start shaving?"

"Oh, little guy you don't want to start shaving. It's a lot of trouble."

I watched as he took his big shaving mug, wet the brush with hot water and swirled the brush around the cup creating the lather. He took the metal safety razor and began in even strokes to remove the soap and whiskers from his face.

I noticed that he would always repeat the procedure on Sundays. "Hey Dad, why do you shave twice?"

"My beard is thick, and I get a closer shave if I go back for a second trip."

On good days my father would lather up my face with the shaving soap and sneak the blade out of his razor and then pretend to let me shave.

No matter what, I loved my dad, Big Tony.

Chapter XVIII

A Move By the Mob

The late sixties brought racial unrest to St. Louis and many other parts of the country. Tempers flared and lives were filled with tension. Despite all the chaos, Tony's schemes and illicit business dealings were making him rich, and along with the money came power.

The thing about money, when you have it there's always somebody who wants to take it away from you.

Three men dressed in expensive suits pulled up in a shiny, new, black Cadillac with Missouri plates, they had planned a late-night visit to the restaurant. This was a sinister looking trio, one large man leading the group, the obvious muscle was dressed in all black and had his right hand buried inside his overcoat, a bulge in his coat offered proof that there was a gun in a shoulder holster. The second man exiting the Cadillac was dressed like a successful businessman, wearing a perfectly fitted three-piece suit, alligator shoes, and a black fedora. He was followed by a short, thin man nervously scanning the area, as if on guard.

Tony, always vigilant himself, spotted the men. He recognized them as part of the mob from Kansas City as they exited the car.

Tony ordered his son Vince, "Stay back behind the counter and be ready for trouble."

"Trouble?" questioned Vince.

"There's no time to explain now, just do what I tell you!"

He alerted Bull Belacino, "Be ready," and met them at the door.

"Can I help you gentlemen?"

The well-dressed man spoke first, "I'm Sam Granda, from Kansas City. I'm here to see Big Tony LeoMorte. These are my associates Willie Spinelli and Carlo Trupiano."

Bull slowly moved in behind the strangers blocking the door, his hand buried in his pocket which was concealing his stainless steel 38 caliber pistol.

"I'm Tony LeoMorte, what can I do for you?"

"Let's sit down," suggested Granda.

"We'll all stand, thanks; I really don't think you're going to be here that long."

Realizing Bull had slipped in behind them, the men looked around anxiously.

"We've allowed you to operate here in St. Louis, and now we think it's time that you showed some respect and cut us in on your operation. We're not greedy, but we think we can offer you protection"

Holding back emotion, Tony replied, "Protection? Protection from what?"

"Damage to your business, all the side ventures you're involved in, and make sure nothing happens to your family."

Now visibly angry, Tony charged the man only to be cut off by the much larger Trupiano.

"You come to St. Louis, my town, and threaten me and my family?"

Tony moved closer to Granda and whispered to him, "I'll make this simple for you, mess with me and I'll beat you almost to death. I might go to jail, but you'll go to the hospital. When you get out of the hospital, I'll be out of jail, and I'll beat you again. You want a war, I'll give you a war. Just remember nobody wins a war, but I'll still be standing, and you'll be buried somewhere."

Vince came charging out from behind the counter. "Don't you threaten my father, ever."

"Who the hell are you," yelled Granda.

Vince proudly responded, "Vincent LeoMorte, first born son

of Big Tony LeoMorte, and I'll kick your ass from here back to Kansas City."

"Get back, Vince, I'm handling this."

Bull now had the muzzle of the snub nose .38 planted in the back of the Kansas City boss, Granda.

Granda, feeling the cold gun barrel in his back remarked, "We can negotiate."

"Here's my offer. Leave now, never come back, and I won't have my man put a bullet in your spine."

"We'll leave, but we will be back. We know where you live. We know everything about you."

The three men moved slowly backwards and exited the restaurant door. Seconds later as Tony and Bull watched from the front window as the car sped away.

"Remember those men, Bull, they're trouble. That type spots any weakness immediately and will prey on you."

Assigning them nicknames as was Tony's custom, they become Sam *the snake*, Willie *the weasel*, and *Cadillac* Carlo.

"If they come back, be ready to fight."

"Do you think they'll try to hurt you?" asked Vince

"I learned from my father a long time ago—they won't come after you, they'll go after what you love the most. We have to be ready all the time now."

On the ride home, Tony asked Vince to keep quiet about the threats. Conflicted about whether to tell Maria, Tony decided to inform her about the conversation that had taken place.

"Vincent, there's no sense in scaring your mother. I'll let her know in my own way."

Later that night Tony engaged Maria in a much different kind of pillow talk.

Lights out, the house was quiet, they were laying in their bed. He said, "We need to talk."

Maria responded, "That's never a good start to a conversation. Did I do something wrong?"

"There was some trouble tonight at the restaurant."

"Trouble? What kind of trouble?"

"Calm down. I have it under control. I'll take care of it. A crew from Kansas City came in and are trying to muscle me for protection money."

"A crew?"

"Three men, bad men, mafia types."

"What did they say?"

"The typical tough guy stuff, nothing to be afraid of. I sent them on their way."

"I could tell something was wrong. You went around the whole house double-checking every door and window to make sure they were locked. Do you think they would ever come here?"

"I don't think they would, but just keep your eyes open, watch the kids, and be careful. I'll keep someone outside the house 24 hours a day for the next couple of weeks."

Extra precautions in place, Big Tony was always on high alert. His gut instinct was that the crew would be back, whether it was overtly visible or under a veil of darkness, they would be back.

After several weeks Tony reined back the extra surveillance around the house but had his bodyguards on call 24 hours a day.

Whenever there was an election or a shakeup at city hall, Tony made sure to support the winning side. He had the city wired and could get just about anything done or slip past any trouble with a phone call or a well-placed envelop bulging with $100 bills.

His standard line for anyone was, "If there's something nobody else can do, or wants to do, call me."

Mary Rose continued her education, but Big Tony was confident enough in her abilities to make her his new accountant. John LaRocca was relieved of his accountant position and given a severance package and a stern warning about keeping his mouth shut.

"I hope you understand you should never ever under any circumstances reveal anything about me, my family, or my business."

"Yes, sir, I understand."

"I've arranged for you to get a job with the city. Don't disappoint me, ever."

"Never, sir."

Mary Rose thought the bookkeeping system was odd. Very few payments went directly through the restaurant, but lots of money was funneled to Metro Financial Management Company.

"Dad, this seems strange the way vendors and people who provide services are paid. Why do we have a separate address for this company in an apartment building?"

"I want you here working with me. I will pay you well as I do Vince, and you just have to trust me. I have my own way of doing things, and everything I do is done for a reason. I trust only family. All the answers you need are found in Psalm 156."

"Okay, I trust you."

Mary Rose noticed the way Big Tony and Vince conducted themselves at Little Italy. Big Tony was mature and smooth, Vince was very flirty with the ladies and a bit of a hothead when there was any confrontation. Often Big Tony had to intercede.

"Vince, slow down, son. These people aren't always right, *but* they're always the customer."

"But Pop, if they're wrong, I'm going to speak up."

"Vince, I need you to conduct yourself properly all the time. There are going to be times I'm not here, and I have to trust you. You can think what you want, but you don't have to say everything you're thinking."

With two family members helping at the restaurant, Tony was grooming his children to be part of his growing dynasty. Maria was doing a great job with each the children, but Dominic was constantly in trouble and leaned heavily on his family name as his shield. Maria was understanding and hesitant to hurt anyone's feelings, and Dominic view this as a pass card to an *anything goes* attitude.

Tony told her, "Somewhere buried in every boy is a man— sometimes it never comes out."

Riding around town in a new car and a pocket full of money was a formula for disaster with Dom. One day in a backroom poker game he was losing heavily and flipped the table over. Cards and cash went flying.

"You punk, you can't get away with that," screamed one of the players.

"One word from me and my Dad will bury you!"

Word got back to Big Tony who confronted Dominic.

"Don't drag me into your fights. You can't bully everybody and then use me to threaten them."

"I can fight my own battles."

"Dominic, you *never* fight your own battles. You start fights then other people have to step in. You're a bully. You always have been, and rarely have I seen a bully who isn't a coward."

The truth hit Dominic like a hard left hook. He turned and left.

Tony turned to Bull, saying, "Have somebody with him all the time. We must keep an eye on him and keep him out of trouble. That kid is going to get himself in deep."

"Got it boss."

Dominic became a regular at all the hang-outs. He practically owned a booth at the Cross-Eyed Cricket, a sleazy joint just down from the bus station—the place wreaked of cheap booze and cheap women. He could often be found there holding court, pretending to be a tough guy. He was booking bets, loan sharking and fencing stolen property—everything a second-rate hood would be doing.

He tried to assume a role as a patriarch of the family on the streets of downtown St. Louis, but everyone knew he didn't have the muscle back up anything. The beat cops let him slide because he was Big Tony's kid.

In a dispute over an unpaid debt, Dominic, backed up by his bodyguard, Vic, got into a fight with a small-time gambler.

"You owe me, and I'm calling in your marker."

"I don't have it, Dom. I get paid Friday, and I can give you part of it then."

"Have all of it here tomorrow at 7:00 or else."

"Or else? Who the hell do you think you are?"

"I'm *Big Dom*, and I run this town."

"Ha, the only thing you run is your mouth!"

Dominic pulled out a switchblade knife and charged the debtor, but he was too slow.

A beer bottle to the head dropped Dominic like a rock and ended the fight. Dominic, unconscious, got a concussion for his trouble, and Vic subdued the gambler with one punch.

Dominic had a two-day hospital stay and left with a noticeable three-inch scar across his forehead.

Tony decided it was time to straighten things out.

"I'm going to call a spade a spade Dominic. You're way out of line."

"What do you mean?"

"What do I mean? I mean I have people coming to me afraid that you're going to get yourself in more trouble than you or I can get you out of. I'm sick of paying off the police to bail you out of trouble. You're a loudmouth, a bully, and you can't back up that trash you're talking."

"I don't need you to fight my battles. I can take care of myself."

"If you don't stop, you're going to end up in an alley with *two in the head*. This is the last time I'm going to tell you."

Tony was ashamed of this *bad seed* and was tired of Maria having to worry about Dominic.

Back to business.

Chapter XIX

Family Tragedy

Somehow Dominic and I graduated high school—him in 1970, me in 71. As was his tradition dad had us both fitted for our lion's head rings. Dom saw his as a sign of invincibility. I saw mine as an outward sign of family tradition.

Daddy's little angel, Angelina, was a bit of a wild child—not to the same degree as Dominic but a little unpredictable and mischievous. Both worried Maria who feared the worst but prayed unceasingly for the best. Maria was the rock of the family.

"I'm proud of you boys but sometimes, Dom, you make it difficult. Dominic you've made it so far without going to jail or getting yourself killed. What do you want to do with your life?"

"I want to be on your payroll. I can collect debts, be your muscle, or even if it comes to it your hitman."

"Dominic, you need a regular job. You're not the badass you think you are. Think about a regular job."

"Little Tony, what about you?"

"If there's room at the restaurant I'd like to work for you part-time and go to law school."

"Law school? That's good! I could use a good lawyer."

Dominic continued to get in and out of trouble, but Tony had a sense that the clock was ticking, and this kid was heading for disaster.

I wanted to please my father, but I didn't want to help him circumvent the law.

In December grandpa Vincent died. The doctor insisted it was pneumonia, but I think it was a broken heart. He had lost the love of his life very early; both his sons were disappointments. One left for California and never came back and the other was leading the mob lifestyle, his oldest son had become what he most detested. His anger and disappointment smoldered just below the surface. He suffered silently, but you could see it in his pale brown eyes, an unspoken sadness. Utmost in my mind was grandpa's story about the lion and Cent'Anni.

The funeral was a spectacle—grandpa would have hated it.

The visitation was at Miceli's Funeral Home. There wasn't room in the parking lot for all the cars, and the overflow parked in a grocery store lot and walked though the winter weather. Miceli's Funeral Home was the place almost every Italian was *laid out*, and many were buried at Resurrection Cemetery.

I remember walking in and seeing grandpa in the bronze casket, it seemed surreal. It could have just been my imagination, but it seemed like there was a faint smile on grandpa's face. I though it odd that it took death to put even a small smile on his face, a smile that life couldn't produce.

There were flowers all over the room—the combination of floral scents was overpowering. There were flower arrangements around the casket stand, and more spilled out into the hallway. People that knew Vincent, and probably more who knew my father, sent flowers as a show of sympathy but more likely out of respect for my father. Nearest the casket people spoke in hushed tones, in the back of the room there were dozens of conversations going on as people from all over visited and caught up on the births, marriages, and deaths from all over the city. I could overhear stories about grandpa that warmed my heart.

When My father walked in, the entire place fell silent. A line formed for people to walk past the casket, stop to say a prayer, shake hands with Tony, hug my mother, and speak to each of us.

"My deepest sympathies."

"I knew your father for years."

"Your father was a good man."

"I came downtown just to buy the bread he made."

"If there's anything I can do, just let me know."

All these and more comments like this were expressed as we stood lined up as a family—my father, my mother, and then each of us children. For two nights hundreds of people filed past grandpa's body. My mother's parents, the Farantellos, showed up—they had long since disassociated themselves from our family because of the reputation of the LeoMorte clan. Even Vito Pagano showed up to offer his condolences.

Father Parisi officiated. As he walked in the grey-haired, aging priest was stooped over and spoke slowly and deliberately. The priest overheard my father telling Dominic while pointing to the casket, "You better straighten your life out or this is where you're going to end up."

Parisi addressed the crowd, "I remember meeting this man and his wife not long after they came to the United States. Hard working, loving, and truly people of God. I know this family, and they are in my daily prayers, and the world is less for having lost this man."

Father Parisi moved in close to my father and whispered in his ear, "You better straighten your life out or this is where you're going to end up."

As the people paying their respects were instructed to exit to form the procession to the cemetery, the family was left in privacy for the final view of grandpa before the casket was closed and transported.

My father said, "I'd like you all to go so I can spend a few moments alone."

I stayed just outside the room waiting to say my own goodbye to grandpa. I could hear my father as he spoke to his own father for the final time.

"I'm sorry we didn't always get along, Papa. I know it was rough on you when Mama died, and you were tough on us, but you were just getting us ready to live in a tough world. I wish we had spent more time together. There were times I thought I hated you, but I never stopped loving you. I know we never said it to each other, but I'm telling you now, I love you."

Tony choked up on his words. "I always wanted you to be proud of me. I know my life is not what you would have chosen, but I wanted to make the best life for my family. Family is everything. I love you Papa. Tell Mama I said hello."

Then he leaned down and gently kissed Grandpa on the forehead, he turned away and stopped to look back one last time and then wiped away the tears from his eyes. I had never seen my father cry.

As I watched my family get into the limousines I moved to the side of the casket and removed my lion ring, slid it into his pocket and waited as the attendant closed the lid.

"God bless you, Grandpa, thank you for your sacrifice and bravery coming to this country. Don't worry about the lion's words, the curse, I think the curse is broken now."

Afterwards the people closest to our family came to the house, brought way too much food, and continued the show of respect along with telling their personal stories about our family. I had noticed men outside walking around all the cars and writing things down. Later, I asked my father who they were. He answered in two words.

"The FBI."

It was eerie and empty once everyone left, we all just sat in our good clothes, everyone in silence. Eventually each of us without speaking retired to our rooms. This was the end of a family era.

Winters in St. Louis can be brutal. This one was harder than most. The house seemed different as Vince had moved out to his own place, and Mary Rose found love and married a successful architect. My father insisted that no matter what, everybody gathered every Sunday for dinner at Villa Cristo.

"My family is everything. We will support each other, and

you should know you'll always be safe here. I would like us to be here together each Sunday for a family meal."

Maria enjoyed the weekly ritual and cherished the time with each of us but especially those of us still at the house.

"You children and your father are my life."

The restaurant had a long list of regulars, among them Bunny Dempsey, who visited throughout the week but never on the weekend.

"Bunny, how's my favorite customer?" Tony said as he pulled her in for a long hug.

"Tony, Tony, how's my favorite restaurant owner?"

Vince stood there waiting to greet the beautiful Irish lady.

"You know, Bunny, I have crush on you!" Vince said, blushing slightly and hoping for reciprocation.

"Yeah, my husband thinks so too. He's never forgotten the evening you kissed my hand. You're what 23 or 24?"

"I'll be 25 soon."

"Well, I'm several years older than you *and* married. The right girl will come along, and you won't give me a second look."

Bunny always got the best of service, and Big Tony always dramatically tore up the bill for her meal and was rewarded with a quick kiss on the cheek.

Tony trusted Vince to handle business and allowed himself the luxury of leaving for hours at a time but rarely took a whole day off. Tony handled the most important business transactions, not trusting important things to anyone else.

"I'm grooming you to take over one day, Vince."

"I can do it now, Pop. I can open and even close. You said you trust family, let me take care of things for you."

"All in good time. We'll get you there. I'd love to take more time off and not have to close the restaurant all the time."

Dominic still required a babysitter. I was busy with school and helping at the restaurant. Mary Rose came in three days a week and was fulfilling her role as a wife and the accountant. Angelina was old enough to drive and was getting passing grades, drawing the attention of the boys, and on the move all the time.

It was a Friday night just before closing time, and the phone rang at the restaurant. It was my mother. My father answered the phone.

"Tony, come quickly! Angelina has been in an accident."

"I'll be right there to pick you up. Little Tony come with me, Vince you close up and go right home."

Bull brought the car around, and as we wheeled away from the restaurant my father said, "I wonder if this is the work of the Kansas City crew? They better pray it's not."

The car sped through the streets lit up only by the streetlights. We pulled up to the house, and my mother was already standing at the entrance. The car barely coming to a stop, my father pulled my mother into the back-seat yelling, "Go, go, go."

"Go where?"

My mother replied, "St. Johns Hospital, the emergency entrance."

"Maria, what happened?"

"Angelina was driving and went off the road and hit a telephone pole, that's all I know."

"Who called you."

"The city police chief. He said he recognized the name and called the house immediately."

The car pulled up, and we had the to wait for the automatic doors to open and almost got run over by a gurney bringing another person in.

At the desk, the night nurse directed us. "Waiting room is down the hallway and to the right."

"Waiting room my ass, I want to know what's going on right now! Where's my daughter?" My father wasn't used to having to wait for anything.

The antiseptic smell common to hospitals hung in the air, and there was a constant humming noise coming from a man polishing the floor with an electric buffer. The silence was occasionally interrupted by coded emergency room communications.

After what seemed like an eternity, a young doctor dressed in blue scrubs and surgical mask came though the double doors.

"Mr. LeoMorte, I'm Dr. Riggio."

"How is my daughter, is she going to be all right?'

"I'm not sure yet, I'm going back in, and I'll update you as soon as I can."

"You take good care of her doctor, that's my little Angel."

"I take good care of all my patients."

My mother stood by, holding onto my father's arm, paralyzed with fear.

"I can't lose one of my children. She's just a baby." Rosary in hand she sat down and began to pray out loud.

After three rosaries, about twenty minutes, the doctor emerged looking distraught.

Tony rushed to meet the doctor. "Tell me, tell me about my daughter," he insisted. Maria moved to his side clutching his arm to brace herself.

"I've got some bad news, maybe you should sit down."

My mother shrieked a horrible cry.

"What is it?" she screamed, "Is she dead? Please, God, don't let her be dead?"

"I was able to save your daughter, but not the baby."

"Baby? What baby?"

"Your daughter was about three months pregnant."

Silence gripped the room as my mother turned away, and my father asked, "A baby. A baby? Was it a boy or a girl?"

"It was a boy."

"And my daughter, my Angelina, what about her?"

"It's going to take a while, but she should make a full recovery."

"A baby."

Chapter XX

Saying Goodbye and Hello

After Grandpa Vincent died, my father seemed to change, ease up a little. He seemed more attentive to my mother and us kids. Learning a lesson from the death of his father where there was an absence of verbal affirmation of love, he greeted Maria each evening with a sincere, "I love you."

After decades of his true feelings being buried, he surrendered to his emotions.

Mary Rose began her own family. First came Lisa with an *Americano* last name, and a traditional Italian look. Big Tony was elated to have another little girl in the family, and Mary Rose juggled work and home very well. She was a great mother, following the example of our own mother.

Our Sunday family celebrations continued, each Sunday at 10:30, everyone was expected to be there. This gave each of us time for church and immediately following to gather around the table which was getting more crowded. Vince had moved again. He was now in the house on the Hill—Grandpa's old house.

Table talk was lively and diverse but rarely about business.

"Vince, how do you like living on the Hill?"

"It's okay, but I'm surrounded by old people."

"Mary Rose, how are you feeling? Work and a baby aren't too much, are they?"

"No, Pop, I like working with you and bringing the baby to the restaurant works out fine."

Continuing around the table like a general addressing his troops, Tony sarcastically quizzed Dominic.

"How about you, Dom?"

"Aw, you know Pop, S.O.S., same old shit."

A stern look from Maria showed her immediate disapproval of Dominic's choice of words.

"Watch your mouth in front of your mother and in my house. I guess we should all be happy we made it another week when you didn't end up in jail. If you continue this path, I can tell you how the story ends, and it's not pretty. Your future is behind bars or someone shoveling dirt on you."

Maria gasped at the thought, saying, "Tony, please!"

Given the weekly routine of a military sense of order going by age, I knew I was next.

"I've enrolled in some pre-law night classes."

"Good Little Tony." At least it's pre-law and not the police academy. Maybe you'll be able to keep us all out of trouble," Tony said, followed by a small laugh.

"And how is my little angel, Angelina?"

"Angel?" Dominic snickered, once again drawing looks from both Tony and Maria.

"I'm good Daddy. Shove it, Dom!"

Maria, hoping to bring peace back to the table commented, "I'm a little embarrassed to say it, but I'm being recognized for community service by the newspaper, the *Globe Democrat*. They thought I should be recognized for my work with the ladies guild at the church, my cooking meals for the mission, and the time I spend visiting the sick at the hospital. I'm not comfortable in the limelight."

"Wow, that's great! You are the glue that holds this family together, and I love you so much. I'm proud of you." High praise coming from Tony, not known to hand out compliments easily.

On Monday it was business as usual—a day off school for me

and I was scheduled to work at the restaurant. Little did I know I had a secret admirer. During the height of the lunch hour, a young blonde-haired girl walked in.

"I'm alone and want a table for lunch."

Feeling bold, I replied, "I'm sure we can find a space for you. I'm Little Tony LeoMorte, it's hard to believe someone as cute as you would be eating alone."

"I'm Carla, and I wouldn't have to eat alone if you could join me. I've noticed you through the window several times when I've come by. *Little* Tony?"

"My father is *Big* Tony, and I'm flattered, but I'm working now, and we're really busy. My father *owns* the restaurant."

"Maybe later or another day then?" she responded confidently.

"Write your phone number on the back of your lunch ticket for me."

"I didn't really want lunch. I just wanted to meet you."

She took the ticket book out of my hand and wrote, *Carla Price 555-843-1823*. She dotted the "i" in *Price* with a small heart—corny but cute.

"Call me. Soon."

What was I doing? I had hardly enough time for school and work much less a girlfriend, but it was nice being pursued.

Later that night, pouring over homework, I pulled the paper containing the phone number from my pocket. *What could it hurt?*

I'd get that answered later, much later.

I dialed the number and wondered as it rang repeatedly if I should hang up or hang on.

"Hello?"

"Hi, this is Tony. Is this Carla?"

"No this is her mother."

"Is she there, please?"

"Do you want to know if she is here, or would you like to speak to her."

Oh, boy sarcasm, my favorite!

"Yes, ma'am, if she is there, I would like to speak with her, please."

Her mother bellowed out, "Carla, it's for you."

After a pause, "Hello?"

"Hi, this is Tony. We met this afternoon at Little Italy."

"I don't remember meeting anyone today," she teased.

"Oh, okay, I must have the wrong number."

"Wait! I'm just kidding you."

"So, Carla, what should I know about you?"

"Well, I recently graduated from high school, I'm 18, and I think you're about the most handsome man I've ever seen."

"You have to get out more and maybe get your eyes checked," Tony countered.

"Oh no, I've walked by several times in the last few weeks and even brought my friends by to check you out. They all agree."

"I was pretty taken by you when you walked in and flattered by your interest. Do you think you're too young for me?"

"Oh no. I'm a mature 18. I know what I like, and I know what I want. And I want you."

"Whoa girl. Slow down. Or are you ready to set the wedding date?"

"Maybe in a few weeks."

"Where do we go from here?"

"Why don't you ask me for a date?"

"Where would you like to go?"

"How about dinner and a movie?"

"Okay, when?"

"How about Friday night? That's kind of traditional date night."

"Oh, are you a traditional girl?" I joked.

"Hardly."

"I can't Friday. I've got to work. Maybe Saturday?"

"It's a date!"

"I'll call you and get an address. Think about where you want to go."

Saturday came, and I pulled up to a small craftsman-style home on the city line in a blue-collar neighborhood. I must admit I was nervous.

Carla must having been peeking out the drapes. I didn't even ring the doorbell, and door swung open.

"Come in and meet my mother."

A short chubby woman extended her hand and said, "So you're the guy who wants to date my daughter."

"I'm Tony, it's nice to meet you," I said as we shook hands.

"Don't lie to me, you just want to pick Carla up and get out of here. I noticed you have soft hands, no callouses, not used to hard work?"

Carla jumped in, "Mom, try not to scare him off already. Are you ready to go?"

"Let's go."

We walked down the cracked, uneven, concrete sidewalk in the dark and made our way to my car. I opened her car door to which Carla said, "Such a gentleman! I knew it."

I jumped in, started the heater and turned the radio down.

I looked over and asked, "Where was your father? I thought I would get to meet him?"

"He left years ago."

"I'm shocked, he left that warm loving woman? Sorry, I think your mother already doesn't like me."

"Oh, it's okay. My mother is a little rough around the edges. I'm not even sure she likes me!"

"Rough around the edges? More like wearing sandpaper underwear. So where do you want to go to eat?"

"Let's go to Steak and Shake and get a hamburger."

"You want to eat in the car?"

"Sure, I told my friends we'd be there. Now they can check you out, see what kind of car you drive, and that kind of stuff."

"Are you kidding?"

"No, not at all."

What was I getting into?

We pulled in, ate and next was a movie.

"What movie did you pick?"

"Whatever is showing at the Starlight Drive In."

"The Drive In? Seriously?"

She said, "Yes," as she slid over on the bench seat to get closer to me.

We arrived, paid, pulled into the back row at her insistence and we barely got parked before Carla scooted over and kissed me on the neck. The rest of the movie was spent with me trying to preserve my virginity. On the drive home I hardly knew what to think. Just as I feared, when we got back to Carla's house she wanted to play tonsil hockey rather than a traditional first date type kiss goodnight.

The next day she showed up at the restaurant, but I wasn't there. I had classes.

My father relayed her message, *Tell Little Tony I had a great time and can't wait to see him again.*

He told me in front of my mother, who instantly asked, "I hope you were a gentleman."

"Oh yes ma'am."

On my next phone call to Carla I suggested we slow it down a little. She took the hint. We began seeing each other regularly. After a few months I began to wonder if this was it? Was this what it felt like to be in love?

"Hey Ma, can I ask you a question?"

"Sure."

"How do you know when you're in love?"

"Do you get excited to see her? Do you get a nervous feeling when you're around her?"

"I do."

"Do you think about her when you're not together?"

"Yes ma'am."

"Do you finish each other's sentences?"

"Sometimes."

"It sounds like you may be well on your way."

We became comfortable as a couple, school was going well, I was becoming confident at the restaurant, and I had a girl who adored me. Life was good.

One day at the restaurant a familiar face shows up with an unfamiliar look—Bunny Dempsey, a very pregnant Bunny Dempsey.

I spot her first and said, "Well congratulations. This is quite a surprise!"

"It was for us, too. We've been trying for a few years."

"Can I seat you in a table or booth?"

"Not sure *we* can fit in a booth. Better make it a table."

"Bunny," Big Tony excitedly called out. "Bunny and baby, we're so glad to see you. How are you feeling?"

"Feeling good and excited for this little one to make an appearance."

"How about a glass of wine?"

"No wine—we don't need a little Irish drunk," she laughed.

"Oops, I forgot. How about milk?"

"Just a glass of water and anything for lunch that's not spicy."

"I'll have the chef make you linguine with browned butter, a few mushrooms, and a hint of garlic."

"Perfect."

Tony delivered the lunch plate to Bunny. "Here you go my dear, piping hot, just like you"

"You are such a romantic flirt; I'm not used to all this attention."

"Let me know if you need anything, anything at all."

"Mr. LeoMorte, you're bad."

Later, after a little casual table talk, Bunny headed back to work.

"Take care of yourself and come back soon Bunny."

"You bet I will. You're the man women dream about."

As Bunny left, Big Tony watched her all the way out the door and stepped out to keep an eye on her until she disappeared from sight down the street.

I saw the look in my father's eyes as he celebrated Bunny's news—she had become a part of the Little Italy family. After seeing that baby bump on Bunny and my father's happiness, I imagined Carla carrying my baby.

It was time for me to take a big step.

Chapter XXI

A Wedding Anniversary
Wedding Bells and a Warning

1977. My parents had been married 30 years and they planned to renew their wedding vows. An 81-year-old Father Parisi, who had become a family institution, agreed to officiate. Father Parisi had performed weddings, baptisms, and funerals for the LeoMorte family.

I had secretly called him and asked him to make it a double ceremony, I was going to marry Carla! I was 24 and she was 21 it was time. I announced my marriage to my family, and we made our plans, plans to spend the rest of our lives together.

Father Parisi communicated his concerns, "Little Tony are you sure about this?"

"Yes Father, I think she's the right girl."

"You *think* she is? You better be sure!"

"I'm sure. I've mapped out our future. I'm making good money working two jobs, and I still catch a few classes every semester."

"There's an old saying, *man plans, and God laughs.*"

"I'm sure!"

My father insisted, "I want my family to stay in the house at Villa Cristo."

"I'm fine with that, plus I can save money that way. Maybe after we settle down, have two or three children to carry on the name, we can get a place of our own."

I was on top of the world.

The big day arrived.

My father and I dressed identically—black tuxedos, black patent, leather shoes, and black satin bow ties completed our look. The brides, Maria in an ivory wedding gown, simple, understated but with a train trailing twenty feet behind her, looked radiant and happy. Carla was a stunning bride in a brilliant white wedding gown befitting a high-class, socially prominent woman.

I was a virgin, but wasn't sure Carla qualified for white.

And so, a double ceremony further cemented my parents' marriage as they renewed their vows and Carla and I walked down the same aisle.

We felt relatively safe as there were armed bodyguards at each entrance and exit. Big Tony had said before the ceremony, "I'll never let my guard down."

As Father Parisi began the mass, the choir joined in with the entrance song of "Amazing Grace." The whole scene was idyllic, sunlight bursting though the stained-glass windows, family and friends extremely well dressed for the occasion, later in the ceremony the echo of the "Ave Maria" bouncing off the ceiling and stone walls would have brought a tear to a glass eye. The double ceremony was moving at a hundred *smiles* an hour.

Father Parisi personalized the ceremony. "I've known three generations of this family. I can say without equivocation, I love the LeoMorte family. Grandpa Vincent and his wife Rosa epitomized the American Dream—they trusted God to guide them to a strange land, they served the Lord, family, and community, they made this world a better place. Now the family with all of you as witnesses is renewing one marriage and starting another. We pray God's blessing descend on them, keep them safe, and watch over them."

The scene was befitting of any Hollywood movie wedding. The reverence of the event was only interrupted by the occasional cry of a baby and the shuffling of the event programs in the pews.

After all the *I dos* were exchanged, both couples strolled out arm in arm to the standard wedding march. I could tell my father was proud. He turned and winked and said, "I'm proud of you."

I lived for my father's approval.

St. Ambrose was packed with people even standing in the back of the church. This was like Italian royalty to the city of St. Louis. Limousines were lined up for a huge reception following the ceremonies. There was even a St. Louis City Police escort.

My father took the microphone. "Welcome to the LeoMorte family celebration. Eat, drink, and dance. Today we strengthened one marriage and started another. We're honored to have you here. If there's anything you need, let us know. Let the party begin." He ended with, "I'll take care of everything." This drew a laugh from the crowd, most of whom had heard him say that under all kind of circumstances.

My father escorted my mother out to the dance floor and half way through the song, "Oh How We Danced on the Night We Were Wed," was booming out off the walls of the VFW hall, my father waved Carla and me out to the floor to share in the spotlight.

I looked at Carla and asked, "Are you happy?"

"I am, I hope you are and that you never look at any other women."

"Why would I do that?"

"Just see that you don't."

I didn't give it much thought then. *Jealousy?* This was new for me.

The celebration lasted into the wee hours of the morning, Carla and I slipped out just after midnight to consummate our marriage.

Off to Florida for a quick honeymoon and then home to continue my job and my schoolwork. I soon had an offer as a paralegal. Taking this job with the prestigious, Italian family law firm of Ruggeri and Ruggeri would be a challenge, one I looked forward to facing. My hectic work schedule became a point of contention at home. I loved the legal challenge and certainly the restaurant duties, but Carla became quickly disenchanted with this way of life.

On a Saturday in September there was rare appearance by Bunny, accompanied her husband Sean and their now five-year-old son, Michael, who they affectionately called, *Mickey*.

A more mature Vince had now honed his social skills and charm as well as ramping back his flirting, but he was still referred to by the staff as *the silver-tongued devil.*

Impulsively Vince rushed to hug Bunny and was intercepted by an angry Sean Dempsey.

"This is the last time I'm going to tell you keep your hands off my wife."

"Relax Irish, I won't steal her away from you."

Pointing his finger into the face of Vince, Sean emphatically yelled, "Last time!"

Bunny, embarrassed by the testosterone-fueled display, announced, "This was a bad idea. Let's go home."

As they were hastily exiting, Sean gave Vince the death stare.

"That guy is trouble, Vince," advised Tony. "I don't need that kind of trouble. Sometimes you go too far."

"Pop, I can handle him."

"You need to dial it way back."

"Pop, we're the LeoMorte family. Nobody can harm us."

Dominic who had been standing nearby joined in the conversation. "I could take that *Mick* jerk anytime. Who the hell does he think he is?"

Big Tony saw this as teaching moment. "You guys calm down. Nobody is fighting anybody. We don't need that kind of trouble."

Tony noticed the bare right ring finger of Dominic. "Where's your lion's head ring?"

"I lost it."

"You lost it, lost it where?"

"If I knew that it, wouldn't be lost," flippantly replied Dominic.

"If you hadn't learned this by now, Dom, I don't let anyone disrespect me or threaten me! Do you understand?"

Dominic stood silently embarrassed about being called out in front of the group that had gathered.

"I asked you a question."

"Okay, okay I understand."

"One day your arrogance, loudmouth, and attitude are going to get you in the kind of trouble you can't escape."

Chapter XXII

The Missing Mysteries

Never a dull moment when you have a family the size of ours. Tony was busy with a network of activities, and money was piling up. Cash heavy Big Tony flashed the cash often. People were always impressed when Big Tony casually peeled off big bucks to cover any purchase and would leave eye popping tips for everyone. Part of this habit was generosity; the other part was to maintain an image of success.

Tony had noticed that Dominic had large gaps of unexplained time; lots of out-of-town time. That concerned my father. He wondered out loud, "Where the hell is that kid going? I have to watch that kid every minute. I may have to assign somebody to him again," Big Tony commented to Bull, Tony's constant companion.

The burly bodyguard replied, "Let me know boss, I can set it up."

Before Dom could be assigned another bodyguard/babysitter ,he was descending deeper into trouble.

Being the younger brother, it was hard to even approach Dominic about anything, but I felt the need to bring it up. "Dom, Pop is worried about you."

"So, my father and little brother are worried about me, ha."

"Pop is afraid you're getting in over your head."

"Getting into what?"

"I know you're smoking weed, I can smell it on you. And you are disappearing for days at a time. We're all concerned."

"Don't worry about Big Dom LeoMorte, I can handle anything or anybody."

"Pop worries about all of us. He says it all the time—*Family is everything*."

"I'm not going to live in his shadow. I'm establishing myself; people will know who I am and look up to me."

"People already know who we are and you know Mama worries too."

"I'm going to go big time. I have plans and connections."

Across town, the Dempsey's were getting Mickey signed up for school. Bunny's schedule was hectic, so it fell to Sean to take his son to the doctor for his school physical and get him the necessary shots. Dr. O'Malley was an old family friend, and Sean had done some remodeling work for him.

Father and son stepped off the elevator to the third floor and entered the waiting room to the doctor's office.

Sean addressed the receptionist, "Sean and my son Michael Dempsey. We're here for my son to get his physical to start school."

"Have a seat the doctor will be right with you."

After a brief wait, Doctor O'Malley poked his head out the office door. "Hey Sean, I'm ready for Michael."

The young boy disappeared into the office as Sean grabbed a magazine and prepared to wait.

After about twenty minutes, the doctor emerged with Mickey, who had a balloon in his hand and a grape sucker hanging out of his mouth.

"Okay, all set. He looks fine. He's up to date on his shots and I'll give you a call in a day or two when his blood work comes back from the lab."

"Great, Doctor. I'll wait to hear from you."

Later that week the phone rang. Sean was home from work, but his wife was still downtown working late.

"Hello."

"Sean, this is Doctor O'Malley."

"Yes, Doctor."

"We've been friends for a long time."

"Yes, we have... is there something wrong?"

"I'm not sure. I have your records here, yours and Bonnie's. I have here that your blood type is O and hers is type A."

"So what?"

"Well Michaels blood type came back as type B. He's not adopted, is he?"

"You know he's not! What are you saying?"

"I'm saying biological parents with type and A and O can't produce a baby with blood type B."

All the blood drained from Sean's face. He demanded, "You aren't to tell anyone about this. No one!"

"I understand. I'm sorry"

My life was hectic. I was splitting time between work at the restaurant, work at the law office, catching a few classes at school, and trying to be a good husband. Even though we had discussed my non-stop schedule before getting married, it was creating a strain on my marriage.

One night the conversation was opened by Carla with the always feared phrase, "We need to talk."

"I'm really tired. Can it wait until morning, or like maybe 1990."

My attempt at humor and deflection was met with an angry stare, a high-pitched voice, and a single syllable response. "No!"

"I never get to do anything. Every day is the same."

"What do you want to do?"

"I don't know, but I thought married life would be different, exciting, and we would be the envy of everyone."

"You have a car, cash, nice clothes, and time to do anything you want. I'm working hard to make a future for us."

"Everybody else travels, goes out every night, lives in big houses—we live in your father's house!"

"We're not everybody—we're *somebody*. We agreed about all this beforehand. Pop wants family close for lots of reasons. We'll have our own house someday."

"I'm sick of this same old routine and living in this house."

"Just be patient. We have a lifetime ahead of us. I'm doing the best I can."

"I need this to get better. I'm bored. It needs to change quickly."

I knew Carla was restless but hoped she would see I was working for us to have a bright future; it would just take a little time. She was going out almost daily, tooling around in her Corvette convertible, having lunch with friends, off to the movies, shopping—always in motion. In the next few months her attitude was changed. She became more demanding and impatient. I thought time would make it better, that time would be my friend.

While I was worried about Carla, I got word from a streetwise guy, a hustler nicknamed Jimmy *the hophead*, street lingo for a *doper*. For a few dollars, Jimmy would keep you informed as to what was happening.

"Hey Little Tony, your brother Dom is getting into some bad stuff and bad company."

"Bad like what?"

He looked around and said, "This is just between you and me—he's graduated from *wacky weed* to *white horse*."

"He's doing heroin?"

"Yeah man, he's hooked on horse, but that's not the worst part. He's dealing too. Word on the street is he's in with this gang from K.C., and he's buying from them and cutting them in on the profit."

"The Kansas City crew? Are you sure?"

"Yeah, he runs up there almost every week. He's in tight with Sam Granda and Willie Spinelli."

"Thanks. Promise me you won't tell anyone else about this. I owe you big time."

I knew Dom was playing fast and loose, but this was serious. He saw him as never really getting past that teenage mentality of being ten-feet-tall and bulletproof. That sense of impending doom hit. *What to do? Do I tell my father or just let things play out? This can't end well.*

Big Tony had been backing away from the business and letting Vince handle things—all except the cash. Little Italy wouldn't be the same if Big Tony wasn't there to meet and greet the customers and oversee some of the critical details. He also needed to maintain his connections all over the city and in local government. Opening and closing were left to Vince, and I was there to help any way I could.

"These are my sons, Vince and Little Tony. Aren't they great looking guys?"

The customers of course would agree and show us, his sons, the respect due a person of my father's stature.

"They turned out to be good men."

"What about your son, Dominic?" was often asked.

Big Tony's standard answer, "Well, two out of three ain't bad."

Vince had become comfortable with the restaurant routine and was doing well. He understood the business, even the shady goings on, and was a good soldier, following directions. The customers and most of Tony's acquaintances knew Vince, but often people sought out Big Tony for help, advice, or when they needed him to wield his power when necessary. Mary Rose had her routine and needed no supervision to keep the paperwork straight—or at least as straight as she could. Daddy's little angel, Angelina, rarely visited the restaurant. She had car and a credit card, that was all she needed.

It was Sunday, 12 noon, and dinner was on the table. We were all in our normal seats—all except Vince. Each loud tick of the grandfather clock added tension to the family waiting at the table. Phone calls to him went unanswered.

"Maybe he's just running late, but on his way.

Maria, at the insistence of Big Tony who was seated at the head of the table, decided to start.

"I don't like cold food. Let's eat."

With each rumble of a passing vehicle, Maria looked out the window and wondered, *Where's Vince?*

"Where could he be? He's never late, and he knows Sunday dinner is a family tradition," Maria said with worry in her voice.

"Pop, I left the restaurant an hour before closing time, and Vince was there. We counted the cash and locked the back door."

"I know, son, it's the same routine as always."

"Do you want me to go by his house and check on him?"

Carla bristled at the idea of having to check on a full-grown man. "He'll be fine. He probably had a late date with some young thing."

"Little Tony, let's you and I go by his house while the women clean off the table and take care of the dishes. Angelina, help your mother. We'll be back in a little while."

We climbed into my fathers black Cadillac and headed for the Hill.

"I didn't want to alarm your mother, but something doesn't seem right. It's not like Vince to miss Sunday dinner and not at least call. That's more like something Dom would do."

"Pop, I haven't told you, but word on the street is that Dom is in with the Kansas City crew and dealing drugs."

"I've already heard that and sent a couple of guys to K.C. to tell Sam the snake and Willie the weasel that if that's true, we have a serious problem. The old timers always said that they don't come after you, they go after what you love. Nobody, and I mean *nobody*, messes with my family!"

I could see the worry on my father's face as he sped towards Vince's house. We ran every red light and shattered the speed limit on the way over.

When we pulled up, the first thing we noticed was Vince's car wasn't there. A check with neighbors just fueled the feeling that something wasn't right—nobody had seen him. We knocked on the door. No answer. I used my key to get in, and it looked like Vince hadn't been home.

"Let's head down to the restaurant."

A repeat of the road race from earlier, and we were soon at the front door of Little Italy.

Vince's car was still in the parking lot. "That's not good!"

I unlocked the door, and we went in. Everything was quiet. We called out to Vince, but there was no sign of anything wrong. We looked around.

"Where could he have gone?"

Tony grabbed the phone from behind the counter and dialed. "This is Big Tony LeoMorte. Is the chief home?"

I knew this was serious if Pop was calling the St. Louis Chief of Police at home.

"Yeah Lou, this is Tony LeoMorte, sorry to bother you on Sunday afternoon at home, but I've got a problem."

I could hear the voice on the other end of the phone.

"What's up?"

"My oldest son Vince is missing. He didn't show up at my house like he was supposed to, isn't at his house, and we checked the restaurant. He's not here either."

"He could just be out somewhere else."

"Nope, something isn't right. Can you have your guys start looking for him."

"Will do. I'm just not sure where to start."

We went back to the house and waited for a call that never came.

Chapter XXIII

The FBI Again

Thinking they were secretly surveilling us, the FBI planned another raid on Villa Cristo. The early morning silence was disrupted by the growling and barking of the newest giant German shepherd that had replaced Rocky. The dog was running the length of the fence snarling as it had been trained to alert Big Tony that there were intruders.

Three cars had pulled up the driveway, the lead car bore the insignia of the FBI, the other two were plain unmarked vehicles.

The banging on the door clearly announced the serious intent of the men that exited the vehicles.

"Open up, FBI. We have a search warrant."

"Hold on," Tony said as he unlocked and unbolted the door.

As quick as the door opened the agents rushed in warrant in hand.

"We've been watching you for weeks and we have a warrant giving us the right to search the premises."

"A warrant based off of what?"

"You think you're so damned smart. In 1970 a law was enacted for people just like you. It's called RICO, the Racketeer Influenced and Corrupt Organizations Act. It's aimed at prosecuting those conducting illegal activities. People like you, Mr. Leo-Morte," the lead agent, Mike Cooper said sarcastically. "You may have the local law enforcement in your pocket but not the FBI!"

"You may remember Agent O'Rourke, he visited you in the past. He insisted on coming along."

"Oh yeah, he was very pleasant."

Cooper explained, "We have the right to search the entire property inside and out."

"You're welcome to look around, but it's in your best interest to let me put the dog in his kennel. He's attack trained, and as you can tell, he is vicious toward strangers. May I?"

"Go ahead, but don't try anything. We're a lot smarter than you, one of the other agents will accompany you."

"I have nothing to hide. I wouldn't have it any other way. I don't want to compromise your search."

Big Tony merely called out to the dog, "Kennel." The giant German shepherd went into the fenced area, and Tony secured the gate behind him.

As the strange man stepped into the yard the dog jumped at the fence, startling the FBI agent.

"He's dangerous isn't he."

"He's the best guard here. He protects everything I value—my family and my home."

Inside, the house was being picked apart. Maria was a fastidious housekeeper and didn't appreciate the tossing of everything from furniture, cookware, clothes, and even under-wear dresser drawers.

"Is this really necessary?"

"Yes, ma'am it is. We're just doing our job."

The FBI agents were relentless. I knew my father was too smart to have anything in the house that could be a problem. My mother was a saint, above suspicion, but what about the rest? Angelina's room was a mess with clothes tossed about, our room was destroyed, and when they got to Dom's room a conference was called, and the door was closed.

You could hear mumbling, but none of the closed-door con-versation was clearly audible. After about 15 minutes the agents emerged with sly grins on their faces. They carried a few paper bags and made their way to the front door leaving their scattered search mess behind.

Lead agent Mike Cooper stayed behind and addressed my Father, "Thanks for your cooperation."

"It was my pleasure."

"By the way I was admiring your big, impressive German shepherd. What's his name?"

With a faint smile, more like a smirk, my father replied, "Rico."

The not so subtle humor infuriated Cooper as he turned, red faced, walked out, and climbed into the FBI marked car.

The very next day the same group returned with their own pair of German shepherds and a fresh search warrant.

My father met them at the front porch.

"Okay, this is now bordering on harassment."

"Take a look at the warrant—it's all legal."

The drug-sniffing dogs were trained to signal a hit on any drug scent. They immediately went to work on the cars and once they got to Dom's car the dogs went wild.

"That's a confirmed presence of narcotics on that vehicle. Who is this car registered to? We need the keys."

Dom's new Cadillac was opened and to a human nose there was just that new car smell, but to the trained, highly developed nose of a dog it wasn't even a close call.

With the whole family watching from the porch, the FBI began to dismantle the car. It didn't take long to find a serious stash of clear plastic bags with what looked like a white powder in the driver's side door panel. The only thing paler than the contents of those bags was Dominic's face.

A field test of the powder proved it was heroin, a lot of heroin. Dominic *and* my father were both handcuffed. They stood on the driveway in front of a horrified Maria.

"Dominic LeoMorte, you're under arrest for possession of illegal narcotics with intent to sell. You have the right to remain silent, anything you say can and will be used against you in a court of law, you have the right to an attorney, if you cannot afford an attorney, one will be appointed for you. Do you understand these rights?"

"Keep your mouth shut, Dominic. Don't say anything to anybody. *Silencio*. Do you understand?"

"I understand."

My mother ran into the house after receiving the instruction of my father who said, "Call Ruggeri, the lawyer."

As my mother was frantically dialing the phone, she asked me, "What should we do?"

"First if anyone is questioned, we should remain silent until there is an attorney present, but remember Ma, I'm only a paralegal. Call Mike Ruggeri."

"Mr. Ruggeri this is Maria LeoMorte Little Tony's mother, Big Tony's wife. My husband and son have been arrested; we need your help."

"Your son Tony has been arrested?"

"No, my son Dominic and my husband Tony. Please help us."

"I'll head down to the police station right now. What are they being charged with?"

"The FBI found drugs."

A long pause was punctuated by a response of, "Don't speak to anyone and advise the rest of your family to do the same thing."

Tony was preparing Dominic for what was to come, he whispered, "They're going to separate us and try to get different stories from each of us. They'll tell you that I rolled on you to get a deal. They'll tell me you broke under pressure and sold me out. Don't believe any of it."

"What else?" A nervous Dominic asked.

"They'll bring in two people to question you to tilt the odds in their favor. They'll try to make you drop your guard by offering you somethng to drink, showing you that they're good guys. As soon as they start to question you simply say, *I can't answer any questions until my lawyer is present.*"

A voice from behind them said, "You two be quiet."

Father and son were transported separately and, after arriving at the police station, they were hustled toward interrogation rooms. There were lots of familiar faces, cops from every level greeted Big Tony and Dominic. About the same time they were being booked, Michael Ruggeri senior arrived.

Typical of Dominic, when they emptied his pockets, he had a comb, a condom, and a roll of cash.

Ruggeri spoke up, "Okay boys I need to see my clients privately."

"You can soon, but not right now."

Just as Big Tony predicted, the FBI agents brought the cuffed LeoMortes into separate rooms.

"Okay Dominic, make it easy on yourself and work with us, and we'll get you a better deal."

"I have nothing to say until my lawyer is present."

"Okay, but you won't get another chance. You're staring down the barrel of 20 to 50 years hard time in a federal penitentiary."

Visibly shaken Dominic still wasn't going for it.

The agents stepped into the next room and immediately tried to pressure Big Tony.

"The kid's already breaking, we'll have him rolling on everybody."

"Then you don't need me."

"We've just been waiting to nail you, now we've got you. No slipping out of this one!"

After intense questioning and getting nowhere, the father and son were brought before a judge for a bail hearing.

The word came down from the judge, "I don't consider you a flight risk, and this is your first arrest. Bail is set at $25,000 each. That's my ruling."

After posting bond, Ruggeri drove Tony and Dominic home. "So, what happened?" the lawyer asked.

"The FBI came to the house armed with a search warrant yesterday and went all through the house and apparently found something in Dom's room. They came back today with drug dogs and discovered a large amount of heroin in the door panel of Dominic's car."

"They have him for possession, and based off the amount,

with intent to distribute. They'll try to drag you into this too, Tony."

"Yeah, too bad they forgot to *Mirandize* me."

"They did?"

"As they were cuffing Dominic, they read him his rights and called him specifically by name but not me."

"They'll dispute that, but we have multiple witnesses to contest that, besides you don't have anything to do with the drugs. I'll file a motion to dismiss soon."

Once they arrived home, Ruggeri left with a promise to call them soon with his plan for criminal proceedings.

A nervous Dominic asked, "Can they get me for this?"

Big Tony dismissed the ladies, including my mother, Maria, to the kitchen.

"It's time for you to tell me everything, I mean everything— every detail, who's involved, and what has been going on."

"Sam Granda came to see me and offered me a deal distributing dope here. He told me I'd be *the man* in St. Louis and make a boatload of money. I'd pick up the stuff in Kansas City and bring it here and set up delivery with a group of high-volume dealers. Easy and clean."

"You idiot. You fell for that?"

"I'd be on my own and making my own money."

"Dealing drugs is dirty business. Did you ever stop to think that any one of those guys could give you two in the head and just take the dope? It's a dirty and dangerous business."

"I owed him $27,000. I was spending money on everything and everybody and using heroin every day myself. I couldn't catch up to get him paid off. He insisted on taking my lion ring as a down payment, he called it his trophy."

"How could you be so foolish and not see that coming? When you roll around with the pigs you get dirty.

"Can't you get me off?"

"These are feds. They're going to make a big deal out of this because of who you are and who I am. It's the rule of the street—they don't come after you, they go after what you love. Now both, the Kansas City crew and the cops got you cornered."

"I'll rat the K.C. mob out. I'll make a deal."

"Haven't you been listening? They'll come after your family if you do that."

"Are you saying I'll have to take the fall and do time for this?"

"It's very possible, and even if you snitch you'll still get some time, and I can't protect you in prison."

Now the true Dom was coming out, and he began to cry uncontrollably.

At the preliminary hearing, the prosecutor Bill McCullough addressed the judge, "Your honor Dominic LeoMorte was found during an FBI search warrant being executed to have a large stash of heroin in his possession, two kilos—over four pounds—of heroin hidden in the door panel of his automobile."

The judge responded. "How do you wish to plead Mr. Leo-Morte, guilty or not guilty?"

Michael Ruggeri spoke out saying, "My client pleads not guilty."

"Now, Mr. McCullough, why is Mr. Anthony LeoMorte here?"

"The drugs were found on his property your honor."

"Mr. McCullough, a even decent paralegal would know you can't hold this man for that. Mr. Anthony LeoMorte, you are free to go."

Two weeks before they were scheduled go to trial the district attorney offered Dominic a plea deal. Michael Ruggeri urged Dominic to take the deal. He pleaded guilty and was sentenced to twenty years in the federal prison at Leavenworth.

Chapter XXIV

The Player Gets Played

It was the summer of 1982. Carla and I barely speak to each other. We're two people sharing the same home.

Carla suggests, "I think we need to go to counseling."

"I agree. I'll make the arrangements. You understand this could take a while, and they can't solve our problems, that's up to us."

"I'm not stupid. I understand how it works."

Once we were in counseling, I watched everything more closely, looking for clues as to how to make my wife happy. I complimented her on her new wardrobe, I note her weight loss and the change on her hair color and style. She bought new, sexier underwear. The renewal energized us both.

Things seemed to be progressing—slowly, but there was less arguing. At least *I* thought it was progress, but I wondered if it was because she just didn't care anymore. I got my answer one Saturday afternoon when I was inside helping to prepare a case file. Carla was outside in a lounge chair talking on her cordless phone. She was smiling and laughing on a call that seemed to go on and on.

She hung up and came inside. "I'm going out for a while."

There was no indication as to where she was going or for how long. That seemed a little unusual to me.

"Where are you going?"

"Out, I'm going out! You know the opposite of in. Is that okay?"

"Who were you talking to?"

"Just a girlfriend of mine."

"I'm going to take a shower, and then I'll be gone for a while. I don't know what time I'll be back."

This new phone had a feature called *redial*. I hit the button, the phone made a varied series of beeps, and a masculine voice answered, "Hello?"

I said, "Hello, is this Mike Cummings."

"No, this is Ronnie Newsome."

"Is this not 555-2790?"

"No, it's 555-3890."

"Must have dialed the wrong number. Sorry to have bothered you." With a shaky hand I quickly scribbled down the unfamiliar name and number. Somehow my world stopped but also seemed to be spinning out of control at the same time. I went into denial trying to convince myself this wasn't happening.

About twenty minutes later Carla came out dressed up in an outfit designed to attract attention.

"Wow, you sure you look nice," I commented.

"Yeah, whatever, see ya later." Out the door she went.

My mind was racing. I looked through our room for clues of a possible affair but turned up nothing. I checked the phone book on a hunch; there was a listing for Ronnie and Crystal Newsome. They lived in the area, but that's all I knew.

I was now keenly aware of every detail of things going on around me. I routinely checked the odometer of Carla's Corvette and watched for any clue as to what was happening. I spied on her phone calls, watched the mail and noted times she left, came back, and what she wore.

Then Carla asked me, "Are you cheating on me?"

"Am I cheating on you?"

"If you are, I could get half of everything you own. A good lawyer could get me more than half!"

"Sorry to disappoint you, but I'm faithful to you."

"Okay, just checking."

Now the game had started.

As fate would have it I had an appointment the next day with my eye doctor. The doc came out of the exam room escorting his previous patient and introduced me to him.

"This is Tony LeoMorte. Tony this is Charles Patterson, he's a private detective."

"Interesting, do you have a business card?"

"I do."

"Nice to meet you, thanks for the card."

I tucked the card into my wallet and went about my business. Knowing the snoopy Carla and her habits, I left my wallet out and pulled the card part way out so she would see it. Sure enough she fell for it, the wallet had been moved. Now to wait.

Before anything came up about the card, I received a phone call from a high school friend of mine.

"Hey man, just a head's up—if you're tom catting, you should be more discreet."

"What do you mean?"

"I saw that convertible Corvette you drive outside Coral Courts—that motel on Highway 44."

"Are you sure it's the same car?"

"Yeah, that custom pinstripe is a dead giveaway, and I've seen it there the last two Thursdays."

"Okay, thanks." My stomach knotted up at this news.

I don't like confrontation, but I have to admit, I'm pretty good at it. When I arrived home, no one else was there but Carla.

"Just so you know, I'm aware of what's going on."

The blood drained from her face. "What's going on?"

"I know where you've been going, what you've been doing, and with who. You accused me of cheating, but you're the cheater!"

"I haven't been doing anything."

There was a roaring in my ears, and I struggled with vacillating between the emotions of anger, hate, and fear—fear of the unknown.

Anger was winning.

"Oh, I think you have," I said as I sailed the detective's business card across the table. "I've been having you followed."

"No, you haven't."

"I have, and I even have pictures, you should have been a little more careful."

She took the bait! Now to ramp it up a bit.

"Does his wife know yet?"

A blank stare in response to my question. Then Carla exhaled. "I haven't been happy for a long time. We live in this stupid house and have no privacy. Any argument, any conversation, even having sex—I have to wonder if everyone is listening."

"That's *making love* not h*aving sex*!"

"No, it's *having sex*, I don't love you anymore."

The door slammed behind her as she left, and I could hear the tires squealing as she drove out of the driveway.

I picked up the phone and called a mutual friend, Dorothy, to find out what she might know.

"Dorothy? Tony. I just had it out with Carla. I know everything." I waited, and she slowly replied.

"I'm so sorry. I wanted to tell you. I felt so guilty."

Another co-conspirator, I thought. "Why did you feel guilty?

"I let her and David use my house. When she said, *He'll never catch me, he trusts me too much*, I knew I couldn't be a part of it anymore."

I dropped to my knees; I felt nauseous, it wasn't one guy it was at least two. How could I not see this?

"She was coming over to meet up with him once a week."

"What else do you know about."

"He's married and has two kids."

"There's another guy too."

"There is?"

"A guy whose last name is Newsome."

"Ronnie Newsome? He works at the Sunset Country Club."

I realized I had been living with someone I didn't even know. I began to plot my revenge. I'd catch them in the act. Then what?

After arriving home and seeking privacy outside she took on a haughty attitude.

"Ronnie and I are going to get married and start a family."

"Don't you think you ought to end one marriage before you start another one?"

"I'm just asking you to keep it quiet. I'll leave and just take the car and some cash. Don't tell anyone."

"You'll leave with some cash, no car. That's cost of cheating."

"Okay, I don't care. I just want out."

"So, his wife doesn't know? Neither guy's wife knows?"

"What?" she responded with a panicked look on her face. Her facial expression and body language showed the shock of knowing I was on to her.

"Yeah, I know about at least two. So, you sleep in the spare bedroom tonight and be gone tomorrow. I'll write you check for $3,000, a thousand dollars for each year."

"I'm not doing that."

"Okay, I'll start calling wives tomorrow."

"Okay, okay. Just don't say anything."

Eight weeks after the divorce was finalized, I received a frantic phone call. It was Carla

"I can't do this anymore"

"Who is this?"

"Carla, your wife."

"I'm sorry, you must have the wrong number. I'm not married. I don't have a wife."

"No wait, listen, after he found out I was getting a divorce, he said he changed his mind about us and was staying with his wife."

"Whoops, man that's tough. You got what you wanted; do you want what you got?"

"I want to come home?'

"Oh, you are welcome to go home—but this *isn't* your home; not anymore. Maybe I should forward your mail to the Coral Courts motel. It's funny, the lawyer asked me when this divorce started, if I would consider taking you back. I told him that would be like throwing up and then eating it. Just imagine if something made you sick the first time and you went back and did it again. How stupid would that be? No thank you."

"I can't do this without you."

"You should have thought about that two guys ago."

"I just need to know where we stand."

"I can help you with that one, you're standing over there, and I'm standing over here. Have a nice life."

You hear music all the time that describes a broken heart, but when you experience that deception, the lies and the betrayal from someone you loved, then you know what a broken heart is. How did I get this so wrong?

In late 1982 Father Parisi, now 83 years old, was hospitalized and fading fast—his heart weak and failing. I took the elevator to the third floor and asked the duty nurse if I could visit his room. She led me to room 308.

"Father it's me, Little Tony LeoMorte."

"Step closer, I can't see or hear very well anymore."

His eyes were red, not bloodshot, just red like many of the elderly people I knew. I took his hand to comfort him and noticed how bony it seemed. The thin skin on his hands was covered with age spots, his face had a little spotty, gray stubble on it and made him look even more frail, almost helpless. I hadn't noticed those things before. He looked tiny laying in that big hospital bed.

"How are you feeling?"

"I'm ready to go home."

"Have they told you when they would release you?"

"No son, my heavenly home."

"Aw, you still have several good years left."

"I'm tired. I've seen it all, done a bunch, and been in the God and people business for a long time."

"You've been good to my family and a lot of other families. We still need you."

"Tony, I've been a good and faithful servant. I baptized God's children, married them, and buried them. My race is run."

"All these biblical references—I remember my father always saying the answers for everything are in Psalm number 156."

"Ha-ha, that sound like something your father would say. You need to blow the dust off your Bible."

"What do you mean, Father Parisi?"

"There is no Psalm 156. There are only 150 Psalms."

I felt stupid and gullible.

"I also wanted you to know that I have gotten a divorce. I caught Carla cheating."

"I do remember asking you if you were sure about this girl when you came to me about getting married."

"I know, I regret not listening closer."

"There is a process you can follow in the church to get an annulment. It takes a while and has a financial obligation to it."

"I'll look into that."

"Father tell me about your memories of my grandparents if you would."

"They were fresh off the boat, and I was newly ordained. They were always solid people. Your grandmother was a devout Catholic, your grandfather not so fervent. I remember years ago your grandfather told me about a dream he had, it seemed to haunt him. I watched your grandfather working hard, I bet I saw him bake a thousand loaves of bread. I can still see in my imagination your grandmother sitting in the back row of pews rolling the rosary beads in her tiny hands as she prayed. She was a good woman."

"Grandpa Vincent told me about a dream—a lion and the one hundred years, Cent'Anni?"

"Yes. He told you too? He must have really loved you and trusted you. He told me he had never revealed the dream to anyone else, it must have been just the two of us."

"He was a good man. I always admired his work ethic, but as family he seemed emotionally distant all the time. He never told me that he loved me, but I guess he did in his own way."

"He was indeed a good man and a product of a rough environment. He never really got over losing his Rosa, your grandmother. He probably was never told he was loved by anyone but Rosa. You should also try to look at it this way, *"The hardest thing to do is give something you didn't get."*

"I remember after he died, we were going through his closet and every gift he got for Christmas sat in a closet unopened. I think he never wanted to depend on anyone else for anything. What a sad existence."

We chatted a while longer, and the priest kept drifting off to sleep. I watched him for a while knowing it may be the last time, and that very night, he was called home.

Afterwards I remember feeling sorry for those who grieved Father Parisi, all that knew him—and later I felt sorry for those who never got to know him.

Chapter XXV

Sweet Music

I've been single twelve years; work keeps me busy and I spend much more time at the restaurant. Some of the same customers I saw as a small boy still come to Little Italy for lunch, dinner and family celebrations. I love seeing the families most of all.

Occasionally Bunny Dempsey stops in accompanied by her son Mickey, now 19 years old, but never with Sean. I haven't seen him in years.

I overheard a brief conversation my father had with Bunny.

"It's been a lot of years since you first walked in here. You were beautiful then, and you still are now."

"It has been a lot of years. You've been a good friend; I couldn't have made without your support. After Sean left it was tough. Poor Mickey he's been without any man in his life, someone to teach him to play soccer, about cars, or be an example of how a man treats a lady."

"That was weird, very strange that Sean decided to just take off and leave you to take care of his son. You can't be both a father and mother to a child. He seems to have done pretty well despite Sean's absence."

"I've cried about Mickey not having his father in his life. I wish his father could have watched him turn into the man he is becoming. I don't know where Sean ended up, but as a master carpenter he could probably go anywhere and get work. It doesn't seem like it, but it's been over thirteen years since he left."

"Yeah, but to not financially support his son, that's wrong."

"I made good money with the modeling agency, but it's not the same. A boy needs his father."

"To be honest, I never cared for him anyway. Too much of a temper, he was a hothead. Maybe you were better off without him."

"His father will never realize what he missed out on."

Over the past years it's so evident that my mother hasn't been the same since Vince disappeared, he was never seen or heard from again. She is quiet and the passing of each of his birthdays and Christmases are especially tough on her. Vince's body was never found and his disappearance with no trace has been like an open wound that will never heal.

My father grieves differently, he got quiet and paranoid. His rage is always just under the surface.

We had never really talked about it a lot, but one afternoon at the restaurant it came up randomly.

"I miss Vince. I've never been able to prove that the Kansas City crew was involved but, in my heart, I know they did something. You know with it being 1998, he would have been 50 years old this year. They better pray I never find out who was involved."

I asked my father, "Do you think they intentionally drew Dom into drug dealing to hurt you, Pop?"

"Tony, they couldn't have pulled that off if Dom wasn't willing. When you get involved in drugs it can never end well."

"I feel sorry for Dom, I thought by now he would have been paroled. I know mom misses him and worries all the time."

"He'll never get out early. The amount of drugs he got caught with, along with his last name, almost ensures he'll do every day of his sentence. He's probably better off in the joint anyway, at least this way I don't have to worry about where he is. Maybe he learned a valuable lesson—when you pick up enough snakes you'll get bit."

Just then a long-time, regular customer came in, Thomasino Certilli, he was a cello player for the St. Louis symphony. He always dressed well and oddly ate the same thing—a sirloin steak cooked medium well, a small salad with oil and vinegar with a side order of fried mushrooms. He was once again impeccably dressed, heavily starched shirt, silk tie in a perfect Windsor knot, perfectly creased pants, wearing thick horned rimmed glasses—a curious little man, but I always liked him.

"Good afternoon Mr. Certilli, how are you today?"

"I'm very well, and yourself?"

"Oh, you know, as grandpa used to say, "*metà e metà*.""

"I never understood that saying, *half and half*. Strange."

"Let me guess, you're going to have a sirloin steak?"

"How did you know that?"

"I pay attention, that's what you always eat. I'll get you order placed."

"I'd like that cooked medium well, a small salad with oil and vinegar, and a side order of fried mushrooms."

We said it in unison, and he looked over the top of his glasses as if he was wondering if I was mocking him.

I left and returned to his table, "I know you didn't ask but I brought you a glass of red wine to go with your meal."

"You're a good boy, Tony, thank you. Hey, for your kindness, I have two tickets to tonight's performance. We're currently doing Rigoletto. The seats are middle, second row, orchestra level, great seats."

"Oh, thanks Mr. Certilli, but I don't know if I will have time. I might have to work tonight."

"I insist. Please."

"Yes sir, thank you so much," I said as I slid the tickets into my shirt pocket.

After his lunch, as he was paying his bill, Mr. Certilli instructed my father to make sure I got off early enough to attend the St. Louis symphony.

My father called me over. "It would probably be good for you to get out a little. Take the tickets Thomasino gave you, get a date, and go to the symphony."

"Aw, Pop I don't think so. I'm not really interested in going or getting a date."

"It's not healthy for a young man like you to be just working all the time. Go enjoy yourself. Get a little culture, meet some people ,just get out and try something different. If you don't, you have to stay and close. Would you rather do that?"

"Now that you put it that way the symphony sounds better than staying here. I'll go back to the house, see mama, and get cleaned up."

"What about a date? You have two tickets."

"Sorry Pop, this kid is flying solo."

I felt so out of place entering the symphony hall and when I got to the seat everyone looked a lot more cultured and well-dressed than I. It didn't help when a matronly looking woman asked about the vacant seat between her and me.

"Is that your seat also?"

"Yes, ma'am, it is."

"No date?"

"No ma'am, no date."

Then the curse of being divorced.

"I noticed you don't have a wedding ring on. Are you single, because I have a wonderful niece that would be perfect for you?"

The conversation came to a screeching halt when I declared, "I'm happily divorced."

The conductor addressed the audience with a welcome and the announcement that the opera Rigoletto was about to begin. The lights dimmed, and the music started. I enjoyed the music—only interrupted by an occasional look of disdain from the match-maker one seat away.

A voice came over the speakers announcing a brief fifteen-minute intermission, and then it happened. I stood up to stretch and turned back looking into the crowd and about fifteen rows up I spotted the woman of my dreams. Petite, black hair that matched a raven's wing, eyes that looked translucent but were an ice blue, and modest makeup which didn't disguise her natural beauty. The *wow* button was going off in my brain. This was uncommon for me. She looked to be at least ten years my junior, and I was instantly drawn to her. My mind raced. Who was she? Was she married? Why was she sitting alone at the St. Louis symphony? I hoped she wasn't from out of town. I hoped she didn't have a can of mace in her purse. I climbed the steps toward her row to introduce myself.

I started a conversation with the dignified looking lady next to her in hopes if not scaring off my dream girl.

"Ma'am, how would you like to have a second-row center seat? I'm leaving soon anyway."

"Why I would love that, how very kind of you."

"Here you go. Enjoy the rest of your evening."

I scooted clumsily out of the way so I could *accidentally* bump into my dream girl. "I'm sorry. I didn't mean to bump into you. Are you okay?"

"Of course, you barely brushed me."

"I'm Tony LeoMorte, it's a pleasure to meet you."

"You really haven't met me yet," she said with a laugh that rivaled the music of the symphony.

Is this lady for real? "Okay, let's formally meet then."

"I'm Catherine, Catherine Collins. What else would you like to know?"

"Since you asked, can I buy you a cup of coffee after the symphony?"

"You want to buy a cup of coffee, huh?"

"Well, I'd like to buy you a two-carat perfect princess cut diamond ring set in platinum. But how about we start with the coffee?"

That a got a full laugh!

"I can't tonight."

"How about tomorrow?"

"Let's make it Friday, that will give me time to do some research on you," she said playfully.

"Uh-oh. Let me help you—I don't like sushi, long walks on

the beach, or Barry Manilow. I'm a Pisces, and I think you're the most beautiful woman I've ever seen."

"Did I mention Barry Manilow is my brother, I love to eat sushi while I walk on the beach, and by the way, your zipper is down."

I panicked but didn't want to look down, so I countered with, "They say it pays to advertise." *Beautiful and witty, wow!* "So seriously, will you really go out with me Friday?"

"Give me your number, and I'll call you. I don't trust you with my number yet, especially after that phony story you told that lady to get her seat near me."

"You knew?"

"Of course, I knew!"

"This is going to be interesting. Is this considered our *first* date?"

"Hardly. I'll meet you Friday at the jewelry store so we can pick out that ring."

Stunned, now I didn't know what to say. I scribbled my home phone number on the back of a Little Italy business card, and as she reached for the card, I took her hand and kissed it gently. Even through her makeup, I could tell she was blushing. "Call me, soon, please."

A few days later I walked into the house at around five o'clock, Mama Maria greeted me with, "Some lady called, Catherine, and left a number for you to call back."

"When did she call? Did she say anything else? Did she sound interested?"

"She called around 3 o'clock and asked who I was when I answered. I told her Maria LeoMorte, I think she thought I may have been a wife or girlfriend."

I wondered if I would look desperate if I called back immediately or should I wait until the evening? To heck with playing it cool, I started dialing with no thought of what I was going to say.

Ring, ring, ring, ring, ring….

Five rings and no answer. *Damn.*

"Hello?"

Now I was tongue tied.

"Hi, is this Catherine?"

"Yes, it is."

"This is Tony, Tony LeoMorte. I met you a few days ago at the symphony."

"Oh yeah, I remember. I have to talk quietly," she whispered. "I don't want my husband to hear me talking to you."

I thought, *What?!*

After a pause she let me off the hook. Laughing, she said, "Just kidding. Did I get you?"

"Uh, yeah. You're just full of surprises."

"So, where are we going on this dream date, Hawaii, Rio, or maybe Paris?"

"I know a great restaurant downtown. Is that okay?"

"Sure, I live at 502 Rock Hill road. I'll be ready at 6 o'clock. Is that okay?

"Absolutely. I'll see you then."

I was nervous as I pulled up to a quaint little craftsman-style home in what looked like a well-established, quiet neighborhood, the streets were lined with old oak, red bud, and sycamore trees; the yard was neat but needed a cut and trim.

She must have heard my car pull up because as I was checking in the glass on the storm door to make sure there was nothing in my teeth, the door opened.

"Hi, am I too early?"

"Nope, you're right on time. You get points for that. But, no bouquet of flowers? You haven't been on too many dates, recently have you?"

"Man, I don't know how to take you."

"You have to take me just the way I am."

I opened the car door for her and she slid into the front seat while I hopped in behind the wheel and pulled out of the driveway.

"You know your neighborhood reminds me of what they say about Florida."

"Oh yeah, what's that?"

"Well, it looks pretty quiet and older; we laugh when we describe Florida as for the newlywed and the nearly dead."

"It's quiet and perfect for me, and I'm neither newlywed nor nearly dead."

"So, tell me what I need to know about Catherine Collins."

She reached over to turn the radio down, "I'm divorced, have one son who's ten, I own a small combination coffee shop/bookstore and moved here from Chicago three years ago. If you ask me how old I am or how much I weigh, I'll kick you in the cubes."

"I'll wait until we go to the circus and let a pro guess your weight and age."

We pulled up to the restaurant. I ran over to open her door and she stepped out gracefully. "Is this place okay? I've heard good things about it."

She looked at the overhead sign and remarked, "Little Italy, huh? You must know somebody here, that's the business card you wrote your phone number on."

"Yeah, I know a few people here."

As we entered the restaurant we were greeted with calls of, "Hey, Little Tony, *Cosa sta succedendo* (What's happening)?"

Catherine realizing the set up said, "So a little home field advantage, huh?"

"I wanted to show you off."

"Did you want to get a drink before dinner?"

"Okay, and we can listen to the music."

We were seated, and a waiter dressed in black slacks and a white shirt asked, "What to drink folks?"

"Catherine?" I ask.

"A strawberry daiquiri."

"A strawberry daiquiri for the lady and a rum and coke for me, light on the rum. Tell the bartender to mix it like I'm driving his daughter home."

The band started playing, "The First Time Ever I Saw Your Face." I took Catherine's hand and led her out onto the floor.

She protested, "No one else is dancing!"

"Good. There will be more room for us."

I pulled her in close, and she put her hand on the back of my neck. It felt so right.

After a few minutes the music stopped, and we sit down to our drinks just as it was announced that our table was ready. I escorted Catherine to our table where a single long stem rose was waiting in her place at the table. I pulled her chair out for her, and she said, "A rose?"

"Yeah. And you thought I forgot the flowers, remember? I called ahead this afternoon and had it delivered. Surprise!"

"I think you said to me, *You're just full of surprises.* Back at you."

We had a quiet conversation over minestrone soup, salad, and ravioli. I was aware of the staff staring at us. I could see a lot of whispering and each in turn going to my father and him nodding in agreement. I could only wonder what was being said.

As we finished our meal, I couldn't stand it anymore and blurted out, "I hope I'm not too old for you—I'm 45."

"So, I guess it's my turn. I'm 33."

I asked, "Are you ready to go?"

"I am, it's been a busy day."

As we left the restaurant, I opened her car door, and she smiled approvingly. "Such a gentleman."

"I was taught to respect women."

I slid my hand over to hers as we drove back to her home, she didn't resist. Once we pulled into her driveway, I exited quickly to get her door again. "I'll walk you to the door."

At the door the uncomfortable question invaded my head, do I kiss her goodnight?

"I had a great time Catherine."

"I did too."

Feeling like a nervous schoolboy, I leaned in and kissed her, a short kiss. She got on her tip toes, leaned in, and kissed me, a passionate, lingering kiss.

I responded with, "If this is a dream, I never want to wake up. That was a wonderful first kiss."

She replied, "I don't know about you, but that wasn't my first kiss."

We laughed together, she opened the door, and disappeared inside.

As I walked back to the car, I thought to myself, *This could be the start of something special.*

Family Life (1998)

For the next two months Catherine and I talked every day, and when her son Oliver was in Chicago with his father, we spent a lot of time together. Having both been single for a while, we were still moving cautiously.

There was an unnatural but somehow understandable tension in the house.

"I'm tired, ready to relax, Maria," my father said.

"I know Tony, I need a break to clear my head too. Vince's disappearance has devastated me, I'm completely lost."

We all noticed Mama smiled infrequently ,and much of the joy she once resonated was gone. Big Tony had grown to hate cold weather. A pall hungover this once happy house, Villa Cristo.

"Let's pack up and go to Florida. The kids can run the restaurant—its' on automatic."

Soon, my parents were all packed and ready to sit in the sun for a few weeks. I drove my father and mother to Lambert Field, the airport servicing St. Louis. With my parents gone, I'd be alone in the house. Mary Rose was in her own home, Dominic was still serving his sentence and Angelina surprised us all by joining a convent, becoming a nun, and being stationed in Rhode Island at an all-girl school.

With Oliver out of town, Catherine came by the house to fix me a home-cooked meal. It was snowing lightly; the roads were getting slick and it was 9:30 PM by the time I pulled into the driveway. As I turned the key on the door, I thought I could smell homemade soup and what I perceived to be cornbread. My mother would have keeled over—cornbread in this Italian house!

Laughingly I called out like the man of the house from a fifties sitcom, "Honey, I'm home."

Playing along she responded, "I'm in here, dear."

I stepped into the kitchen. "Boy, is it nice to see you here," I said as I slid my hands around her waist for a tender hug and quick kiss.

"I thought you would enjoy a nice, hot meal, not something from the menu at the restaurant that you would have to eat standing up or running back and forth from customers to kitchen."

"Wow, a homecooked meal, a fire in the fireplace—this is great. I definitely could get used to this."

We sat across from each other at the small table in the kitchen, and she watched as I slurped my soup.

"I think you're getting as much *on* you as you are getting *in* you."

"The cornbread goes great with the vegetable beef soup. Do you think we might need to add cornbread to the menu at Little Italy? Maybe garlic cornbread?"

"I doubt that it would be received well by the regulars."

A question was begging to be asked, "So what do you want to do?"

"When?"

"With the rest of your life."

"Where the heck did that come from?"

"I often look at you and wonder. Plus I want to make you happy."

"I've been a wife and a mother, now a business owner, it hasn't left a lot of time for anything else."

"What hopes and dreams do you have?"

"Some crazy stuff. You sure you want to hear this?"

"Positive."

"Okay, here goes. I want to ride in a horse drawn carriage, at night, in the snow. I want to go to the ocean and swim with the dolphins. I'd like to hike and horseback ride in the Rocky Mountains."

"That's it?"

"I'd like to learn to fly fish—I've watched other people do it, and it looks like fun."

"That's your list?"

"Was I supposed to say, *create world peace?*"

"No, I like your dreams."

I could see out the window the snow was coming down harder. We stepped toward the window together. I hugged her gently from behind, and she took my arms and wrapped them tighter around her.

I whispered in her ear, "That snow is really piling up now. I know this sounds forward, but would you like to just spend the night here instead of driving home?"

"Will you be a gentleman?"

"Of course."

"Well, hell no, then I'm not staying."

She laughed, and I didn't know what to think. While we had become close, we hadn't consummated the physical side of our relationship.

"There's four bedrooms you can pick one."

"I'm going upstairs to take a shower, is that okay?"

"Sure, there's everything you need in my bathroom. The one at the end of the hallway on the left-hand side facing the street. I'm going to clean up a little in the kitchen."

I watched as she glided up the steps, she always moved like a dancer—fluid, effortlessly, and graceful. I began to wonder what would happen next. Was this the night we made love for the first time? I feared rejection or damaging our budding relationship. My two biggest fears were failure and rejection. I could face both at the top of the stairs.

I waited nervously, sitting on the bed, when I heard the shower stop, then the whirring noise of the blow dryer. After a few minutes the door opened, and I could see Catherine had raided my closet. She came out wearing one of my favorite shirts, old, soft from years of wear, a faded black-and-red checked flannel shirt. On her it looked like a night shirt. With just a small light illuminating the room, she looked like a dream, an apparition floating toward me. After what probably was an audible gulp, I wondered again was it time?

All doubt was erased as she moved close and started unbuckling my belt. I was excited but nervous. I didn't take this lightly. Two people become almost like one, this was a gift. Giving yourself to another person in a way that only you can give is sacred.

She stood in front of me and slowly unbuttoned each of the six buttons on the borrowed shirt seductively. "Is this okay?" she asked.

"It's more than okay." I felt my entire body tingle. Even my butterflies had goosebumps.

I looked like a circus clown clumsily ripping off one shoe, my shirt, a sock, hopping on one foot fighting a knotted shoestring and all the while this woman is looking adoringly at me trying not to laugh. She eased into the bed wearing only a sheet and a smile.

I kissed her on the forehead and on the side of neck—small, slow kisses.

"I just want to make you happy," I declared.

She responded, "Can we freeze time, you know, make time stand still?"

"Would that we could."

We spent the next hour exploring each other and making what could only be called sweet love, mixed with an unbridled passion I had never known before. At that moment we weren't aware that there was anyone else on the planet. It was like a dream, an erotic dream, yet sacred. We were truly lost in each other.

We were for that time two bodies transformed into one—one soul, one heart, and forever changed. Exhausted I whispered to her, "To say I love you just doesn't seem like enough."

"I hope that's not just pillow talk. I love you. I feel safe with you."

"I've never felt closer to anyone than I do to you right now."

"Tony, I hope we can always feel this way. I admire your

strength and yet you can be tender, your confidence without being arrogant. I watch the way you treat people—it makes me love you that much more."

"I fall in love every day, but it's always the same, it's always with you. We're such a good team!"

"I've learned to trust you. That's big for me."

"I knew life could be good. I would have never imagined it could be this good."

Her eyes were closing, and the delivery of her words came slower.

Physically spent and totally satisfied, Catherine fell asleep with her head resting on my chest. Each time she exhaled I could feel the warmth of her breath as my chest hairs moved like tall grass in a prairie breeze. Her rhythmic breathing was like a barely audible metronome.

I prayed silently that I could keep this feeling forever. I wanted to stay right here, not have the sunrise any time soon. I watched her sleep. She looked so peaceful, her hair reflecting a radiant soft glow from the lamp on the nightstand.

She fell asleep, and I fell in love.

Chapter XXVII

Secrets Revealed (2004)

The phone rang at Villa Cristo. Maria answered. "Hello?"
"Hello, is this Mrs. LeoMorte?"

"Yes, it is."

"This is Bonnie Dempsey; I've met you a couple of times at the restaurant."

"Yes, I remember you. How are you?"

"I'm okay. I was wondering if there was a time soon that I could come to see you. It's very important and nothing I would like to discuss over the phone."

"Why yes, is this evening okay? Should we say 7:30?"

"Oh yes, thank you. I'll see you then."

Maria was apprehensive. She wondered, *What could this lady possible want?* Big Tony had spoken of her but nothing in detail. This was unusual for any of the restaurant customers.

Maria watched the clock nervously and tried to busy herself with mindless tasks around the house. She got a pot of coffee ready to serve her unlikely guest. Around seven o'clock Maria stationed herself at the front window. She was anxious to hear what this might all be about, especially from this relative stranger.

Big Tony's Cadillac pulled up unexpectedly. He climbed out of the car and sent Bull away with just a wave.

"What are you doing home this early?"

"I got a call from one of my customers, Bunny Dempsey, well really *Bonnie*, but I call her *Bunny*. It's a long story. She called saying she was coming by to see both of us, that she had something she wanted to talk about."

"Do you know what it's about?"

"I have no idea. She's been a customer for a long time, but I haven't seen her in years."

About that time a red sports car pulled up, and out stepped the lady with the mysterious message.

Before Bunny could ring the bell, Big Tony met her at the door. She leaned in to hug him—Maria hadn't expected that.

"Mrs. LeoMorte, I'm Bonnie Dempsey. Thanks for seeing me."

"Come in; let's sit down. Can I get you a cup of coffee?"

"That would be great. Maybe it would calm my nerves."

Maria left for a moment, then returned carrying a tray with coffee, cream, sugar, and a spoon.

"Thank you."

"Father Parisi had nothing but nice things to say about you, and I can see why."

"Oh, you knew Father Parisi?"

"I only saw him three different times, but yes, I knew him. The first time I met him it was just outside the restaurant. He was coming out as I was going in. We introduced ourselves, and I had a conversation with him. I was instantly comfortable with him and asked if I could come to visit him and get some counseling. He agreed, and we set a date for a few weeks out."

Tony and Maria were listening intently, wondering what could have possibly been the purpose of this very unexpected visit. Tony was getting nervous, beads of sweat broke out on his forehead and he began tapping his foot on the floor. He hoped his heartbeat wasn't audible.

"I have some news for you—I'm afraid it's bad news. I received a box and a letter." Bunny then pulled out a familiar ring—a lion's head ring. "This was your son Vince's ring."

Big Tony grabbed the ring from Bunny as Maria gasped and began to look unsteady, like she might pass out.

Big Tony demanded in a thunderous voice, "Where did you get this?" He quickly moved to Maria's side to hold her up.

"It came in my mail with a letter." I can read you the letter if you want me to." Without waiting for a response Bunny unfolded a single sheet of paper, slipped on a pair of glasses and began.

"Here's a souvenir for you, I took it off the finger of your lover, Vince LeoMorte. I wanted to kill his father, but he always had bodyguards around him, so I waited. I waited in the parking lot of their restaurant and grabbed Vince at gun point and forced him into my car and made him drive across the Mississippi river into Illinois. I walked him down to the edge of the river and took his wallet, his watch, and this ring so he couldn't be identified. Then I shot him and dumped his body into the Mississippi River. It was high and muddy, and it would assure he was never found. Later I took the diamonds out of the eyes in the ring and sold them. I thought you should have it now. Now he's lost his son like I lost mine. Good-bye Bitch!"

After a long pause, Maria, in a shaky voice, said, "I don't understand any of this."

Bunny explained, "Sean wasn't my son's real father. He thought it was Vince, or maybe Big Tony."

Maria cast her eyes toward Big Tony, eyes full of hurt and doubt. Bunny seeing the disbelief in her eyes asked, "Can I explain please?"

Maria through tears said, "Go ahead."

"For nine months I carried a baby and a secret."

"The second time I saw Father Parisi was when I went to see him for counseling because I was infatuated with your husband. He was good looking, rich, and powerful—that's an overpowering aphrodisiac for any woman. I met Father Parisi at the church, we went out into the garden area behind the priests' house, I was starting to talk when it began to rain, we ran into the house, no one else was there. As I told my secret Father Parisi hugged me to comfort me—an innocent hug and our faces brushed into an accidental kiss, and then we got carried away. He broke his vow of chastity and I broke my vow of marriage. I went home immediately ashamed and afraid. I had sex with my husband Sean for three days in a row as if it would erase my indiscretion. Years after my son was born it was determined Sean couldn't have been the father."

More tears trickled down Maria's face. She understood in the way only another woman could of the torment Bonnie had suffered with all the secrecy surrounding the taboo of her sin.

"The third time I saw Father Parisi was the same day Little Tony went to see Father Parisi in the hospital, I almost passed him. I waited with Mickey in the parking lot for him to leave. Then we went to Father Parisi's room, he was barely able to recognize me, and he had never seen Mickey. He had lost a lot of weight, the room wreaked of a combination of antiseptics and sanitizers. I introduced them.

"Mickey said, "So, this is your Father Parisi that you always talked about."

"I took a deep breath and said, "No, this is *your* father…Father Angelo Parisi."

"They both looked at me in horror.

"Mickey whirled around asking, "Did I hear you right?"

"Father Parisi laid there speechless, tears slowly made their way down is hollow facial features. As he turned toward me, I resisted, looking away in shame. He exhaled loudly, it sounded almost as if he had the wind knocked out of him.

"I explained further, "This is Michael, *Mickey* I call him. You would be proud of him. He's a good man, kind, gentle, and even got an academic scholarship offer and an athletic scholarship offer to Notre Dame. He was the valedictorian of his class and a high school All American soccer player. He's getting a degree in theology."

"The priest could scarcely lift his hand but reached through the rails of the hospital bed to hold the hand of this child turned man, unbelievably his son. He asked Mickey to lean over and he whispered to him. Mickey shook his head, yes, to acknowledge the words the priest, his biological father spoke. Father Parisi kissed Mickey's hand and pulled it close to his chest.

"I leaned in and said, "I'm sorry I didn't tell you sooner. I let my fear and conscience stop me hundreds of times. You had a right to know."

"He nodded, yes, slowly and raised his shaking hand to make a sign of the cross toward me, an indication that he forgave me and was in a way granting me absolution.

"Mickey moved to the other side of the hospital bed; his face contorted with emotion. Father Parisi reached for both our hands, placed them together as to unify us all and then closed his eyes for the last time.

"As we left the hospital, I thought, *We were two imperfect people who made a perfect baby that turned into a good man.*"

Bunny continued her story, "The drive home was quiet—I only hoped two things, that my som would understand and forgive me."

Bunny looked at Maria and spoke, "Directly or indirectly I've brought immeasurable misery to your life. No words can describe my sorrow from one mother to another for what has happened. I'm begging for your forgiveness"

Tony asked, "Where did the letter come from?"

She said, "It was post marked, Dublin, Ireland. I'll leave it here if you want me to." Maria nodded, and Bunny left.

Without another word Big Tony climbed the steps to his bedroom and let out cries of anguish that didn't even sound human. He questioned why those secrets and this seemingly unavoidable curse followed him?

After an hour downstairs, Maria climbed the steps and went to what used to be Vince's room. She looked around at his pictures, high school trophies, and the clothes left in his closet so many years ago. At least now she could put her son to rest in her head. As gruesome as it was, she now knew what had happened.

Maria later found Tony face down on the bed, still sobbing. His eyes bloodshot, he was drained physically and emotionally.

He had no more tears to shed. They stared at each other, fell into each other's arms, and wondered how they could go on.

"This doesn't even seem real Tony, it's a nightmare. I'm not sure I can bear any more."

Tony looked into Maria's eyes and said, "I've always been faithful to you, I would never betray you, I love you, always have and always will."

"Family is everything."

Chapter XXVIII

Time Takes Its Toll

Time does not *heal all wounds.*

Maria had much of the life drained out of her, the sting of loss was no stranger to this woman. What meant the most to her had been destroyed, disappeared, or was distant. Being emotionally spent eventually eroded her physical health, at 82 years of age she was diagnosed with breast cancer. She dwindled away despite the best doctors and care. She succumbed to the disease in 2011.

Through his sorrow, Big Tony hoped that his Maria had found in death what she lacked in life—peace. Their 63-year marriage had certainly been a roller coaster ride of life. Blessed with beautiful children that sometimes turned ugly, they supported and tried to guide each of them.

Dominic was eventually released. Prison had changed him mentally and physically. Gone was the brash attitude and the overconfident pseudo-gangster he imagined himself to be. While he still showed that edge of attempted intimidation, he was like a barking hound with no teeth. Big Tony had mercy on him and set him up with a trust that doled out $3,000 a month, enough to get him by, but not so much that he could live the *lifestyle.*

His only means of entertainment was the Friday night poker game he hosted. Dom was now living in the home on the Hill, Vincent's old home, and he worked as the daytime manager of a small, B-class, hole-in-the-wall Mexican restaurant near Forest Park called *Park and Beans.*

On a visit to the house, the old Dominic resurfaced when he

was outside playing with the two guard dogs. We had two more German shepherds from the same litter who never seemed to get along, so we named them J. Edgar and Al Capone. Dom impatiently said, "Hey, Little Tony, these dogs are stupid. I'm trying to teach them to roll over, and they can't get it."

Not trying to hide my disdain for my prodigal brother, I explained, "You have to start with the most basic premise—to train a dog, you have to be *smarter* than the dog."

"Maybe you're forgetting who you're talking to."

"Don't try the tough guy routine with me, it'll ruin your vision."

"How the hell is it going to ruin my vision?"

"Because I'll black both your eyes. Didn't prison time teach you anything?"

Pop came outside. He stooped over to pick up a tennis ball. I watch as the *old warrior* transcends into being a kind, gentle guy just playing fetch with his puppies.

Soon we were joined by Mary Rose's grandson, Robbie, who called out to Big Tony, "Hey, Gran-Tiny, can we play ball?"

I laughed at the nickname that stuck because the little guy couldn't learn to pronounce Grandpa Tony.

He called back, "Sure kid, get that old broom handle over there. You can use that for a bat. That's what we did when I was a kid. We called it stick ball."

The boy strolled over and made a stop at the dog kennel. Swinging the gate closed behind him, he and yelled, "Look Gran-Tiny, I'm in jail."

We looked at each other and laughed. My father, through his chuckle, said, "As a family we had to fight to keep *out* of jail. This kid thinks it's funny."

I urged him, "Come on out here Robbie, bring your bat."

Pop was pitching, Robbie was batting, and I was catching. Robbie took a dozen swings and could not connect with the broom handle/bat and soon tired of the game.

"I'm going inside. Mom said she would make me some grape Kool-Aid, and I can pretend it's wine like you drink, Gran-Tiny."

"Catch," Big Tony called as he launched a weak throw toward me.

"Coming back to ya." I sent the ball back. And then I wiped a tear from my eye. Somehow I realized I had never played catch with father in all my life—until that moment. Such a small thing. Such a gigantic thing.

Robbie ran out, and speaking through a purple-stained smile said, "This is fun." Big Tony took time to play with his grandkids that he didn't take with us, his own kids. The little ones didn't fill the void left from the death of Maria, but they're visits did allow temporary relief from his sadness of waking up without her.

I tried to make life pleasant for Catherine. I learned all her sizes and the style of clothes she liked. It was a Friday ritual that I would bring home a sweater, a scarf, flowers, chocolate or some surprise to show her I was always thinking of her and truly loved her.

"You don't have to bring me something every week."

"I do it because I love you."

"You show me every day that you love me. It's the little things you do. Pulling my chair to seat me in public, opening doors, getting the car door, all those things mean so much and are priceless."

"I guess I learned from those around me that buying things shows you love someone, but I see what you're saying."

"Do you know what my favorite thing you do is?"

"What is it?"

"I love it when you go to the bedroom and climb in on my side and warm up my side of the bed before I get there. That costs nothing but is so sweet and considerate."

That's the way it was for years. We often included her son, Oliver, when we made plans. We booked a quick summer vacation to Montana—Oliver agreed to come along and looked forward to getting away. He had discovered a passion for fishing and especially fishing with a fly rod. TV shows and magazines depicted the purity of casting in mountain streams, and Oliver was on a quest to catch the trout that swam in seemingly every creek, stream, and river in the state. We felt like family, and Oliver, who had taken up permanent residence in St. Louis, lived on his own but visited often with only an occasional trip to see his father.

Flying over this rugged western state gave us all a preview of the landscape and certainly was a departure from the concrete jungle that was St. Louis. I recalled my father speaking of a Missouri farm that belonged to his surrogate father, Tommy Russo. I connected this mile-high visual with the freedom Big Tony probably felt and found in the Missouri outdoors. With just a short stay planned we drove to Billings, Montana, where Oliver was anxious to wade the cool Big Horn River.

While Oliver was *flicking flies*, Catherine and I breathed new life into our relationship. Surrounded by rugged but beautiful mountains and surrounding prairie land, with business and traffic miles away, we enjoyed each other throughout the days and the nights. The trip provided temporary relaxation for us. We took a vacation and it turned into a vocation for Oliver.

"I want to move here and become a fly-fishing guide," he announced.

I offered the voice of reason to this young man I viewed as my own son. "Whoa, it's all new and seems like a good idea now but winter brings thigh-high snow and sub-zero temperatures."

"I know that."

His mother chimed in. "What will you do in the winter months?"

"I'll find work I can do online."

"Ah, the adventurousness of youth."

We were flying back the next day, and reluctantly Oliver climbed aboard the small jet still talking about his future plans. We changed planes in Denver for the direct flight back to St. Louis. Neither of us was able to sleep in the cabin of the plane, but Oliver was another story. He was snoring loudly, sleeping like a man with not a care in the world. Flying first-class offers the room and the quiet necessary for sleeping.

A flight attendant approached us, and I asked, "Would you be serving anything to eat on the flight?"

She answered, "I'm working coach."

I smirked and said, "I'm not a coach."

Unamused, she said, "I've been on my feet all day, in two-inch-high heels and five cities. Would you like something?"

"Yeah, I'd like to be ten years younger, three inches taller, and have a 34-inch waist."

Catherine turned toward the window trying to pretend she wasn't with me.

Now it was on. "What do you weigh, about 230?"

"Are you kidding, I'm in perfect shape."

She came back with, "I suppose, if you count round as a shape."

We were better entertainment than the inflight movie.

"Please make sure your seat backs and tray table are in the upright position."

I asked, "Does that mean we're landing soon?"

"No, I just like saying that for the ten millionth time."

"Hold on," I said as I reached into my pocket and pulled out a $20. "Here's your tip."

"I didn't do anything for you."

"Exactly, I'm just overjoyed that you weren't assigned as our regular flight attendant. I try to like everybody until they give me a reason not to like them. Don't push it."

She snatched the twenty and headed back to the coach section.

"Well, that was embarrassing," Catherine said as she elbowed me.

We heard the announcement from the pilot, "We're about ten minutes out of St. Louis, we should be landing on time."

Catherine leaned over to me and asked, "Would you ever want to move? Get away from the city, start all over again?"

I sat there realizing I had never really considered relocating. "I'm not sure Catherine. My family has been there for decades. Why would I move? I guess I also hate the idea of giving up what my grandparents risked relocating."

Catherine continued, "There's so much more of the world to see, things to experience."

After a brief pause, I responded, "Would it be disrespectful to their sacrifice and all the hard work they put in to make a home in St. Louis? I love the house, my father is getting old, well *is* old, I can't imagine leaving him at this point. He's always said, family is everything.

Days and months seem to click off much faster. In 2013 Big Tony turned 91. Hard to believe—91 years old.

He seemed to age considerably each day, a shell of the man he once was.

"Little Tony, my Little Tony, I'm so tired. Feel vulnerable and alone. In my private movements I wonder if I made a difference in the world and my family?"

"Are you kidding Pop? You're the standard I judge other by."

"That's nice of you to say. You know I pray more often now. I hope God hears the prayers of this old man. I did a lot of bad things, a did some good things too, but for the wrong reasons. I'm tired."

I watched my father closely, drinking in the days we had left and the memories that I treasured. He drank more wine and took longer naps. Often I sat and just watched him sleep.

Chapter XXIX

The Whispers of Autumn

My father was sleeping alone in a king-size bed. We checked his blood pressure regularly, his pulse beating like the second hand on a wall clock. I often caught him staring at the picture of Maria, his wife of 63 years, that was sitting close to him on the nightstand.

"How you are feeling, Pop?"

"Like I'm 91. One foot on a banana peel and the other one in the grave."

"Aw, you'll probably outlive me."

"Oh, *Little Nino*, Little Tony, don't even say that."

"I want you to talk to your brother and your sisters, tell them I need to see them while we still have time. *Comprendere* (Understand)?"

"Yeah Pop, I'll take care of it."

I placed a long-distance call to Connecticut. By sheer luck my sister, the Sister answered. "Hey Angelina, this is Little Tony."

"Is everything all right?"

"Yeah. Pop asked me to call you. he wants to know if you can come home for a few days?"

"I can't. We're in the middle of getting final grades out and have a fundraiser scheduled next week."

"Maybe he can just talk to you over the phone? Hold on let me ask him." I called into his room, "Hey Pop, do you want to talk to Ange now?"

"Sure, that'll be fine."

I brought the phone into him. "I can leave the room so you can have privacy."

"No stay," was his reply.

"My little angel, how are you?"

"I'm good Pop, how about you?"

"I'm getting ready to see your mother in heaven."

"No, you'll make it to a hundred."

"I know you can't stay on long, but I wanted tell you first how much I love you and hope you can forgive me if I've offended you in any way or wasn't the father you needed?"

"No Pop, you were great. I think I owe you the apology, I was wild and caused you and Mama a lot of worry and sleepless nights."

"You were always daddy's little angel. I'm ready to spread some money around. I want to give you an inheritance, big bucks!"

"Pop, when I joined the convent, I took a vow of poverty."

"Maybe you can hide some cash under your mattress?"

"Oh no, no, I can't do that. Let me check with Mother Superior Sister Monica to see if we can accept a monetary gift for the school. Is that good with you?"

"Sure, get with your brother Tony, and he'll take care of everything."

"I have to go Pop; you hang in there. I'll be there when you blow the candles out on your hundredth birthday. *Ti amerò per sempre* (I'll love you forever)."

He handed me the phone, and took a deep breath fighting back tears. "Call Mary Rose and Dom, tell them to come here tomorrow. Wait, *ask* them. Before you call them, I want to give you something. Step over here."

I stepped over to his bedside. He had lost weight and the lion's head ring he had worn for so many years slid easily off his finger. "I want you to have this now so there's no fight with your brother over who should have it. LeoMorte, the lion—I always loved this ring. There's a secret I've known for years. When your Grandpa Vincent came over to this country our name got accidentally changed from DeoMonte to LeoMorte at Ellis Island. I only found out when I enlisted in the army and it was on my birth certificate, that made it my legal name. I always loved the association with the lion."

I swallowed hard for two reasons, the meaningful gesture of giving me the ring and because I knew the other secret, the secret Grandpa Vincent revealed to me. Did I dare tell my father now in this tender moment or carry the secret entrusted to me?

"I love the ring pop, especially because it was yours. When I was going to school, I learned a word that's appropriate for this ring."

"What is it?"

"*Talisman,* Pop; it means a ring or something like it that has magic powers and brings good luck."

"It's just a ring to me. I believe in God, not luck. I'm not sure how lucky I've been."

"Maybe God brought you luck. Think of all the good things that happened in your lifetime. I'll wear it proudly."

I noticed the ruby eyes had faded and showed a few chips and that the gold had worn smooth in several places. I leaned down after I put the ring on my right hand and kissed this once powerful man who now was physically weak and frail.

"Your wedding band has gotten thin, Pop"

"It's like me, old and worn out. Sixty-three years of marriage to your mother, with all the bad things I did, I never strayed from her. I never loved anything or anybody as much as her, she was an angel on earth. After she died, I didn't want to take my wedding band off, I felt like I was still married to her. Family is everything."

"I know, Pop. You've said that a thousand times."

The next day it was Dominic's turn to visit. He walked up the stairs and tentatively into Big Tony's bedroom. "I'm here Pop, what did you want?"

"What the hell is wrong with you? That's how you greet me? Where did we go wrong with you, Dominic?"

"You think I didn't know Vince was always your favorite?"

"Don't you dare talk about your dead brother with disrespect! I loved all of my children."

"It was always everybody but me. Dominic was last in line. Anyway, what did you want to see me about?"

"I know my time on earth is short, I want to settle my affairs before anything happens, I should have done this years ago. I know you struggle with money, I'm changing your trust fund monthly allotment, with conditions. Soon instead of $3,000 a month, you will get $5,000 a month. There are two stipulations—one, if you go back to jail, you get zero."

Dominic interrupted, "I'm not going back to jail."

"And two, if anything happens to your brother Tony, you get zero. So, you better pray he stays healthy and nothing happens to him."

"What is that about?"

"In the Bible, Cain and Abel. You can read it yourself. Have I made myself clear?"

"Clear."

"Is there anything you want to tell me?"

"No Pop, nothing. Can I go now?"

"Go."

As Dominic hurried out of the house, I heard Pop call. "Tony, come up here."

Climbing the steps and down the hall I found my father sitting on the side of his bed. "What are you doing up?"

"I'm tired of laying there. Your brother is an idiot and a disappointment."

"Did you call me up here to tell me that?"

"No. Come down the hallway with me."

I took his arm and supported his weight as he shuffled down the hall to a window looking out over the backyard.

"When we bought this house, I had a secret hiding place built." Big Tony looked around as if someone could hear him talking.

"Who are you looking for, Pop?"

"The walls have ears."

"What does that mean?"

"It's an old Italian saying. What we say now stays inside these four walls."

"I understand. What is it?"

"You see that doghouse inside the kennel? It is built to slide back," he said as he put his hand up to shield his eyes from the sun.

"Slide back?"

"Yes, there's a space in the concrete under that doghouse with a sealed stainless-steel box. In that box is a lot of cash, a *lot* of cash. There're millions in that box! Don't ask me where it came from. After something happens to me, take $250,000 and go to a company I started, Metro Financial Management, deposit that money and send a cashier check to Angelina's school in Connecticut. Tomorrow I'll tell your sister Mary Rose, she will be getting $2 million when I die. It must be spent slowly, so as to not draw attention. Do you understand?"

"I get it Pop, but my law background tells me that's not all legal."

"I devoted my life to making sure my family was well taken care of. I did it in life—I'm doing it in death. There's almost another $6 million in there. That's for you. Same thing, spend it slowly, use it to make a secure future for you and Catherine. She's a good woman."

Just then we heard the front door open," Anybody home?" It was Mary Rose.

"We're up here. Come on up."

Mary Rose was breathing hard after her trip up the stairs. "How you are feeling, Pop?"

Big Tony struggled to turn around and headed back to his bedroom. "I'm great, ready to go dancing," he said sarcastically.

"Tony said you wanted to see me."

"Yes, I want to tell you how proud I am of you, my daughter the CPA. You married a great guy—a square John, but a good guy."

"Pop, a square John—*Cos'è quello* (What's that?)"

"It's not bad, a guy that plays by the all the rules, a straight arrow."

"I'm very happy, I've got a great husband, good kids, and grand-kids that I adore. Those little ones, Robbie and little Lisa, bring me so much joy, and they love their "Gran-Tiny.""

"And I love them. I'm setting up my wishes for after I die. I want to make sure you're taken care of; you've been good to me and you were good to your mother. I remember how happy we were after you were born. We already had Vince and then our first girl—you were always pretty and well mannered. Anyway, I'm tired and ready to lay down again."

"All right, Pop, I'll bring the grandkids by to see you soon. I love you, let me know if you need anything."

Big Tony slid out of his slippers and sat down swinging his legs up onto the bed. I covered him up with his old flannel blanket—much like a small child he always wanted that blanket. I knew the reason for that—it was the blanket he and Mama had on their bed when she died. I think he felt closer to her when he had it pulled up to his chin. He also took her pillow and hugged it at night, it had long ago given up her smell.

"Let me show you something else. Your mother and I decided we wanted to be cremated when we died. Some of her ashes are in the urn in our room, I did that so I could be close to her. But years ago, I went to Larry Valenti and bought the wooden bread paddle Grandpa used. I took it to a friend who was a cabinet maker and had him make this box."

Big Tony opened the box that had three sections in it, each with a piece of glass that could be opened and secured with two brass latches. "These ashes in the middle are some of your mother's. I want some of mine to go in the first compartment."

"What about the third compartment, what's that for?"

"That's my mother's rosary and my fathers wedding ring. The other is a dried flower from your mother's memorial service." He choked up as he spoke of his sweet Maria.

As he closed the lid, I noticed the lion's head carved into the top of the memory box. I didn't know how to feel about that, all I could think was, *Cent'Anni, 100 years.*

"Little Tony, my son, it's important to me that you know I'm proud of you and that I love you."

It's almost like he knew, in a matter of weeks he would be gone. I walked up to say goodnight and found him with Mama's pillow tucked between his arms and a small but distinct smile on his face. I imagined he saw her as he was passing from this life, at least that's what I wanted to believe.

If anyone had a life to celebrate, it was Big Tony LeoMorte. I once heard someone respond when asked who he was, *I am many men.* It showed as messages grieving his loss poured in. I told Catherine about a few of the notes I received and conversations that came up:

Your father helped me without being asked, he gave me money knowing I could never pay him back.

The shoemaker from the old neighborhood told me that when his wife died, my father contacted the funeral director and covered the cost of the funeral.

People came into the restaurant and cried, each with their own story about how much Big Tony meant to the community. He knew and helped three generations of Italians and other ethnic locals.

I remember the last conversation I had with him.

"Son, I didn't do everything right, but I did the best I could. In life you can't give what you don't have. I took the gifts I was given and tried to make the most of them. I made lots of mistakes."

"I know Pop, spending time with you, I learned a lot about you. I know you *bent* the law a lot, but I also knew if I needed you, you would be there. I knew your childhood was tough, Grandpa Vincent couldn't be father *and* mother—and truthfully wasn't even much of a father, but he had it rough too."

"I'm not asking for a free pass; I just want you to know I tried to protect my family and give them everything they wanted."

"We had what we wanted but not as much of what we needed,

your time. You and Mama were a good team, we were well-fed, clean, and safe. We lived in a nice home and given chances that you weren't. The hardest thing to give people, even family, is what you didn't get. You did great, Pop. You gave us the greatest gift."

"What was that?"

"You were a good husband to our mother."

"I would change a few things if I could, but that I cannot do. It's like the Frank Sinatra song—you know that one?"

"No, Pop, I don't know."

"You know, oh, what the hell is it? Huh, "I Did It My Way," that's it. I did it my way! Do you think I was a good father?"

"Let me ask you two questions, Pop. "Do you think you did better than your father?"

"I do."

"Did you do the best you could?"

"I did."

"Nobody could ask for more than that."

I just didn't want him to be in pain or afraid, but he was both.

I climbed in the bed with him—it seemed like such a natural thing to do. We talked until he fell asleep, and I laid there and just looked at him. The scars and wrinkles on his face were like a roadmap of his life. I watched his chest rise just so slightly and fall, hoping none of these were his last breath. I wanted to keep him a while longer. He stirred slightly and opened his eyes.

"You know, Pop, in the weakest part of your life you showed your greatest strength."

He settled into a peaceful sleep.

In some ways it was my best day and my worst day both in the same day.

I remember coming home with Catherine after the service. I could almost always visualize my mother and father as I went from room to room. While it was a little lonely and quiet, it was comforting to think about all that happened in that old house, the memories living on in each room, the familiar squeaks in the wooden floor, and knowing his spirit lived on in me were a comfort in my private moments. Catherine closed off the bedroom that my mother and father shared, and it became somewhat of a shrine with little mementos scattered around there and throughout the rest of the house.

There were times when I thought I could hear her laugh or his cough. I'd imagine seeing their shadows coming down the hallway or entering the rooms.

Reality set in eventually. They were gone.

Chapter XXX

Fear Drops, Remembrances, and Rainbows
Cent'Anni

Years passed and Catherine and I enjoyed the family home. It did at times seem big and quiet, but Villa Cristo was our home now—it had weathered many storms and held so many secrets. Mary Rose lived in a quiet subdivision in the county. She had a home business as a CPA. Years ago, we legitimized the business at the restaurant. Now everything was legal at Little Italy. The customer base had changed with a lot of business coming from outside the city. It was considered *cool* to have prom dates, wedding rehearsal dinners, and family reunions at Little Italy. We retained generations of families loyal to the restaurant and to our family—and occasionally the FBI would send a couple of agents in under the guise of eating lunch, but we knew they were scoping out the place. They never give up.

Once when a pair of agents were preparing to pay their meal ticket one asked sarcastically, "Do you have an FBI discount."

Without hesitation I replied, "Yeah, the FBI special. You can avoid paying taxes."

While in Montana, Oliver met Amber, a young lady from Idaho who was in Billings to attend Montana State College. Amber, like many college students, held down a job while going to school. She was a waitress at a local hangout, Big Sky Bar and

Grill. They dated for a year and married soon after. A daughter, Caroline arrived and four years later little Thomas, named after Amber's father, completed their family.

Amber had never been to the big city and yearned for the supposed excitement that comes with living in a metropolitan area. A restless Amber suggested, "Let's move from here; let's go someplace where the children can get a good education, where there's more to do, some sort of culture."

"I lived in St. Louis and visited Chicago often, but I love the peacefulness of Montana, the streams, mountains, and open air. I can't earn any money as a fly-fishing guide in a city!"

"We don't have a future here. It's time to move on."

So, they packed up and made the migration to the Gateway to the West, St. Louis. Amber loved the hustle-bustle atmosphere of the city; Oliver still had the longing for the rugged life offered by the west.

We reinstituted the tradition of the Sunday dinners, but as I feared, it was not the same—oh, it was the same table, but different people. Mary Rose had her own family and though they came over occasionally, she had her own version of Sunday dinners at their home. Dominic was invited but never came.

Catherine kept the memory alive—we always played vinyl records on an old turntable, albums that spun decades ago with songs from opera tenors Mario Lanza and Enrico Caruso filled the room with music familiar to me but with words she didn't understand. It didn't matter. It was about reliving memories.

"I enjoy our Sundays; it's comforting to me to recreate what we had in this house for years. Sometimes I close my eyes and I can, at least in my mind, see everyone here. It warms my heart but sometimes makes me sad. I should have appreciated it more at the time."

Catherine came over and sat next to me on the couch which now was more worn out than antique. "I just want you to be happy."

"This house is special to me. Everywhere I look I can tell you a story that impacted my life. Even the backyard had its secrets and memories."

I took Catherine by the hand, we walked over to the back window and looked out. You could see the two old dogs, muzzles almost completely grey—J Edgar and Al now mostly tolerated each other and seemed satisfied to lay in the shade of a big oak tree. Most of their exercise came from chasing the occasional rabbit that slipped through the fence. The large yard that hosted parties and playtime had healed from the worn-out spots where no grass grew because of children and grandchildren playing.

"This house, that yard, holds lots of stories." I sighed as I reminisced.

Catherine smiled and said, "I enjoy your family history—well most of it."

"There was sadness, but there were good times too, and many life lessons."

Our reflection time was interrupted by the sound of spaghetti sauce bubbling in an old pot. The aroma of my mother's recipes could always be smelled all over the house. Garlic has a way of doing that.

Seeing with Catherine's fresh eyes, the house did show its age, but in ways that endeared it to me. I explained many of the nuances.

"Look, here's where the pantry doors were marked with ink marks on the frames. We stood there so Mama could measure our height. I was only three feet tall. The marks started to run together as Mama continued the ritual of measuring us and inscribing our names on a regular basis."

The glass door handles barely turned or locked anymore.

"Here's another reminder," I said, pointing to a cracked tile in the kitchen floor. "That's where Dom threw a soup can at Mary Rose. So many stories in this place."

Regardless of how many people came for Sunday dinner, I couldn't erase the old seating arrangement from my mind.

"Hey Catherine, I remember Pop always sat at the head of the table, Mama at the opposite end, and kids lined the long table. They had a strategic placement so they could make corrections. It was almost the same with church seating, kid, parent, kid, parent, kid, and then the older ones."

I laughed as I recounted, "Dominic always had a place alongside Pop because he was constantly being corrected, and Mary Rose never needed to be corrected so she earned a spot at the end of the pew."

Catherine couldn't hold back. "None of that worked out too well with Dominic did it?"

Though we rarely managed Sunday dinners, sometimes we could coordinate everyone's schedules and gathered for a baseball game and watched the Cardinals play. It was a time of renewal and relaxation as we all could forget the day to day grind and immerse ourselves in the game and add to the family memories.

Oliver and Amber were frequent visitors, and we enjoyed the time with the little ones. Thomas at nine months old was fun, but Caroline won my heart. I was her *Poppy*. When she would visit, she always knew there would be a stash of cookies, and *Nana* Catherine was a pushover.

In a shy, barely audible voice as soon as she walked in, she would ask, "Nana," *pause for dramatic effect*, "may I please have a cookie?"

One time Catherine responded, "Caroline, you eat so many cookies you're going to turn into a cookie."

My response was, "That's her new name—Cookie." Everyone in our family had to have a nickname!

One evening while I was reading, Catherine called out from down the hall, "The kids want to drop Thomas and Caroline off so they can go out."

I yelled back, "So, we're going to have Tom Collins and Cookie for dinner?" I waited. There was no reply. Which means, *You're not as funny as you think you are.*

Catherine appeared at the doorway. "And they would like for them to spend the night."

Having already tested her mood, I merely replied, "Yes Dear."

She poked her head around the corner again and asked, "You know, I was wondering; we have more time now and the money—is there anything *you'd* like to do?"

"Yeah, maybe travel, take a vacation."

"Where?"

"Ireland, maybe Ireland—Dublin, Ireland."

The conversation was interrupted by the doorbell. The Collins kids had arrived.

They entered in a whirlwind like only little kids can. "Nana, can I have a cookie."

"I already have them out, and I'll pour you a glass of milk."

"Chocolate milk?"

"No, white milk."

Oliver and Amber didn't stay long. They were ready to start date night and made a quick exit, calling out, "We'll see you tomorrow afternoon around three o'clock. Love you both and thanks."

Thomas was asleep for the night and Cookie soon followed. Having little kids in the house, fed, ready for bed, and outfitted in pajamas adds a tranquility to a home.

As we prepared to sleep, Catherine asked again, "What else would you like to do?"

"I know you'll think this is crazy, but I'd like to write a book."

"Really. A book? About what?"

"A book about my family's life—but I don't think anyone would believe it."

Lightning flashed and thunder rolled in the distance—another summer storm. We always slept lightly when we had the grandchildren in the house. This night would be no different. My mind wouldn't be still.

As I tossed and flopped around in the bed Catherine asked, "What's wrong?"

"My mind just won't shut down. It's racing. I'm reliving lots of family moments. Maybe it's the full moon."

"Try to relax, think happy thoughts, count backwards from 100. That always help me."

I dozed, catching 30 minutes here and 30 minutes there. I got up a half dozen times to look out the window. The storm has set in. At six AM the little human alarm clock went off. Cookie was standing by the bed.

"Poppy, I'm scared."

"What are you scared of, Cookie?"

"The rain, thunder, and lightning. It scares me."

"Let's go see what Nana has for breakfast."

The smell of bacon hit first. That's enough to know that Catherine will have eggs, toast, and orange juice for me and my little shadow. Sure enough, she has the baby on her hip and a fork in her other hand.

"Good morning, Miss Cookie."

"Hi, Nana. Can I play after we eat?"

"You and Poppy can play. I have to take care of your brother. He needs to be changed and get a bath."

A plate of half-eaten breakfast sits in front of Cookie, and I picked through her bacon and slug down the rest of my black coffee. We made our way down the hall and into my office. I opened the closet where I keep a tattered cardboard box.

"All right, what do you want to play with?"

She walked over and dumped out the box. "Everything."

In the pile is a big ten-piece puzzle with only nine pieces visible. There's a bag of wooden blocks, the kind with numbers, letters, and farm animals on the faces. The blocks show evidence of use from many little hands—corners are worn off, colors are faded, and cracks in the wood—all proof that they've been used and abused. A box of crayons has spilled out, broken, peeled, and some that are nothing but nubs. The refrigerator is already loaded with juvenile art ripped from the coloring books.

"What do you want to play with first?" I asked, as we both assume a prone position on the cold, oak office floor.

"Let's color."

She grabbed the remnants of a red crayon and scribbled across the face of a dog in the coloring book.

"Wait, you have to stay in the lines and pick a real color for the dog."

Cookie looked at me with childhood innocence and asked, "Why?"

"That's just the way it's supposed to be."

"Why?"

"You know, I'm not sure. Just do it the way you want to. You'll have rules to follow soon enough."

Satisfied with the answer, she started the red scribbling again.

I looked around the room that was once my father's office and saw reminders of him and the secrecy that often followed him. A few old pictures of ancestors, his army picture, and small treasures that only made sense to him. I saw sharpened pencils—knowing that he had sharpened them struck me, as did those little notes in the top middle drawer of the desk. He never used his lack of formal education as an excuse, he wore it as a badge of honor when he achieved success. *Honor.* That was large with my father, and from what I remember, my grandfather.

As I reflected a loud clap of thunder struck, and lighting flashed across the darkened sky. It startled Cookie, and she jumped into my arms. "I'm scared, Poppy."

I held her close to comfort the little, flannel-pajama clad child. "It's okay. It's only a storm outside."

Her fright brought a tear to my own eyes, and as we stayed cheek to cheek, little *fear* drops trickled from her eyes. I felt a single tear fall from my own face and mingle with the tiny tears streaming down her chubby little cheek. I would do anything to protect this child, now I knew more than ever what my father meant when he said, *Family is everything.* I now understood that this innocent child and others who were not of my blood—were of my soul.

A flood of emotion washed over me. It was like I could feel my father's presence in that very room at that very moment.

A loud knock at the front door. *Who could that be this early in the morning?* I wondered.

Catherine came to the office door. "There's a man here who says he needs to see you. He said it's important."

"Tell him to wait outside. I'll be there in a few minutes."

I looked out the rear office window and pointed. "Look over there, Cookie. Do you see that? It's a rainbow. That's God's promise that everything is going to be all right. Nothing in the world is more powerful than a promise from God."

Again I could feel my father and a sense of relief. I walked slowly toward the wooden memorial box made from my grandfather's bread paddle, ran my hand over the image of the lion's head, opened the lid, and peered at the contents for what must have been a full minute—ashes from my father and mother, and the rosary my grandmother treasured, grandpa Vincent's wedding band, a dried flower—and I knew what my father was telling me.

The tightening in my throat was a precursor to the tears now dripping from my eyes, I slowly slid the lion's head ring from my finger and laid it in the box, now resting near the other family relics. As I turned away, a feeling of peace like I had never felt swept over me, I noticed the desk calendar indicated it was August 10, 2021—*Cent'Anni, one hundred years.*

About the Author

Joey Monteleone

Joey Monteleone is a multimedia communicator who has spent decades working in TV, radio, and print media. Part of the 2017 Legends of the Outdoors inductees, he's boated more than 48,000 bass with 1,500 weighing in at over five pounds.

In addition to being a seasoned fishing guide, Joey holds a third-degree karate black belt, is a three-time Eastern USA fighting champion, and is an in-demand speaker at seminars.

Joey has cracked the code for catching trophy fish from any kind of waters from all over North America. He is well versed in catching almost every species of freshwater fish from every type of watercraft imaginable. With more than 60 years' experience, he displays a marked reverence for the resource. He shares his passion for introducing new anglers to the sport he loves in his books, *I'll be Tennessean Ya* and *60 Seasons: A Fishing Guide.*

The Secret of the Storms is his first novel.

Joey lives in Rock Island, Tennessee. Contact him at:

fishjoey@gmail.com

Also by
Joey Monteleono

I'll Be Tennessean Ya'
60 Seasons: A Fishing Guide

Also Available From
WordCrafts Press

The Restless Earth
by Alan Cockrell

Ring the Bell
by Gerry Harlan Brown

One on One
by Michael Kelso

Better Off Guilty
by Lindsey Lamar

www.WordCrafts.net